Front cover design by Donika Mishineva

www.artofdonika.com

"The best thing you could do is master the chaos in you.

You are not thrown into the fire.

You are the fire."

**M. Indigo**

# Chapter One

# The Woman and the Zebra

Cape Town had fallen, and Tambamba had taken its place.

The coastal village sat where the South African city once stood. In the centuries that had passed since Cape Town's destruction, its ruins were crushed into the earth and its existence eradicated from record. This, too, was the case with every country and city that once existed centuries ago in a civilisation referred to as the humanoids. Nowadays, each rural village was indistinguishable from the next, and only one authority ruled the planet: the Holy State of Borea.

Perry Benson despised living in Tambamba. The voice recorder in his neck and the tracking device in his foot confined him to a life of monotony. He did not even choose where or how he travelled each day: every morning, he sat in a mechanical wheelchair that took him to work. This was the main reason, Perry suspected, that his belly was quite plump, and his cheeks were rather chubby.

On one particular Tuesday, Perry twiddled his thumbs as the automated wheelchair carried him down the single track from his workplace to his assigned dwelling. He pushed back the straggly blond fringe hanging over his eyes and smiled back at his wife, Mabel, who sat in the wheelchair behind his.

'That was wonderful, wasn't it darling?' said Mabel.

'It certainly was,' Perry lied.

'All occupations under the Holy State of Borea hold equal importance, of course. But how lucky we both were to be randomly assigned as Eradicts for the rest of our lives.'

'That's right,' agreed Perry, while silently wishing that the state had assigned him to a different occupation nine years ago. Even now, as his wheelchair arrived in Tambamba, his fingers were covered with blisters from the difficult hands-on nature of his work.

Dozens of houses outlined all four sides of the central village square. Each was an identical white pyramid with a black door at the front. These structures were arranged in several rows, stretching for kilometres back into the great coastal plains that surrounded Tambamba.

'Hello, Janice!' called Mabel, waving at a brunette woman across the village square.

'Good evening, Mabel. Eradiction for you today?'

'As always! We gladly do any job the Holy State of Borea assigns to us.'

Perry rolled his eyes, but thought of the voice recorder in his neck, and said: 'It is our pleasure. Are you looking forward to attending Recreation Day tomorrow, Janice?'

'Absolutely! I love celebrating the Holy State of Borea.'

'Me too! We will see you then, Janice. Have a great evening.'

Perry waved as his wheelchair halted outside his house, on the outskirts of the village square. He rose from the vehicle and stood beside Mabel.

'May we all remain loyal to the Holy State of Borea,' they said in unison. The door opened in response to their voices. Mabel entered the house and rushed upstairs, but as Perry followed her inside, a scream echoed across Tambamba.

Perry halted, stunned by the unexplained noise, and looked across at the screaming woman. She pointed past the final row of houses at a second woman, standing in the grassland and stroking a wild zebra that had stopped to rest nearby.

Perry gulped to suppress his horror.

'Get away from there!' boomed a man arriving in the village square.

'Yeah, stop touching that animal!' cried Perry, surprising even himself with his sudden outburst. 'What's the matter with you?'

The woman looked up and laughed. She continued to pet the zebra as if nothing were amiss. How wrong she was. How could anyone be so brazen? Perry shook with fear as he glanced up at the late-evening sky and spotted a black aircraft making its way towards Tambamba. Currently, the vehicle was just a distant spot, but Perry knew that several Demiurge were inside. He sprinted inside his house and slammed the door behind him, before racing to the nearest window and looking out.

The aircraft landed in the wild grassland behind the village. The law-breaking woman peered over her shoulder as six Demiurge in black uniform emerged from the vehicle. They chased her as she sprinted away, still laughing, and raced past Perry's window across the village square.

One of the figures launched a spear that connected with her arm. The woman collapsed; her eyes widened as blood gushed from the fresh wound. She writhed on the ground and looked up at Perry, standing at the nearest window, as the Demiurge surrounded her. Batons flailed as she shrieked and screamed, until her blood-covered body became limp on the cobbled pavement.

The Demiurge carried the woman back to the aircraft, saluting the villagers waving from their windows.

'Is everything all right, darling?' said Mabel, appearing at the bottom of the stairs. Perry choked back a sob and stared at the pools of blood covering the ground outside.

'Of course,' said Perry, a tear glistening in his eye. 'Everything's fine.'

# Chapter Two

# Recreation Day

Perry sat at the bottom of the stairs in his house, his head in his hands. Mabel read state-approved literature at the kitchen table, a satisfied smirk on her face. A voice had boomed through their house intercom several minutes earlier, announcing the state's victory over the woman who touched a zebra.

'I wish I had been there to see it,' said Mabel as Perry walked into the kitchen. She smiled at him between two dimpled cheeks, and toyed with her frizzy auburn hair. 'She deserved to die.'

Perry nodded, and scratched the back of his neck. He sat down at the table and helped himself to a large portion of the only food available in Borea: seaweed, oats and beans. Once he had finished his meal, he excused himself to bed.

When Perry woke the next morning, Mabel stood by the bedroom window. Her freckled nose was highlighted by the morning sunlight streaming into the room.

'Good morning, darling,' she said.

'Good morning.'

'It is a beautiful day. How blessed we are to live in

Tambamba, under the Holy State of Borea. May I ask you a question?'

'Of course.'

'This evening, when we return from Recreation Day, would you like to copulate?'

'I don't know,' said Perry. 'I think I'm going to be quite tired.'

'You haven't even got out of bed yet, and you already know that you're going to be tired? You are not worthy of the Holy State of Borea.' Mabel stormed out of the room as Perry sighed and rolled out of bed.

'Good morning, Perry Benson!' greeted a voice from behind his mirror.

'May we all remain loyal to the Holy State of Borea,' he said. Turning to confront his reflection, he noticed that there appeared to be a bird's nest on his head. Dirty blond hair stuck out in every direction, and his straggly fringe rested on his light brown eyebrows. Standing beneath the bird's nest was a pudgy figure, not at all unhealthy or short, but could nonetheless do with losing a bit of weight.

'Would you like to read *The Borean Bible*, Perry Benson?' asked the bookshelf.

'Yes, please.' Three words in black lettering flashed onto the wall opposite the bed.

*The Borean Bible*

Surrounding the title were articles detailing worldwide happenings from the past twenty-four hours. One article showed the face of a Demiurge, while another interviewed a young girl attending her first Recreation Day.

Perry lifted his index finger and jerked it towards the first article. The writing disappeared, replaced by the enormous head of a woman with vivid pink hair and large eyebrows. She had harsh, unattractive facial features, and stared down her nose at the camera.

'May you all remain loyal to the Holy State of Borea,' said the woman.

'Until the end,' Perry muttered in response.

'The Holy State of Borea is all powerful. The humanoids that lived hundreds of years ago destroyed the natural world, and we have rebuilt it. By preventing you from interfering with animals or plants in any way, we have saved you from your greatest enemy: yourselves. The Holy State of Borea has preserved the earth forevermore.'

*But at what cost?* thought Perry.

'Our journey is not complete. The safety of the natural world cannot be taken for granted, and there are people living in Borea who still do not comply with the state's regime. These people, known as the Crolax, have mental and physical disabilities. This causes them to think differently to normal humans. The Crolax believe that all people should have freedom of speech, thought, and movement, just like the pathetic humanoids who almost destroyed the planet.

'That is why, when the Holy State of Borea first came to power, we eradicated all Crolax from the earth. But some still exist, unidentified, amongst you all today.

'If you suspect that someone you know thinks differently to the rest of society, then hand them in. If you know someone who is not devoted to satisfying the Holy State of Borea, and does not agree with everything we do, then hand them in. Between your diligence, and our voice recorders, we will locate these traitors, and eradicate them.

'May you all remain loyal to the Holy State of Borea.'

The woman's face disappeared from the wall, as Perry said: 'Until the end.' The familiar sensation of fear, isolation and vulnerability filled his heart. He was one of the people that Borea sought to weed out and destroy: he, according to the state, had a mental or physical disability. What other explanation was there for his disloyalty to the regime?

Perry went downstairs to eat breakfast.

'Good morning, Perry Benson!' said the kitchen light.

'May we all remain loyal to the Holy State of Borea.'

After eating, he walked to the front door and stepped into a circle engraved in the floor.

Shiny metallic rods emerged from the wall. One poked at Perry's eyes to remove residue from his previous night's sleep, while another hovered in front of his mouth and emitted a cleansing spray. A third rod tugged at his left sock, while two others tore off his pyjama bottoms and jumper. A sixth covered his now naked body with a new set of clothes.

Finally, the rods retreated into the walls and Perry confronted his reflection in the mirror next to the front door. His shoes, trousers, and jumper were all coloured a dreary shade of grey. Above this, the red light of a recording device flashed through the skin of his neck.

Mabel appeared in the hallway and the pair left the

house. They each sat in a wheelchair and were carried out of Tambamba, along a track that ran through the gigantic coastal plains. Thousands of animals grazed across the landscape, beneath a serene blue sky.

'Are you excited for Recreation Day, darling?' asked Mabel.

'Of course,' Perry replied, without looking at his wife. Even after nine years of marriage, he failed to understand how she could adore a state that quashed her freedom. What's more, her fervour seemed to grow stronger as each year passed.

Perry had married Mabel under unfortunate circumstances. The Holy State of Borea's laws meant that all citizens were required to live with their parents until marriage. Perry's hatred for his mother and father had caused him to marry at the age of eighteen, but there was no choice in whom one could marry; citizens registered their willingness, and were randomly assigned a partner.

Thankfully for Perry, the state had assigned him and Mabel accommodation in a different village to his parents. He had not seen his parents for nine years, and hoped to keep it that way.

'Look over there, darling! Look at that beautiful cheetah. And look over there! That's an impala. Do you see it, darling? Do you see it?'

'I see them, Mabel, and they are beautiful. Really beautiful.'

Six gigantic pyramids appeared on the horizon, bordered on all sides by an enormous black gate.

'May we all remain loyal to the Holy State of Borea!'

screamed Mabel, throwing her head back and striking herself on the cheek. She was both worshipping Borea, yet flagellating herself for being unworthy of such an honour. Her squeals transformed into wails. Perry grimaced at her absurd reaction, but, remembering the voice recorder in his neck, he likewise started to scream.

His wheelchair stopped in front of the gate. A list of words was projected in front of his face, and he used his finger to scroll down in mid-air and push forwards on the word 'Secular'.

'Please identify yourself,' said the gate.

'My name is Perry Benson, and I am a dutiful citizen of the Holy State of Borea.'

'Have a blessed day, Perry Benson.'

His wheelchair edged through a doorway, before navigating left towards a distant pyramid, reaching the foot of the structure, and entering.

Despite having been here before, Perry was amazed at the pyramid's size. The roof sloped upwards from four directions to meet kilometres above in the centre, and all four walls were painted a matte black. A stage was positioned in front of the farthest wall.

Perry's vehicle aligned itself in an engraved circle in the floor, and a podium hoisted him to the air. He stared at the back of the heads in front of him until darkness engulfed the arena and excitement infested the crowd.

Perry ducked, ready for the arena roof to cave in. Surely no structure could withstand such ferocious levels of sound. Nonetheless, he, too, yelled rapturous approval.

'May we always serve you! May we always serve

you!' he shouted. In the wheelchair beside his, a young girl with red pigtails screeched: 'Weed out the Crolax! Weed out the Crolax!'

A light shone on the stage. Two dancers pranced into view – one was a pale man, and the other a beige-skinned woman. Both were dressed in furry white gowns strapped to their chins and flowing to the floor. The figures faced each other and covered their heads with the bodice of the gown.

They danced in perfect synchrony beneath the white sheets. If one gown bowed its head, raised its knee or pirouetted, the partnering gown replicated the movement. With each step the crowd breathed a collective gasp, and several voices expressed their wonderment.

'How do the gowns move like that?'

'What's causing the gowns to move?'

'I thank the Holy State of Borea for using its technology to bless us with the wondrous self-moving gowns.'

With both dancers forgotten, the crowd was transfixed by two sheets moving of their own accord. This continued for several minutes until, high above the dancers, a baby was lowered from the ceiling.

Perry narrowed his eyes and yawned. He was too far away to be certain, but suspected that a string was attached to the baby, lowering it to the stage.

'The beautiful, flying baby must be protected!' roared a deep voice several rows ahead. Nearby citizens howled their approval. The baby floated onto the stage, remaining motionless as the gowns danced behind it. Finally, the dancers rolled their gowns back down their head and thousands of cries echoed through the arena. The masses had no idea where these figures had come from.

Both dancers waved and smiled at the flummoxed crowd. The magical baby floated up into the ceiling, and the performance concluded. Seconds later, two new dancers took to the stage, and the cycle repeated itself. This continued eighteen more times: each time the masses were shocked to witness two sheets moving of their own accord, a magical baby floating down from the sky, and to then learn that the dancers were hidden beneath the gowns the entire time.

Upon the conclusion of the final performance, light was restored in the arena. Many people shook their heads and widened their eyes as though emerging from a trance. Perry's wife turned to face him.

'The majesty of the Holy State of Borea is truly unparalleled, don't you think?'

'Absolutely. How do you think the magical baby lowers itself from the ceiling?'

'Well, the Holy State of Borea has methods of achieving things that citizens could never comprehend. It is not our duty to try to understand it, darling, it is our duty to worship them for letting us glimpse their sanctity!'

'I am fulfilled,' said Perry.

'I love you,' said Mabel.

The podiums lowered, and thousands of wheelchairs left the arena into the pinkish hue of a gorgeous sunset.

A claxon reverberated across the landscape, and four words appeared in the air in front of Perry's wheelchair.

'The Eight Holy Laws!' boomed a deep male voice,

coming from each citizen's wheelchair. Many people whooped and punched their fists. The lettering morphed into a longer sentence and the man read:

each citizen has the right to be implanted with a voice recorder at birth –

Citizens in every direction roared their approval. Perry cheered along with them, knowing that he must do so after each law. The voice read on:

each citizen has the right to be forbidden from inter-fering with nature and animals –

each citizen has the right to be implanted with a movement tracker at birth –

each citizen has the right to parent a maximum of one child –

each citizen's child, exceeding their first, has the right to be killed at birth –

each citizen without a partner at the age of thirty has the right to be assigned one –

each citizen has the right to have their life terminated at the age of sixty –

each citizen's body has the right to be ground into

dust upon death and integrated into the soil –

Perry sighed upon the conclusion of the final law, but his relief did not last long. The three sticks of bamboo depicted in the Borean state emblem appeared in the air where the laws had just been.

Perry shut his eyes and clenched his jaw. He felt scared, faint and lost. A ringing sound filled his ears and the blood rushed out of his head. His lungs swelled to twice their normal size. His muscles ached. He kept his mouth shut to not alert the voice recorder, and regained control of his body as the emblem disappeared.

'… so that's always an incredible moment, too. But the baby! Oh, the floating baby! Have you ever seen anything so magnificent in your entire life, darling? Of course, you haven't. There's absolutely nothing the Holy State of…'

Mabel had not noticed Perry's strange behaviour. His body always reacted like this when confronted with the Borean emblem, although Perry did not know why. It reminded him that he was different from the other citizens. No one else lost their hearing or struggled to breathe when confronted with the three sticks of bamboo. Perry was alone in this abnormality. From childhood, his fear of bamboo highlighted his mental isolation, and hatred for Borea's repressive, totalitarian rules followed thereafter.

He was still regaining his breath when his wheelchair arrived in Tambamba. Mabel greeted a neighbour across the village square, as Perry turned away, and wondered how much longer he could survive in Borea.

— Chapter Three —

# Eradiction

Perry did not sleep in his bed that night. He sat in the kitchen, wondering why he was so afraid of bamboo, and how much longer he could hide this abnormality. His fear had existed since early childhood, but he had trained himself to shut his eyes and mouth whenever the state emblem appeared. His lapse in concentration, earlier that evening, brought it all rushing back. He was isolated from the rest of the world. He wanted to get out.

Mabel babbled the next morning as the Bensons headed to work. They arrived at the Eradiction factory twenty minutes later.

As an Eradict, Perry's job was to destroy evidence that the humanoids ever existed. While the Demiurge openly referred to this former society in speeches made on Recreation Day and in The Borean Bible, they wanted all items proving their existence to be demolished. Therefore, Eradicts spent their days reviewing items from the humanoids, explaining why those objects were evil, and destroying them.

Perry doubted that this monotonous process was truly necessary. He felt convinced that all items from the humanoids had been destroyed when the Holy State of Borea took power centuries ago. Why eradicate cities and countries, but not the objects that existed within them? *Surely*, he thought, *the items he was employed to destroy were replicas.* In his mind, Eradict factories only existed to keep Borean citizens busy, and make them feel valuable in erasing the humanoids from existence.

'Here we are, darling,' said Mabel as the pair arrived at the factory. It was an enormous building with hundreds of windows spaced along the front wall.

'Please identify yourself,' demanded a voice coming from the black entrance doors.

'May we all remain loyal to the Holy State of Borea.'

Perry entered. The entire factory consisted of one hall. Throughout the room were thousands of citizens seated at rectangular desks. Each workstation had a huge chute above it that dropped objects in front of the citizen.

Perry's vehicle pulled up at a desk. In the wheelchair beside his was a pencil-like woman, prattling about something known as a 'fiction book'.

'… children were often distracted for this reason. By idolising make-believe stories and characters that did not exist, they were unable to focus their efforts on …'

To Perry's left, meanwhile, a muscular man with short brown hair grunted and snorted as he tore apart something known as a 'cushion'.

A stringy, glistening silver ornament landed on Perry's desk.

'This is an ornament known by the humanoids as 'tinsel',' said Perry. 'They used it to decorate trees placed inside their houses. Tinsel is an extremely evil object because it encourages the cutting down of trees, which is a disgraceful thing to do. The humanoids particularly used tinsel at a period known as 'Christmas', during which they celebrated the birth of a holy child born to save the world. This, too, makes tinsel an object of pure evil, as the only holy thing in the world is the Holy State of Borea.'

'Thank you, Perry Benson,' said a voice hidden inside his desk. 'Please dispose of the object.'

Perry increased the volume of his grunts as he gashed at the tinsel with his hands, giving the impression of someone determined to destroy the anti-state poison. In reality, his zeal stemmed from anger at the Demiurge, rather than the humanoids – channelling his frustrations in this way made the job more tolerable.

'Thank you, Perry Benson. You have successfully destroyed the tinsel. Please wait for your next assignment.'

The desk surface opened and the tinsel fell inside.

'Good morning, fellow citizen!' said the pencil-like woman on Perry's right. 'My name is Eliza. What is yours?'

'Good morning. My name is Perry.'

'I feel obliged by the Holy State of Borea to say, Perry, that your destruction of the tinsel was truly awe-inspiring. You are quite the specimen!'

'Thank you. It is my honour to rid the Holy State of Borea of all evidence of the humanoids. You, too, destroyed your fiction book most admirably.'

'A specimen like yourself *must* produce a ripe offspring,' continued Eliza, narrowing her eyes. 'Do you have a child?'

'No, not yet. My wife and I shall copulate tonight, to satisfy the Holy State of Borea.'

'You are a magnificent specimen, and I'm sure that you will nourish the state soon.'

Perry forced a smile and thanked her, while wishing that she would stop calling him a specimen. An oval-shaped ball fell onto his desk and he raised his voice towards the chute.

'This is an object known by the humanoids as a 'rugby ball'. It was an extremely evil creation, used for a recreational game known as 'rugby'. This wicked object encouraged humanoids to partake in recreational physical activity, and therefore spend less time preserving the natural world. That's why the rugby ball was one of the evillest objects ever created.'

As Perry destroyed the ball, the muscular man to his left spoke up: 'You're very dedicated, aren't you, sir?'

'I live to serve the Holy State of Borea.'

'My name is Britton,' said the man, staring around the hall. 'It's magnificent, isn't it? Have you ever thought about the magnitude of what the Holy State of Borea is achieving? I mean, a factory such as this would have been unprecedented under the humanoids – they seemed to spend all their time lounging around and destroying the natural world. This quantity of people would only have been seen together at recreational events, nowhere else. Even this conversation would have been unlikely, as the humanoids only spoke about matters concerning the destruction of the natural world. Fascinating, to think how citizens have evolved under the Holy State of Borea. How grateful we all must be!'

He spread his arms wide above his head and looked up to the roof of the factory.

'Yes, indeed,' Perry muttered.

Various objects fell on Perry's desk as the day wore on: a book titled 'Alice in Wonderland'; a DVD player; a pile of glue; and many objects besides. At the end of the day, Perry waved to Eliza and Britton.

'Goodbye. May we all remain loyal to the Holy State of Borea.'

'Until the end!' Eliza and Britton called back together.

Perry's wheelchair emerged beneath a grey, gloomy sky. Clouds smothered the setting sun, casting the region into darkness and rinsing Perry in showers of rain. When he arrived in Tambamba, he took no notice of his surroundings, but instead cringed at the declaration of a woman seated in the wheelchair behind his.

'What a delightful deluge of rain to wash away the sins of the humanoids!'

Perry arrived at his house grateful to be sheltered from the rain outside. His gratitude was replaced by confusion, however, as he discovered two, rather than one, wheelchairs waiting outside the house.

'May we all remain loyal to the Holy State of Borea,' he said, rising from his vehicle.

Once indoors, the metallic rods changed his clothes.

'Mabel?'

'Up here, darling!'

She sounded happy, which was not a good sign. Perry

climbed the stairs and saw a small man standing by the toilet. He wore a trench coat hanging down to the floor, hovering just above a pair of well-polished shoes. His dark hair was pushed back to reveal an enormous forehead and his eyes were angry and alert. A notebook rested in his hand.

'May we all remain loyal to the Holy State of Borea,' said Perry.

'Until the end.'

'He is here for our bi-annual Stabilising, darling!' said Mabel, skipping out of the bedroom and throwing her arms around her husband's neck. 'Isn't that wonderful?'

'It is my job to reassure the state of your unwavering loyalty to the regime, Perry Benson,' said the Stabiliser. 'This is a compulsory process for all citizens."

'We understand, of course!' assured Mabel.

The man turned back and pressed his nose against the toilet seat for several seconds. 'Seems to be in order. What did you think of the Secular dancing on Recreation Day, Perry Benson?'

'Magnificent,' Perry replied.

The man marched through the hallway and stepped downstairs. The Bensons followed, sitting at the kitchen table as the Stabiliser scribbled something in his notebook.

'Can I help at all?' asked Perry, feeling disconcerted.

'No. Let us begin.' As the man said so, Perry squirmed in his chair – the state emblem, with its three sticks of bamboo, was printed on the back of the notebook. He jumped up from the table and stumbled out of the room, choking and coughing as he fell down at the bottom of the staircase. His lungs squeezed together and his head span. The entire world shrunk, and only Perry and the state emblem remained. He sat down on the floor and restored himself to calmness, before trudging back to the kitchen several minutes later.

'Is everything all right?' asked the Stabiliser. Perry's wife glowered.

'Yes, fine,' said Perry, feigning a smile. 'I just felt overwhelmed by the majesty of the Holy State of Borea.'

'Quite natural,' said the Stabiliser, surveying Perry up and down. 'Well then, to pay homage to the Holy State of Borea to which we all serve, let us begin. I feel no need to hear the confession from your wife, Perry Benson, for she shows the utmost reverence for the Holy State of Borea. I do, however, have great interest in hearing your own confession. Please go ahead. I shall be watching closely.'

Perry took a deep breath before speaking.

'My name is Perry Benson. I live under the Holy State of Borea, in a village called Tambamba. The Holy State of Borea was founded long ago, before anyone can remember. Religious worship, homosexuality and headwear are three examples of forbidden practices in the Holy State of Borea.

'There are two reasons for which a citizen may leave their house: to work, or to attend Recreation Day.'

The Stabiliser scribbled in his notebook.

'Work takes place in the Holy State of Borea every day between Thursday and Tuesday. The Holy State of Borea may use any method necessary to monitor and ensure a citizen's loyalty to the regime.'

A smile lingered across the Stabiliser's bottom lip as

he stopped writing.

'If an individual is unmarried at the age of thirty, the Holy State of Borea will randomly assign them a partner with whom they must co-exist. Once married, two individuals may never terminate their marriage. Parents are only permitted to bear one child, and they have a choice of twelve male names and twelve female names to which they may assign their child.'

The glinting smile vanished from the Stabiliser's face and was replaced by a definite frown. He glared at Perry and scribbled in his notebook. Perry glanced over at his wife, who looked irate. Had he said something wrong?

'Two individuals are eligible to marry if they are aged within three years of –'

'What is a disability?' cut in the Stabiliser, glaring at Perry.

'Something that makes a citizen act out against the state. Having a mental or physical disability is the ultimate evil.'

'When may those with disabilities be allowed to live in the Holy State of Borea?'

'Never. It is for everyone's safety that they are removed from existence.'

The man stopped scribbling and put his notebook away. Perry's confession was over.

'Well then,' snarled the Stabiliser, 'everything appears to be in order. I shall be leaving. Keep up your dutiful service.'

There was no emotion in these final words, and the Stabiliser marched past Perry and out of the house before he had the chance to wish him a good evening. Mabel stormed from the room.

What had Perry said to make the Stabiliser doubt him? He tried to think, and recalled a negative reaction following his statement that 'parents are only permitted to bear one child'.

Of course, it was obvious: he used the word *only*. He must not imply that any law is a negative thing, or that Borean parents were somehow limited.

The state would now monitor him. If he wanted to continue living in Borea, he must be sure not to misspeak again. But Perry was unbothered by this, and resented the world in which he was forced to live.

He hated that the Demiurge killed its citizens for being born with a disability. He hated that the Demiurge tracked and listened to everything he did. He hated that the Demiurge arrested people just for stroking an animal.

Did he really care if his disloyalty was discovered? Did he care if they locked him up, or worse? His life was a prison sentence, and he did not want to continue existing under the pretence of being free. Borea confined him to a labyrinth of suffering and repression and pain.

'I demand that you copulate with me!' screamed Mabel, reappearing in the kitchen. 'Now!'

Perry gulped, pressed his lips together, and nodded. As he walked upstairs and entered the bedroom, the lights in the house dimmed. Repetitive, methodical music drummed throughout the room. The music was easily recognisable: 'Yearn at the lightest day', a song performed in the singing arena at Recreation Day.

"When the Holy State first came to be…"

Perry's wife sang along to the music. Light exposed every spotless corner of the room.

"… Borea sets me free!"

Mabel undressed. Each string of fibre loosened from her waist and slid down her body, like a snake shedding its skin.

"If ever a Crolax comes near me…'

No more clothing touched his wife's skin. Her naked body blurred until only a series of circles and rectangles stood opposite Perry. He looked down to see that his clothes had also been removed. The drum beat louder. The glaring light sharpened.

"… Bestowed upon a tree!"

His wife slithered into the far corner of the bed, hazy and blurred yet indisputably gesturing for him to come closer. His feet stepped one in front of the other as the rain spattered outside.

"If the Crolax ever tries to flee …"

Two rectangles pointed upwards in front of him, parallel to

one another. He moved his body in between them, obedient and dutiful.

"… Batter it on the knee!"

Blinding light burned against the walls and a misty white took over the room. Soundless grunts coursed through the walls of the building, but Perry shut his eyes. A pained sound came from his mouth.

The bed shook against his body. The water hammering against the window merged with his own imagination. He heard an animalistic squeal. Finally, the muffled white eased against his eyelids, and he saw two rectangles contracting against the bed, moving away from his body.

Applause filled the room. The sound of Borean citizens whooping and cheering could be heard. The light sharpened throughout the room until Perry was finally in control of his senses. He shut his eyes, pulled away from the bed, and crawled across the floor. It did not matter where he was going – he just wanted to be away from his wife.

Perry knew, now, that it would require sacrifice to be elevated above the labyrinth of Borean life. He picked up his clothes and slipped them back over his body. On the other side of the room, serene against the bed, Mabel's naked body sat upright against the frame.

'You would really be better off grunting a bit more quietly during copulation; I couldn't hear the holy state music. Although, I was honoured by how quickly you shut your eyes during the proceedings. The Holy State of Borea tells its citizens to close their eyes and envisage the state emblem during copulation, and you did so right away!'

Perry felt himself wretch, and ran from the room.

'How was your day, Perry Benson?' said the staircase bannister.

'Shut up,' he mumbled, racing across to a mirror in the hallway and facing his sweaty reflection. He could not take it anymore. He shut his eyes and thought of a happier place, but none came to mind. Only the outline of bamboo was visible, etched against his eyelids. His heart pulsed through his chest. His blood pounded through his veins. He could not hide his abnormality any longer. He could not hide that he was different from everyone else.

The sound of footsteps drew closer as Mabel got out of bed. Perry pushed back his fringe and took a deep breath. It was irrational, and he was going to die, but there was only one thing he could do.

'I do hereby denounce the Holy State of Borea.'

— Chapter Four —

# The Igloo

Sirens blared through the Bensons house as metallic rods converged on Perry's body, lifting him up and slamming him against the wall. He was locked beneath an iron grip. The alarm continued for some moments, until yielding to a robotic voice blaring over the intercom.

'Until the end. Until the end. Until the end.'

Mabel appeared, hopping from one leg to the other, flailing each arm closer to striking him yet barely avoiding contact. She spat in Perry's face.

'Until the end. Until the end. Until the end.'

The lights dimmed throughout the house as the metallic rods gripped tighter. A resounding smash signalled more entrants into the property, and Mabel backed away. Faceless men and women streamed down the corridor, uniformed in black. They surrounded Perry as the rods clutching his body let go, allowing new rods farther along the wall to take over. He was transported towards the staircase and down to the ground floor.

'Until the end. Until the end. Until the end.'

The rods dropped Perry at the front door, and the Demiurge picked him up. They marched him outside, ridding the natural and logical world of the venom infiltrating its ranks as he was carried into a black aircraft.

He was dropped inside the vehicle as someone stepped up from the rear. It was a middle-aged man with short bristles of black hair.

'Until the end,' he said, withdrawing a needle from his armour. Perry blinked as the man injected it into his arm. His vision became hazy, then black, as he stared at the roof of the black aircraft about to take him to an even blacker future.

\*\*\*

Perry's head fell back against a hard surface. He opened his eyelids, but could not see beyond a reflective white light. His entire body shook, vulnerable to a chilling air. The ground beneath him was white, as were the walls surrounding him.

He was sitting in an igloo.

Perry jumped up and ran to the entrance, but it was covered with metallic bars. His body shook from the snow all around, and as he looked down, he saw that he was completely naked. He span back around and saw a white, rectangular table in the centre of the igloo. He shrieked with glee and jumped onto it, lying down to avoid the freezing snow.

'Ouch!'

The surface was ridged. Small, unnoticeable spikes pointed up from the table, cutting into his back. He leapt up as his blood dripped onto the snow. The cold seeped into his muscles, leaving him paralysed as he realised where he was.

This was the state prison. He was here to be tortured. This was where he would die.

He paced around the igloo, trying to keep the blood pumping through his freezing loins. He glanced between the bars, and saw snow stretching for kilometres. Only now, stepping closer, did he realise that he was looking at hundreds, if not thousands, of other small igloos. He could not see the entrance to any of them – they were all facing the other way. But as Perry forced his teeth to stop chattering, he heard the screams and shouts of prisoners in the surrounding igloos.

'Help!' cried Perry. He saw a distant figure walk between two igloos. Its black uniform was silhouetted in a fine silver mist. 'Help me – please!'

Perry's shouts were drowned out by the other prisoners' screams, echoing as though they were standing next to him.

Perry pressed his face against the bars and looked upwards. Far above, beyond a swirling mist, was the roof of an enormous dome. The igloos were all inside the structure. Was the snow beneath his feet even real?

*You're overreacting*, Perry told himself. *You can only feel the cold because you aren't wearing any clothes. You have to stay strong, and hold on, until someone comes for help.*

But Perry knew, as he repeated these words in his head, that it was nonsense. No one was coming to help. This was the last room he would ever stand in. The state had left him here to die.

The distant figure marched between the thousands of igloos, its head gazing side to side. 'Come over here! Help me!' yelled Perry, as it halted a few metres away.

It was a man with dark brown hair and hazel eyes. His face was pale and his eyebrows were furrowed. A black thread ran between his lips, sewing them together, but Perry instead gazed at the body of the man, which was covered in a smooth, shiny suit of armour. Engraved across the chest was the word: 'Stitcher'.

The Stitcher stepped up to the bars of Perry's igloo and held out a sharp silver knife.

'Who are you?' said Perry. The Stitcher blinked, but did not respond, and Perry stared again at the thin, black stitching encircling his mouth. 'Can you – can you talk?'

The Stitcher shook his head. His ears turned increasingly red in the freezing room, as Perry wondered whether the armoured suit was moving independently of the man's head.

Perry took the knife. The Stitcher marched away, but his head peered back, straining the corners of his lips sideways and fighting against the black thread trapping his mouth. Finally, he became silhouetted in the silver mist.

*This is the state's message,* Perry thought, looking at the knife. *Kill yourself, before we do it for you.*

He swallowed the bile rising in his throat and threw the knife to the other side of the igloo. The blunt end bounced off the wall, and Perry was struck with a sudden idea. He picked up the weapon and thrust the blade into the wall. It did not cut through the snow. He tried again on the bars covering the entrance, but they did not break. The knife had only one purpose. The state wanted Perry to kill himself.

'I'm going to die in here, aren't I?'

'Yes, that's correct,' replied a voice. Perry covered his face as the back igloo wall filled with colour.

A video was projected onto the wall. A teacher walked back and forth at the front of a classroom. Perry recognised the scene from his days at the Learning Centre: the school all Borean children attended until turning eighteen years old.

'Hello?' said Perry, but the woman could not hear him. She stared at the students sitting in front of her.

A young boy, at the back of the room, raised his hand. He sat in a wheelchair, like the other students, and had a sweeping curtain of blond hair covering his eyes.

'Yes, Perry?' said the teacher, walking to the boy's wheelchair and frowning.

'Sorry, teacher, but I do not understand the task.'

'What don't you understand, dear?'

'I don't understand why we have to do it.' The young boy lowered his brown eyebrows. 'You said that we should write why the Crolax are bad, but I do not think that they are bad.'

A gasp ran throughout the class as the students shared nervous glances. They leaned back on their chairs to hear the conversation at the back of the room.

'What do you mean, Perry?'

'I mean, is it really so bad if the Crolax are different? I am different from that girl.' The young boy named Perry pointed at a girl on the other side of the classroom, who had short dark hair arranged in a bob. She crouched down at Perry's words and shut her eyes. 'And what about him?' Perry continued, pointing at another young boy with auburn hair. 'I look nothing like him. Does that mean that I should be arrested, or he should?'

'You ask too many questions, Perry Benson,' growled the teacher. She kept her spine perfectly straight and strode to the front of the room.

In the igloo, the older Perry gasped. He did not remember the specific conversation being shown on the igloo wall, but he recognised the woman standing at the front of the classroom. She had been his teacher at the Learning Centre for his entire childhood. This meant that the boy named Perry at the back of the classroom was a younger version of himself.

The woman tutted and shook her head, addressing the class in a much louder voice. 'Let us be clear: the Crolax are evil. It is because the Crolax were allowed to exist in the humanoid society that the world was destroyed. The Holy State of Borea protects us from the Crolax. Do you understand, Perry Benson?'

The younger Perry nodded his head, and the igloo walls changed colour. The Learning Centre classroom disappeared, and was replaced by thousands of long, black podiums. Perry recognised this scene vividly, as he had been here only two days prior. It was Recreation Day in the Secular dancing arena. Beyond the thousands of podiums were two white sheets, dancing on a stage at the front of the room.

'How do the gowns move like that?' shouted one voice in the crowd.

'What's causing the gowns to move?' yelled another.

'I thank the Holy State of Borea for using its technology to bless us with the wondrous self-moving gowns!'

The video panned slightly, focusing on a row of wheelchairs lofted on podiums near the front. Each citizen, regardless of age, gender or appearance, stared wide-eyed at the dancing sheets. On the farthest podium to the right sat Perry.

The audience whooped and cheered as the dance routine concluded. The camera panned farther right onto Perry. He clapped along with the rest of the crowd, but rolled his eyes.

'Why are you showing me this?' Perry demanded of the empty igloo, as the colours shifted again.

This time, Mabel slept in a bed, alongside Perry. He turned in his sleep, mumbling under his breath. The sound was amplified as the camera zoomed in on his twisting body.

'Down with Borea. Down with Borea. Get me out of here.'

In the igloo, Perry shut his eyes as his teeth chattered. His limbs felt out of control, shaking in the icy chill as he thrust a finger into each ear and waited for the video to stop.

The wall changed colours again.

Perry and Mabel sat at their kitchen table, facing a man with a long coat and polished shoes. He wrote in a notebook, on the back of which was the state emblem. Perry's former self jumped up from the table and stumbled from the room. He arrived in the hallway and fell down, gasping for air.

The video vanished from the igloo wall.

'So, you've been watching me, have you?' said Perry, crouching in the snow. 'Not just tracking my voice, not just tracking my movements – you've been watching my every move. That's what you're saying, isn't it? You knew I was disloyal, all along.'

The screaming continued from surrounding igloos. Perry eyed the knife on the other side of the room, and wondered how long the state would torture him. Would he be stuck here forever, until he killed himself?

Perry's body went stiff over the ensuing hours. The dome was not as cold as he had first thought: he was being tortured, but the fake snow was not chilly enough for him to get hypothermia in a few hours. It would take a day or two, at least.

Perry tried sitting on the table in the middle of the igloo. He perched on the edge where the spikes were least numerous, when a robotic voice boomed through the dome.

'An announcement from the Holy State of Borea,' said the voice. 'The winner of our daily competition has been selected. Crolax number twenty-seven thousand, five hundred and fifty-five, your time has come. Submit yourself to the Holy State of Borea.'

An icy silence filled the dome as Perry peered between the bars. Ten silhouetted Stitchers marched in unison about one hundred metres to his right. They stepped up to an igloo, surrounded it, and removed the metal bars. Then, as a harrowing shriek filled the enormous dome, a naked, frail older woman was dragged across the snow and thrown to the floor.

'Shame!' bellowed a deep male voice from the igloo next to Perry's, as the Stitchers whacked the woman with batons. 'Shame! Do it yourself – do the dirty work yourself. Don't get robots to do it for you, you cowards!'

The ten Stitchers moved methodically, yet each one's head faced the opposite direction. They all wore metallic suits, just like the one that had handed Perry the dagger.

The frail woman collapsed in the snow and the Stitchers lifted her over their shoulders. They paraded her back across the dome, marching past Perry's igloo. He looked at the Stitchers' faces, and while their bodies lofted the woman above their heads, their eyes were sunken and red.

Perry turned away before he glimpsed the woman's body. He beat the floor with his fists, furious that his time on earth would end like this. The freezing cold was settling into his limbs, and he felt his feet sinking into the snow. He lay down on the ridged table, his body being absorbed into the spiky surface. It did not cut deep into his skin – only enough to cause discomfort. He closed his eyes and shut out the shrieks from the nearby igloos. It was slightly warmer up here, and he kept his body rigid as he drifted off to sleep.

His slumber was filled with images of sharp daggers, floating babies, and monsters covered in snow. He jolted awake every few minutes as he rolled onto a spike. On one of these occasions, he noticed a dark shadow looming across the opposite wall, and bolted upright from the table.

A figure stood outside the igloo door. It wore the same metallic suit as the other Stitchers, but with the addition of a huge circular helmet. Perry gasped as it pulled out two sharp blades of rock and cut away the bars crossing the entrance.

The Stitcher stepped inside. Perry clambered back against the igloo wall, terrified, as the figure pulled off its helmet. A dark-skinned man smiled down at him, rubbing his bushy goatee. He did not have a thread running through his lips, and spoke in a gentle whisper.

'Come on, Perry. Let's get you out of here.'

Perry gaped at the broken bars and the sharp rock in the unknown man's hand. He was unsure whether he was hallucinating or dreaming.

'Please don't hurt me.' Perry's teeth chattered, and he pushed back his long fringe as the unknown man smiled down at him. 'I don't know who you are, but please let me die in peace.'

'I'm here to help you, Perry.'

'No you're not,' said Perry. 'You're a Stitcher. I know that.'

'I'm not a Stitcher.' The man crouched down in the snow. 'I am here to rescue you, and to take you to Hades Forest.'

'Hades – where? I'm sorry, but you have made a mistake. I don't know who you think I am, but I – hold on!'

The conclusion popped into his brain, fully formed and finally offering an explanation. This man was making no sense, and that was because he was lying. He was a

Demiurge, sent here to trick him. Perhaps he was luring Perry to a torture chamber, or a prison worse than this one.

Perry jumped up and sprinted for the igloo exit, but the man pushed him down.

'Don't make a scene. I'm here to break you out of this prison. My name is Dolphin.'

Perry shivered. 'You're rescuing me?'

'That's right.'

'Isn't someone going to come?' said Perry, pointing at the open doorway. 'One of those Stitchers?'

'No, of course not. They don't suspect that I'm an imposter. Just come with me, Perry, and I'll explain more on the boat.'

'Boat? There's a boat?'

'Of course there's a boat,' grinned Dolphin. 'Did you expect me to come in here without an escape plan?'

'Well, I didn't expect you to come in here at all.' Snow crunched beneath Perry's toes as he stood up. He glanced at the doorway, considering whether to trust the man, when an icy chill blew into his face. Finally, with a look down at his purpling toes, Perry nodded.

Dolphin stepped out of the igloo, dragging Perry behind him as though he was a captured prisoner. The pair trudged through the snow towards the edge of the dome.

'Help me! Help me! Please.'

Perry glanced sideways at a young girl reaching out of her igloo, begging him to rescue her. He bit his tongue and marched onwards. He did not want to raise any suspicion.

'I hope you die. I hope both of you die.'

An elderly man from another igloo had spoken. His

skin was purple around his sunken eyes, and he lay in a heap on the floor, moaning and trembling.

As the edge of the dome neared, Perry shortened his steps and glanced back at the elderly man.

'There will be a time,' said Dolphin's muffled voice from beneath the helmet, 'but this is not it.'

The pair passed one final igloo and reached the enormous dome wall. Dolphin stepped up to it and placed his hand against the surface. A small rectangular door appeared in the wall, which slid upwards to create an opening through which they both walked. Perry gaped back as the doorway closed behind him.

He turned around, and looked out across a vast ocean. Sand crumbled beneath his feet, and he stepped forwards into a gorgeous midday sunlight. There was only a few metres between the edge of the dome and the ocean shoreline.

'Where are we?' said Perry. He had never seen the ocean before; he had only learned about it in the Learning Centres. Dolphin removed his helmet and squinted back, smiling through his furrowed goatee.

'Somewhere in the South Pacific.'

Perry's rescuer strolled across the sand and climbed into a long, smooth blue boat. Camouflaged against the ocean, Perry had not noticed the vehicle, but ran his hand along its exterior as he climbed inside.

Dolphin pressed a button on a dashboard at the front of the boat, and a thin, transparent screen rose out of the hull and locked the pair of them inside. Perry continued to shiver as Dolphin pressed another knob on the dashboard. Two propellors appeared on either side of the boat, and a steering wheel rose through the dashboard, as the vehicle shimmied into the ocean and set off across the waves.

'Now then,' said Dolphin, turning around and handing Perry a razor-sharp axe. 'You're going to need this.'

— Chapter Five —

# Dolphin's Tale

Perry shivered as the sun beat down over the South Pacific ocean. His body was numb and stiff, slowly adjusting to the temperature of his new surroundings. He held an axe with a wooden handle and rock blade behind his back, cradling it and peering through the transparent glass as the boat travelled across the waves.

'You can relax now,' said Dolphin, handing Perry a bowl filled with a white, fleshy substance. He steered the boat's wheel with his other hand. Perry had already tied a sheaf of vines, leaves, and twigs, provided by Dolphin, around his crotch, and now bit into the strange food.

'What is this?' he murmured between bites.

'Fish.'

Perry spat onto the floor, coughing and gagging. 'Why didn't you tell me? I've never eaten an animal before!'

'It seemed like the best way to cross that hurdle. Keep eating, Perry. It'll help.'

Perry left the fish on the floor and watched the gentle, sparkling blue waves passing beneath the boat. 'How do you know my name?'

'This vehicle has many impressive features. One of

them is this.' Dolphin pressed a pink button on the dashboard and a list appeared in front of Perry's face, projected by some invisible device into the air. He scrolled his finger downwards, and the list showed thousands of names, with coordinates matching each person. 'This provides detailed information on every Crolax, including which igloo they are in.'

Perry poked the side of the boat. 'What is this thing?'

'It belongs to the state. Well, not anymore, but it did.'

'So, um… where exactly are we going?'

'Ah, yes. Of course.' Dolphin smiled. 'We are going to Hades Forest. But you won't understand what that is until I tell you more about myself, and why, and how, I've just rescued you from the state prison.'

Perry looked away from the list of Crolax and held his breath as Dolphin started speaking.

'I used to live in Borea, just like you. I grew up under the state's regime, and was taught to obey its every command. But I was disloyal to the Demiurge. I disagreed with the lack of freedom granted to citizens. I believed that there had to be a better way. Eventually, I denounced the state, and was taken to the prison that we just left.

'Back then, the prison was slightly different. It wasn't a simulated snow dome that froze the Crolax to death. Instead, it was a scorching desert.'

'Were you locked inside a hut, like the igloo I was in?' asked Perry.

'No. Every prisoner could roam freely around the dome. There weren't any Stitchers in there. It was so hot, though, that every Crolax lay in the sand, waiting to die. It was completely silent, even though thousands of people were inside the prison.

'I went over to a group of five people, sitting together at the edge of the dome. One was a young boy, one was a very fat lady, and the other three were adult men. No one spoke, they just glanced over their shoulders at me. I sat with them for several hours, thinking, before finally speaking up.'

'What did you say?'

'That we were united by the same cause. That if we worked together, we could find a way out of the prison.

'We discussed a plan. All around the dome, there were people charging into the wall, throwing their bodies against it and trying to break through. But this didn't work. I knew that we could not exit the dome through the sides, and it was impossible to climb up to the roof, as there were no ridges on the wall. If there was any chance of getting out of there, we had to go down.'

'Down?'

'The six of us clawed through the sand. There was metres and metres of it, but I knew it had to end somewhere. I don't know what we were expecting – we just hoped for the best. We kept digging as the heat increased in the dome. Finally, when we were just about to give up, two Stitchers marched through a doorway into the arena. They both had batons in their hands. They walked towards us and drew back their weapons.'

'Why?'

'Clearly, the Demiurge had seen what we were doing, and they didn't like it. I think that there was something beneath the sand that they didn't want us to find.

'I tackled one of the Stitchers to the ground. It fought back, and the second punched me, but there were six of us against two of them. We overpowered the bodies and held them down with the help of four other strangers. I ordered the others to carry the Stitchers to a dome wall. Then, I pressed one of their gloved hands against the surface, and a door appeared. I stepped out and found myself on a beach.'

'The same beach we were just on?'

'Yes. There was a boat moored on the sand, which had just been used by the Stitchers. I looked across the ocean, and saw dozens more boats headed towards the beach. More Stitchers were coming, so I jumped in the boat and called for the group of five to join me.

'On the boat's dashboard, there was a flashing purple button with the words 'Automated Destination' written beneath. I pushed it, and two levers sprung out of the inside of the boat. One fixed itself to the floor on my right, and the other to the floor on my left. I pressed the left one, and the boat shifted backwards in the sand. I pressed the right lever, and it climbed forwards out of the sand and across the ocean.'

'Did the other Stitchers intercept you?'

'No. I'm sure you've noticed, Perry, that the Stitchers' heads aren't in control of their bodies. They are just the Demiurge's minions, and they do whatever they are told via satellite signal. Stitchers are only programmed to carry out a limited number of instructions. There was no allowance for our unprecedented situation.

'Next, a steering wheel rose through the dashboard. I guided us across the waves, away from the dome where hundreds of Crolax were now streaming onto the beach. Looking back, I saw the Stitchers arrive on the island and massacre the Crolax. No boat came after us – they had all been instructed to kill as many prisoners as possible.'

Dolphin paused, and a tear dropped onto the floor.

'We travelled for three days and two nights. I learned the names of the other people: the young boy was called Colby. The three men were called Diablo, Yasha, and Crank. The woman was called Tovia.'

Perry raised his eyebrows. 'But those aren't Borean names.'

'They made up new names for themselves. No one wanted to identify with Borea. Next, we found supplies hidden beneath the floorboards of the boat, and shared them around.'

'Supplies?'

'For the Demiurge, in case they ever used the boat. That's why there was an option to turn off the automated location.

'We travelled until we found land. I saw a small shape on the horizon one morning, and headed towards it. It was an island made up of a huge forest stretching for thousands of metres. We carried the boat into the forest, and spent the next few days rationing our supplies.

'Eventually, after talking more and more to my five companions, it became clear that I was surrounded by the most violent people I had ever met. These were not passive rebels against the state. They wanted blood.'

'What do you mean?' asked Perry.

'I wanted a peaceful life, Perry. I had never engaged in combat before. But, when I spoke to the others about what they wanted our next step to be, their response was unanimous: to take on the state, and wage war against them.

'I did not like this idea. Escaping the dome had exhausted me, and I suspected that it would not be long before the state found this marooned island that we were stranded on, and killed us. Nonetheless, I was outvoted five to one.'

'But you were the only reason these people were free in the first place,' said Perry. 'Surely you had the right to overrule them.'

Dolphin smiled, but his lip quivered. 'Let's just say that my companions made it clear, in no uncertain terms, that they would take matters into their own hands if I did not agree.

'We did not speak to each other for the rest of that night. I woke up several hours later, surrounded by panicked shouting. A shape had appeared on the beach, walking towards the forest with a baton in each hand.

'The six of us ran forwards and fought the Stitcher. We struggled at first, but then Colby punched its head, which was that of a young girl. With every blow to the head, the body crumpled to the ground, until the little girl was finally killed. The Stitcher's body fell down, and moved no more.

'We searched the rest of the island, and the ocean, but the Stitcher had come alone.'

'Why?'

'Like I said, the Stitchers are programmed by the state.

I think the Demiurge sent one Stitcher to every island across the ocean, to defeat us, wherever we were hiding. It might've worked if we hadn't discovered that killing the head of the Stitcher is the way to destroy its body.

'Next, we carried the deceased Stitcher's boat, moored on the sand, into the forest. We now had two boats, rather than one. We then tried to pull the Stitcher's armour off its body, but couldn't do it. So, we built some sharp instruments – spears, axes and so on – and used these to separate the armour from the body. Eventually, after hours, we succeeded. Beneath the armour was the young girl's body, but she was stiff and dead, so we threw her into the ocean.

'Colby put on the metal glove from the armour, and found that it expanded to fit his slightly larger hand. Furthermore, it did not control his body as it had with the Stitchers in the prison. Clearly, we had destroyed the suit's technology. Colby put on the rest of the armour, and we all sat down to discuss our next move.

'My five companions were fascinated by an unimaginably reckless plan. They wanted to return to the state prison, and rescue more prisoners. In their eyes, that was the only way of building up an army that could take on the state.

'Naturally, I said that returning would be suicide, but I was ignored. The others theorised that we could use the Stitcher suit to break back into the prison. We already knew that entry was gained by pressing the metal glove against the dome wall – and now we had the suit in our control, we could do this ourselves.

'Five of us stayed on the island and hunted animals for

food, while Colby set off across the ocean.

'We waited nearly ten days, but Colby eventually returned with a young girl. He reported that no alarms had been set off during his heist, but that he had encountered an unexpected obstacle. The inside of the dome was no longer a scorching desert, but a freezing landscape filled with igloos.'

'Was that to provide extra protection, because of the breakout you caused?' said Perry.

'Definitely. Colby said that each prisoner was in a different igloo, with bars across the entrance. So, improvising, he had gone back outside and collected two sharp rocks from the shoreline. Then, he used these to cut away the bars covering the young girl's igloo, and took her outside with him. To the rest of the prisoners in the dome, they suspected that she was being taken to her death, or some other ghastly fate. No one suspected a thing.'

'What happened next?' asked Perry.

'After the success of Colby's journey, my companions formed a plan. Colby would return to the dome once every thirty days to rescue a new prisoner. This would allow us to build up an army.'

'So, is that why I'm here?' said Perry. 'Am I one of the prisoners being rescued, and recruited to join the army?'

'Well, not exactly. You see, in the month that followed the first rescuing, a schism formed on the island. My companions entered premature, but heated, discussions on how to dispose of the Demiurge once we captured them.

'Colby and the young girl believed that the Demiurge should be murdered. Diablo believed that they should be tortured. Yasha believed that they should be enslaved. Tovia believed that they should be systematically raped. And Crank believed that they should be directly usurped – that we should claim all their possessions for our own, and rule the world in their place.

'As the days went by, I became increasingly ostracised. The group stopped sharing food with me; they threatened me with death if I took too much water. Meanwhile, what started as a light discussion about how to punish the Demiurge had since created a deep divide in the group. Each person felt passionately, and hated anyone who disagreed with their solution.

'I sensed an opportunity, and acted. I deliberately exacerbated tensions in the group. I spoke to Diablo privately, saying that his idea was the best. I then separately told Tovia, Yasha, Colby and Crank the same thing. Slowly, all six of them warmed to me and vied for my affection. Each person got jealous when another was friendly to me, and in only a few days, I became the most respected person in the group.

'Finally, I gathered everyone around the campfire one night and made a proposition that appealed to their ruthlessness. I suggested that, to settle the dispute, there be a five-way fight between Diablo, Yasha, Colby, Crank and Tovia. Whoever wins, would get to decide on the final treatment of the Demiurge.

'Everyone agreed, but, showing their violent dispositions, requested higher stakes. Each person wanted to form their own private army – a tribe – with which they could take on their four rivals. In only a few days on the island, my companions had become distracted from the real enemy: they now sought to kill each other.

'Internally, I thought that this was a ghastly idea, but I knew that to deny these individuals the chance to rise to the top of the pile would result in me being killed, too. So, as the impartial party, it was decreed that every month I would be the one who travelled to the state prison and freed a prisoner. I would then assign each one to either the murder, torture, rape, slavery or thievery tribe.'

'Thievery?' asked Perry.

'Crank's tribe. He wanted to take the Demiurge's possessions for his own, and steal their position as leaders of the world.' Dolphin's shoulders slumped. 'That's why you are here, Perry. To join the thievery tribe, and fight with them in a battle to the death against the four others.'

Perry gulped as he wriggled his toes and stretched his neck. Any feeling returning to his muscles immediately disappeared. *Surely*, he thought, *Dolphin was not serious.* He had never fought anyone before. A sharp ringing filled his ears, and he slumped backwards.

'Listen, Perry. I'm not a bad person. I want the best for everyone – especially those who have faced persecution from the state. But life is never so simple. I had to do what was necessary to keep myself alive, and now you have to do the same. With those five leaders, it was inevitably going to end in conflict. I just found a way to keep myself alive while that happened.'

'Can't I stay with you?' muttered Perry.

Dolphin shook his head, and pointed ahead: 'Look – that'll be them, now.'

Perry glanced up, feeling extremely ill and wishing that he were still in the state prison. An enormous island approached, with five people standing on the shore. Perry looked at the half-eaten fish on the floor, then at the tribe on the approaching beach, and vomited into the corner of the boat. Dolphin did not turn around, but moored the vehicle onto the sand and pressed a button on the dashboard. The screen retreated into the body of the boat, as did the steering wheel. He then picked up a wooden mask hidden beneath his seat. It had the face of a Dolphin carved into the front, and he placed it over his entire head so that no skin was visible.

Perry clambered out and gaped at the unknown men and women. They did not wave, cheer, or acknowledge his presence in any way.

A bald man with beige skin stepped forwards to greet Dolphin. 'My Lord.'

'Look after him, and fight well,' said Dolphin from beneath the headgear. He turned to Perry. 'Farewell, my friend. I hope we meet again someday.'

And with one final nod, Dolphin dragged the boat across the sand and disappeared into the forest.

# Chapter Six

# Hades Forest

Perry stood on the beach, shifting from leg to leg as the hot sand burned the soles of his feet. He glanced up at the five strangers, staring at him without expression. Finally, as he went to open his mouth and speak, a jet of water crashed him to the floor.

Liquid squeezed up Perry's nose, and he flailed his arms left and right to bat away the flood.

'Don't move.'

Perry peered up as the water stopped. The tribe marched towards him.

'Told 'chu 'dis thing'ud come in handy!' cheered a swaying woman, bouncing across the sand with a wooden apparatus in her arms.

'Stay still,' said a second woman.

'Ya' king is doin' you enough of a favour just comin' out to rescue ya' – we could leave ya' for dead, y'know.'

Perry blinked away the remaining water and observed the latter two speakers. The former was a young woman with smooth olive skin and bright silver hair tied in a bandana. The other was a stern-faced bald man with beige skin, a thick goatee and scars across his face.

'I don't want any trouble,' muttered Perry, 'I really don't.'

'Oh, honestly, just be quiet,' hissed the silver-haired woman.

'Yeah, we've got to get ya' out of here,' said the stern man.

'I don't want to die,' whispered Perry, squeezing his knees together and rocking across the sand. 'Please don't kill me. I don't want to die.'

'Did ya' not listen to Dolphin? We're not here to kill you. You're part of our tribe.'

The olive-skinned woman flicked a mealworm balancing on her finger at Perry's face. He choked as it landed in his mouth.

'That's better,' she smiled.

'We should get him out of here, before someone sees,' said a third woman. The rest of the group mumbled their assent, picked a long wooden plank off the floor behind them, and used it to lift Perry into the air. They balanced it between their shoulders as Perry caught his breath, but said nothing.

'This isn't going to work,' said the bald man, leading them into the humid forest. Perry, who had his eyes shut, heard him turn back. 'Turn him over.'

'Why?'

'His belly is stickin' out. Anyone could be watchin' right now. I don't want them seein' how fat he is.'

Several hands rolled Perry over. He moaned for a few seconds but then fell silent. The five figures commenced hushed conversation, when a thin, slippery object touched his cheek. He flinched as the woman holding the back-right corner of the plank whispered in his ear.

'It is important that you eat, to maintain your energy.'

She coughed and then, with a sneeze, raised her voice to ask another warrior an inaudible question. Perry opened his eyes and saw that she had given him a fish, like the one from the boat. He ignored it as the group walked on.

Even though it was after noon, the forest grew dark as the tribe travelled. Perry peered between cracks in the wooden plank and saw creatures blinking at him from every direction. The entire forest was filled with animals, scuttering through the undergrowth.

Finally, light burst through the trees and the group reached a circular clearing. Perry was thrown onto his back, facing his new surroundings.

Palm and coconut trees reached high above a rounded cave with five tunnelled entrances. While the clearing was vast, the cave took up half of the space. Each entrance tunnel was pitch black inside.

A movement in the corner of Perry's eye brought his attention to a new structure. A rough-looking Iberian ibex ran along a bridge built high in the emergent layer of the forest. But this was not the only bridge; a comprehensive and intertwining network ran across one another, held up by vines tied to nearby trees. So transfixed by the cave, Perry had not seen this assembly of wood, yet it was now impossible to miss. One bridge carried far to Perry's right-hand side, steeping and curving downwards from the trees and providing a useful walkway.

The stern-faced man grabbed Perry by the shoulder and thrust him down a tunnel towards the main cave.

The tunnel was short, dark, and possessed by an impairing smell. Mould and slime lined the walls. The group pressed behind him, and a few steps brought them to a large slab of rock with hundreds of diamond-shaped handles across it. The stern-faced man stepped forwards and twisted one of the handles. The stone door was pushed aside and, with a last look backwards, the man grabbed Perry by the hair and dragged him into the cave.

The strangers stood in a line. The bald man and silver-haired woman frowned; the skinny woman who had given him food stared at her reptilian feet. The slurring fat woman drank from a wooden bottle. The fifth warrior, a burly black man with spiked pink and turquoise hair, gazed at a fly hovering centimetres from his face. They were all silhouetted by the flames lining the cave walls, and each wore a sheaf of leaves around their crotch, with an additional bunch around the breasts of the women.

'What's ya' name, kiddo?' said the bald man, chewing a beetle.

'Perry.'

'Village?' said the silver-haired woman.

'Tambamba.'

They both circled him, sizing him up as a pack of hyenas might a meal. Only now was Perry able to fully regard the rest of the cave.

It was not at all what he had expected. A flowery fragrance drifted through the room. Various armchairs and beds were dotted around the cave, each carved from wood.

Instead of a cold, hard surface beneath Perry's feet, he stood on a soft, matted carpet of interwoven vines. The circular cave wall held burning flames atop stone torches, each surrounded by ledges. The vines across the floor continued up the walls in many places, creating different ladders to each ledge. At the centre of the room was an enormous Juniper tree, stretching almost twenty metres to the roof.

'Tell me, kiddo,' said the bald man, 'why do ya' look like that?'

The silver woman extended one of her ears.

'Umm...' mumbled Perry, pushing back his fringe. 'Well, my father was rather fat, and my mother had quite a lot of –'

'Kirito thinks that the new person looks like a dog,' said the high-pitched voice of the burly man. Several warriors sniggered. Perry was not sure who 'Kirito' referred to.

'Yeah, he does,' said the leading man. 'You look like a dog, don't ya', kiddo?'

This time, Perry identified the man's rhetoric; he was being dared to disagree, and treated it as such. The silver-haired woman stepped up to his face, pushed his hair back and sniffed his ear.

'He smells like a dog.'

All laughed except the skinny woman and the leading man, the latter of whom stepped forwards to confirm the woman's judgement. Perry stood rooted to the spot, hoping that he would not be killed.

'Yeah. You do, don't ya', kiddo?'

Perry did not respond. The pair walked back to join the rest of the group and turned to face him once more.

'Please don't kill me,' said Perry.

'Kirito thinks that the tribe leader should tell the new person the Leagros warriors' names.'

The tribe leader chewed the beetle even harder. 'I am the king of Leagros,' he said, stroking his goatee, 'and you can call me Crank.' He looked along the line, gesturing for them each to say their names.

The skinny woman sneezed before introducing herself as: 'Avanti.'

'Chintu,' growled the silver-haired woman with the bandana.

'Kirito,' said the muscular black man with fluorescent hair.

'Saskat,' slurred the swaying woman, fiddling with the leaves around her breasts and untying them from her body. Two enormous bosoms appeared, hanging down and moulding into her unbelievably fat body. She winked at Perry and sucked on her finger.

'You now find ya'self in the Leagros tribe of Hades Forest,' said Crank, stepping forwards into the firelight. 'Avanti will explain to you, in greater detail, who we are up against. Make sure ya' pay careful attention.'

The skinny woman moved forwards. 'We won't be leaving the cave, and will start with Leagros.'

'Liven up!' smirked Chintu, flicking another meal-worm into Perry's hair. He recoiled, and gave her a loathing look which she returned with increased ferocity. Saskat blew on a small whistle and pressed her breasts together.

Crank scooped up a beetle from the floor and chewed it as Avanti went on.

'I am going to tell you everything you need to know about our tribe: Leagros. You need to remember everything I tell you. If you don't, there is a strong likelihood that you will die. The first thing you need to understand is that Leagros operates within a theme.'

'Theme?'

'Each tribe has developed its own fighting style, according to what they believe to be the rightful future punishment for the Demiurge. In Leagros, we steal our opponents' supplies.'

'What do the other tribes do?'

'Our opponents all believe that it is more important to dominate your opponent than kill them. They manifest this in different ways. It is their belief that if you maim your opponent physically and mentally, without killing them, then you impregnate yourself into their psyche forevermore. This is more powerful than death.'

'How?' said Perry, still waking up yet determined to catch on. 'How can anything be worse than death?'

'Humans recover from a broken toe or sprained ankle,' said Avanti, 'but penetrating the mind of your victim – living in their brain – is far more powerful. If they can no longer see a cave without screaming for fear; if they can no longer see a man with black skin without crying on the floor and begging for death... that is a far more effective way of defeating your enemy.'

'Why don't you guys fight in this way?' asked Perry.

Crank spat on the vine carpet.

'We have our own methods. Leagros puts the odds in our favour by stealing. Entering the camps of other tribes and taking their supplies means that they are driven back into the forest. When their food is taken, they go and hunt some more. When their weapons are stolen, they design a new one using forest resources.

'By taking their supplies, the four other tribes re-enter the forest to regather what they have just lost. This means that they encounter more warriors from other tribes. The more this happens, the more conflicts there will be, and the more warriors will die. By the end, the other tribes' numbers will dwindle and Leagros will still have all our warriors alive.'

'That is, if you don't get us all killed,' said Chintu.

Perry ignored this final comment and clung onto the relief that, by the sounds of it, he would not have to kill anyone. The other tribes would do it for him.

'This doesn't mean that Leagros won't kill when necessary,' assured Chintu, retying her bandana. 'It just means that it's not our preferred method of operating. Either way, it doesn't matter, 'cause we're the best warriors in Hades Forest.'

'Besides Leagros,' Avanti went on, 'there are four tribes in Hades Forest: the slavery tribe, the rape tribe, the murder tribe and the torture tribe. Each has their own distinguished style of fighting, and each is stationed in a different part of the forest. I'll now take you through all four tribes, one-by-one, so you know what we're up against.'

'And none of them kill their victims?' asked Perry.

'None of them kill their victims. First, we have Feysal,

otherwise known as the slavery tribe. This tribe consists of six extremely tall and muscular black men. They are stationed at the northern border of the forest in a region known as Halcyon. They live on top of a small hill, meaning that fighting there puts us at an instant elevation disadvantage.

'Feysal's goal is simple: to capture and enslave. As already discussed, the four tribes focus on inflicting psychological damage, and Feysal is no different. Once captured, they take you back to Halcyon, tie you up and force you to do humiliating and degrading things. This enslavement continues until you agree to pass over crucial information on how Leagros operates: hunting times and strategies, ways into the cave, and so on. Once they have extracted every ounce of information, and ruined you psychologically, they kill you.'

'Sorry to interrupt,' said Perry, 'but can I just ask – how do you know all this? Warfare has only just started.'

Chintu kissed her teeth.

'All four tribes have tested and perfected their methods on animals over the past year,' explained Avanti. 'They also discuss their methods – something that benefits us, as we have several hideaways stationed throughout the forest which allow us to listen to their conversations.

'It is also important for you to consider each tribe's fighting style, so you can have optimum success against them. Feysal, for example, fights through hand-to-hand combat. They are the tallest and strongest warriors in the forest, and use this to their advantage. Every warrior wields a blunt-force weapon which can be thrown at opponents.

As a result, Feysal warriors often fight in two stages: first, they throw their weapon at the opponent. Second, they follow up with a series of punches and kicks. In this sense, their arsenal is twice the size of ours; their natural strength is a lethal backup, even if their main weapon fails.'

Perry took a deep breath as his brain imagined an enormous, multi-limbed ogre.

'Got all that, kiddo?' growled Crank.

'Kirito thinks that the fat man will benefit from crocodile juice,' said Kirito, handing Perry a rock-made bucket of clear liquid. Before he could drink from it, however, Crank snatched it away.

'You'll drink when ya' king says so.'

'Next up we have Taveron, otherwise known as the rape tribe,' said Avanti, sneezing and glancing between Crank and Kirito. 'All their warriors are female. Taveron is stationed in a cove beneath a waterfall on the south-east border of the forest. The cove is known as Corinthian Cove, but the wider south-east region is referred to as Blackstream. Taveron seeks to capture and rape their victims.'

'How?' asked Perry, bile rising in his throat.

'They strap large blocks of wood to their coccyx and insert them into their victim's body. While they don't receive direct sexual pleasure from this act, the domination of another person is deeply arousing for them.'

'But, you said...' Perry's voice tailed off, and he cleared his throat. 'You said earlier that these tribes have been practicing on animals.'

Avanti nodded.

'It's not pretty,' said Chintu from the back wall, showing her first sign of humanity.

Perry pushed back his fringe and placed his head in his hands as Kirito re-placed the bucket at his feet. This time, Crank did not object, and Perry drank, hoping that he would never witness such a debased exhibition of the human condition.

'Once,' Chintu said, 'we saw Taveron rape this beautiful little parrot. Can you guess what the bird did next?'

Perry felt certain that he did not want to know. 'Left the island?'

'Killed itself. It stumbled around for a few hours, flapping its wings, before flying up to this tree branch at the top of the forest and launching itself off. It didn't flap its wings on the fall down or anything.'

'Kirito would not like to be caught by Taveron.'

'As you might expect,' Avanti went on, 'you need to be a capable swimmer to fight in Corinthian Cove. Depending on where you approach from, you either have to navigate through the river or the waterfall. Fortunately, both mine and Saskat's weapons lend themselves to this.

'While Feysal prefers short-range, hand-to-hand fighting, Taveron prefers long distances. Their style is indirect and more intelligent than Feysal's. Individually they are perhaps less remarkable, but they work effectively as a team. Taveron attacks in waves: they have moves, follow-up moves, and follow-up moves to those follow-up moves. An arrow flies at you from the right; an arrow flies at you from the left; and as you step backwards to avoid them both, a snare lifts your foot into the air.

Taveron loves a booby trap. Not only do they fight from a distance, but they position various snares and trip-wires in locations throughout the forest that only they know about. Even if you are on the opposite side of the forest to Blackstream, you could still fall victim to one of their traps.

'Thirdly, we have Orynx, otherwise known as the murder tribe. This tribe wears animal masks in battle: a kitten, puppy, bunny, chick and hamster. Orynx is stationed on the east border of the forest, on a small d-shaped island made by a tributary from the East River.'

'D-shaped?'

'The run-off river forms a meander – like a curve,' she explained. 'The island in the middle is known as the Isle of Bees, so named because of the enormous beehive at the top of each of the three main trees on the isle.'

'Is this tribe led by Colby?'

'Yes, but he now identifies as 'Bunny'.'

'And I assume these guys just kill you straight away?' said Perry.

'The fat man is quite wrong,' said Kirito.

'Orynx has no interest in capturing one victim – they seek to capture two. Both victims are taken back to the Isle of Bees, where they are instructed to fight to the death. If you win, Orynx allows you to return to you tribe.'

'What? They let you go?'

'Yes. Orynx seeks to mentally scar the victor to such a point that you do one of two things: kill yourself, or compromise your tribe's ability to fight.'

'How?'

'By being so haunted when you later face Orynx in combat that you have a panic attack and make the rest of your tribe vulnerable. It is important for you to understand that a tribe with five strong warriors is more effective than a tribe with five strong warriors and one terrible one. In the latter scenario, the sixth warrior compromises the rest of the tribe, who spend too much time worrying about the sixth to focus on what they're doing themselves.

'By allowing you to re-enter the forest, Orynx hopes to kill three, four, five or six warriors from your tribe in later combat, rather than just yourself.'

'And how do they fight?' asked Perry. 'What's their strategy?'

'Orynx only has five warriors, and they are much younger than the other three tribes. Each one is shorter than yourself, and they use this to their advantage: Orynx likes to fight in the trees. They are small and light on their feet, making them inaudible in the branches. They are also adept at climbing, as their favourite pastime is to scale the three trees on the isle without disturbing the beehives. Perhaps you can guess the next thing I'm about to say?'

'They sound energetic,' Perry thought aloud.

'Correct,' said Avanti. On the back wall, even Chintu looked impressed – Perry smiled at her, but her thin lips hardened in response as she searched the floor for another mealworm to fling at him.

'Orynx are the fastest runners, the best climbers, and have the most impressive stamina in the forest. There is no downtime on the Isle of Bees. They are either hunting, climbing trees, running laps of the isle or challenging one another to duels. Even during the night, you will find two, maybe three of them awake and training.'

Perry pictured five sabre-toothed hamsters running non-stop around a rotating wheel.

'The fourth tribe is Vemlin, otherwise known as the torture tribe. This tribe consists of both men and women, with a man named Diablo as their king. Each warrior, except for him, is disfigured.'

'Disfigured?'

'Body parts missing; major limbs twisted; that sort of thing.'

'Why?'

'Diablo ordered that the Vemlin warriors distort or remove a body part several months ago, to prove their loyalty to him. He resents Dolphin's power. I think he aims to usurp him, one day.

'Vemlin is stationed at the centre of Hades Forest, in a region known as Arklow. The forest is different there than on the rest of the island: the trees are thicker, taller and more densely packed. There is an outer layer of bamboo trees which border this central region. The animals are also more lethal in this part of the forest, so you need to be alert.

'Vemlin seeks to capture, torture and kill their victims. They do this at the centre of the colony of fireflies that travels around Arklow.'

'Why there?' asked Perry. 'Doesn't the light reveal their position?'

'Diablo insists on it. He's arrogant, boastful and proud, and treats it like a challenge – he's showing the stricken tribe where their warrior is, but daring them to be stupid enough to retrieve them. Not only does Vemlin monitor the edges of the area, in case anyone jumps in, but they also believe that no one will ever get that far. The Arklow creatures are so lethal that Vemlin thinks it impossible to enter the region without being attacked, or making so much noise that Vemlin is alerted to their presence.

'Vemlin doesn't have a clearly defined strategy for how they torture their victims. It depends on what mood they're in, and the physical weaknesses of their victims. Inevitably, the torture involves the dismemberment of limbs or crucial body parts.'

'Has this got anything to do with their own disfigurement?' Perry said, feeling sick.

'Kirito suspects so,' said Kirito.

'Vemlin are proficient at fighting in all circumstances. Generally, though, they prefer to fight in the dark. Vision in Arklow is worse than the rest of the forest, so Vemlin tries to do one of two things in combat: draw their opponents into the centre of the forest, or keep fighting into the night.'

Avanti sneezed, spluttering snot down her chin. She then looked down at her feet, and stepped back into line. Crank nodded at her.

'Got all that, have ya', kiddo?' he snarled, the beetle churning in his mouth.

'You better have remembered every word, or you'll be dead,' said Chintu.

Saskat raised her wooden container and poured more liquid down her throat. She stepped forwards into the firelight, her arms outstretched.

'C'mon, sexy – let's calm 'chu down from all 'dat rubb'sh.' She shimmied her way towards Perry, dropping her drink to the floor as her rolls of fat jiggled.

'Um,' stuttered Perry, 'could you –'

'Cut it out, Saskat,' said Chintu, strutting past. Crank took no notice of this action, however, and turned to the rest of Leagros.

'Scoutin',' he said. Everyone seemed to know what this meant, for they collected different weapons and departed through the five tunnels. Moments later, as each enormous stone slab pulled shut, Perry was alone.

The Leagros warriors were gone for some time. Despite their hostility, the cave became more ominous when no one was in it. Perry fretted that one of the four rival tribes may figure out how to enter Juniper and attack him. He spent the passing hours in an armchair, staring up at the Juniper tree – he dared not risk enflaming Crank's fury by touching the food supplies.

When Leagros returned, Perry was in an exceedingly bad mood. It was surely nightfall by now, and visions of slavery, rape, murder and torture flashed through his mind.

'Food!' cried Kirito, leaping onto the supply pile. Various shapes dribbled down from the mound and rolled across the carpet, with some berries giving a definite squish under Kirito's weight.

'You idiot!' roared Crank, tugging on his goatee. 'Ya' just ruined my favourite…' He leaned down to retrieve a squashed grapefruit from the floor. 'My favourite…'

'Fruit?' suggested Avanti, eyeing Crank.

'Yes, that's right,' said Crank. 'Fruit.'

'Grapefruit,' said Avanti.

'Yes. Grapefruit…'

Avanti gathered some stray nuts from the floor and tossed them to Perry. He looked at her with unease.

'Cashew nuts are good for you.'

It briefly occurred to Perry that he had not seen Avanti eat since his arrival in the forest, but he was too hungry to mention it. The cashew nuts were large and brittle under his teeth, with a texture unlike any he had tasted before. They filled him up much better than his usual meal of oats back in Borea.

Perry excused himself to bed as soon as he finished eating. Only now did he consider his terrifying new reality.

Did the Leagros tribe know that he had never fought another person in his life? Was that why they were treating him so horribly?

Animals shrieked in the forest outside, reminding him of the danger still to come. And as he shut his eyes and drifted off to sleep, Perry dreamed of the Borean life he had left behind which, beyond the cave walls enclosing him in Hades Forest, seemed very far away indeed.

— Chapter Seven —

# Spiders and Screams

Perry woke the next morning to a collective murmur hissing through the Juniper cave. His vision was impaired by a silver object lying across his face – a rotting fish, he soon discovered – which he left in place, to not disrupt Leagros' conversation.

'So what if I care? I say we kill him.'

'He might come in handy.'

'Killing the fat man would be the wrong thing to do.'

'*Oh*, when will you get this into your head? There is no right and wrong anymore. The usual laws, the usual morals, don't apply in this place. All that matters is survival.'

'That doesn't mean we have to abandon our true selves.'

'What true self? When did any of us get the chance to explore our true selves in Borea? We're fighting for the chance to find our true selves, when we get out of this forest and take on the state.'

'Are ya' suggestin' we kill him ourselves, or leave him out in the forest?'

'Ourselves. Out there, he could come back and get

revenge.'

'Ahem.' Perry placed the fish on the floor and rose from his mattress. Avanti stared down at her feet as Kirito and Saskat turned away. Crank's face remained unchanged, however, and Chintu glared at the unwanted warrior. 'So… what are you guys talking about?'

'Just tribe stuff,' shrugged Chintu. For once, she averted her eyes, and Perry's knees weakened as he stared at five people plotting to have him killed.

'It's time for ya' trainin',' said Crank, gesturing to a dark corner of the cave. Perry did not move, flitting his eyes between the Leagros warriors and waiting for one of them to attack him. His heart pounded as the floral fumes intoxicated his senses and Avanti guided him into the designated corner. Perry glanced behind her back, but did not spy a knife tucked within her sheaf. A pile of string was arranged on the floor, waiting for him – would he be instructed to hang himself with it?

'Chintu, you can take this one,' said Crank. She retied her silver hair and nodded as Crank chewed his beetle, pointing the rest of Leagros towards the exit. Avanti gaped at Perry as she moved away. Saskat stumbled across the cave and Kirito waved a long wooden pole through the air. At last, Crank shut the cave door behind them, and only Perry and Chintu remained.

'Please don't kill me.'

'We're starting here, 'cause it's the easiest and you're basically useless. This is called string – it's been plucked from a horse's tail.'

Perry retreated across the cave, arms outstretched.

Chintu had not attacked him yet, but would surely do so now they were alone.

'Oh, honestly,' Chintu said, rolling her eyes, 'for the sake of my sanity today, can you *please* just get over this sorta' stuff? I get the whole sweet-little-angel-who-doesn't-want-to-hurt-a-fly thing, but all the other tribes are killing animals. If you don't get used to it soon then it's gonna be a whole lot more difficult when you're expected to kill a person.'

He blinked, unsure what she was talking about, but crept forwards. Chintu turned back to the string and explained that it could be used to create something called a snare. Perry nodded along for the following hour, slowly understanding that, if he were to be killed, she was not going to do it today.

'There's different types of snare, and they can be put at different heights and locations. The simple ones, found in the middle of the forest, catch the victim's ankle and dangle them upside down in the air. More complicated ones, found in the east of the forest, seize the victim's arm and hang them horizontally. String can also be used to create tripwires, which knocks over a warrior mid-battle.'

'What's the point of tripwires? Surely you'd just get back up again?'

'*Ingenious* though your thinking is,' she drawled, 'tripwires do more than that. First, they bring a warrior to the ground, which gives Taveron a few crucial seconds to capture them. Also, if the warrior carries a sharp object, they could fall on it and be skewered. In most cases, though, a tripwire is put in front of a deep hole which Taveron covers with leaves and grass. That way, the person falls into the hole and is trapped there for Taveron to collect.'

'How does Taveron collect the person who falls down the hole?'

'Eurgh! Why do you ask *so* many questions?'

'You said yesterday that I need to understand everything!'

Chintu sighed, when one of the five doors opened and the four Leagros warriors entered.

'Finally!' exclaimed Chintu, skipping across the room, 'someone take over – I was literally about to kill myself.'

'More questions?' growled Crank, grinding a beetle between his teeth. Avanti stopped alongside Perry.

'What do you want to know?'

'I was just, um, just wondering: once a tripwire drops someone down a hole, how does Taveron retrieve them?'

'Every night, a Taveron warrior named Yozora checks the holes for victims.'

'Doesn't doing that on her own make her vulnerable? As in, couldn't we just memorise her usual route, and intercept her?'

Avanti raised her eyebrows at Perry's suggestion.

'We don't intercept because Yozora camouflages herself. She's not easy to spot.'

'Right then, kiddo,' said Crank, striding over with a smirk. 'Time to get dancin'.'

'What do you mean?'

'Dancin', kiddo. Dancin'.'

Leagros climbed the various vine ladders across the Juniper wall and glowered down at him. Saskat winked as her breasts glinted in the firelight; nonetheless, she stood without a flask in hand.

'Time for a treat, I think,' said Chintu. 'This one prepares you for both Taveron and Orynx. As you already know, Taveron fights at long-range and Orynx fights from the trees. This means that their weapons come from above. Therefore, we're all gonna throw weapons at you from up here, and you have to avoid them. Ready? Three, two, one…'

A whizzing sound shot over Perry's right shoulder. Kirito, high up to the left, launched a blunted arrow at him. Instinct rather than anticipation enabled Perry to dodge it, and he jumped to his toes, alerted for the next one. Several more arrows flew in unison, darting at his paunchy body and forcing him to collapse to the ground to evade them. As Leagros attacked with greater vengeance however, so too did Perry's ability to avoid them improve. He soon learned to ignore his breathlessness, and was miraculously apt at weaving between the missiles. No sooner did one weapon shoot past his body than a second, third and fourth were launched from an adjacent ledge.

Leagros moved between the ridges, determined to create a new angle from which their prey would suffer. The shadows on the cave walls performed a melodic dance, with each flourish of the arm threatening to knock Perry senseless. After some minutes, a blunted spear grazed his neck, but he sprang backwards onto his heels to avoid being struck.

Ten minutes later, the attackers exchanged their spears and arrows for slingshots. They placed stones, rocks, wood and dead spiders in them. The smell of insects dampened Juniper's aromatic scent, but Perry was too preoccupied with the sudden increased speed of the missiles to notice. His legs sagged as the exercise wore on, and a lapse in concentration resulted in a wooden block striking his head. He crumpled to his knees, clutching the wound and yelling as the surrounding cave blurred. Blood stained his hair but, besides Avanti's sympathetic frown, the other warriors remained unmoved. Kirito span a dead spider on his fingertip.

'The real thing will be much worse,' said Chintu, dismounting her ladder. 'You know the different cave ledges, but in the forest, Taveron and Orynx could be hiding anywhere.'

'Onto Feysal, sexy,' said Saskat. 'You're now to fight Crank, one-on-one, without weapons.'

Perry gulped and peeled his bloodied hands away from his scalp.

'Not so thrilled about that, are ya' kiddo?' said Crank, strutting around the Juniper tree and spitting the beetle onto the carpet. Beside him, Kirito hummed and kissed the spider, cradling it, while Avanti eyeballed the floor.

Perry ambled to his feet, certain that he had misheard. He started to object, when Crank hurtled at him, teeth bared. Perry sprung his body away from the king's grasp and willed new life into his jaded knees. His opponent launched a follow-up attack. Perry leaned into the collision, but Crank swerved and propelled into the cave wall, using it as a launch pad to fly towards Perry and kick him in the face.

Perry crashed to the floor, adrenaline coursing through his ears as he swung his legs around in one swift movement. Crank hurdled the move and extended his arm into Perry's chest. He collapsed once more, but used his lowered position to push off his hind legs and drive into Crank's torso. The Leagros king fell backwards into an armchair as they scrambled from the furniture and rolled across the carpet, tussling and tugging and wrestling.

Perry rolled on top, pinning Crank down and aiming a blow at his left ear. He missed, and Crank headbutted Perry in the nose. The king sprung on top as Perry wriggled and flailed, preventing his opponent from a clear strike by bringing his elbow up into Crank's jaw. They each leapt up and stared at the other, fists clenched and veins throbbing.

'Time up!' called Chintu.

'Why?' snapped Crank. 'I was about to murder him!'

'Calm down,' warned Chintu. 'He's in Leagros, remember.'

Crank muttered as the glazed look vanished from his eyes. He skulked into a far corner of the cave.

'For the record,' said Chintu as Kirito placed a bucket of clear liquid at Perry's feet. 'While Crank is a prolific warrior, he isn't half the size of the Feysal warriors. You'll need to be better when you come up against them.'

Perry's chest throbbed, as did the bridge of his nose. Flecks of blood now decorated the carpet. Several minutes passed without anybody speaking. Yet despite his giddiness, Perry sensed all five Leagros warriors staring at him, waiting for his submission. He refused to give it to them. He was determined to see this through.

Next, Crank demanded that Perry do fitness exercises as preparation for mounting the Halcyon hill. The ensuing two hours exhausted Perry's body. His overweight exterior wailed in protest as he lifted blocks of wood with his legs, completed an exercise known as 'press-ups', and ran circuits of the cave. Midway through, Chintu departed the room in protest at his shoddy form.

'Why am I doing this?' he gasped after the first of these tasks.

'Halcyon is on top of a hill, so ya' need to be fit.'

'Can we at least extinguish the flames?'

The Leagros king scowled as his response.

By the completion of these exercises mid-afternoon, Perry was ready to collapse. He was wary of showing vulnerability to the rest of the tribe however, so crouched against the cave wall and forced a smile. The tribe scowled at him. Avanti looked fretful at the sweat dripping from every part of his body.

'Kirito noticed that the tired man runs in a strange way,' said Kirito. He stared at Perry's legs, as though waiting for them to reveal why they moved in this way. Perry did not respond – if he stopped breathing for one second, he thought he might die. Kirito, with an inquisitive look, once again placed a bucket at Perry's feet.

'Crocodile juice.'

'What do ya' think you're doin'?' demanded Crank's voice across the cave. 'Today's training is not over.'

'Not even for you, sexy,' chimed in Saskat.

'Surely I can have a break?'

'No.'

Crank dragged Perry to the farthest cave wall as Chintu re-entered the cave holding the fluffiest, most adorable bunny rabbit Perry had ever seen.

'Don't look so relaxed, kiddo,' said Crank, taking the bunny from Chintu and dropping it on the floor. 'Kill it.'

'What?' said Perry.

'Kill it.'

'What? No!'

'Don't ask questions. Kill it.'

Crank's ludicrous demand evoked a perverse laugh from Perry. Surely the king was joking. He stood, conjoined with the wall, gaping at the small bunny on the floor. It was a blinding snow-white, not much larger than a clenched knuckle, with electric white hair puffed out on every side. Any evidence of a mouth, chin or nose was hidden beneath the fluff.

'Kirito thinks that it is important for the fat man to know how to kill an animal,' said Kirito, 'as Orynx will make him kill another person if they one day capture him.'

The bunny seemed unaware of its new surroundings. It sat on the vine carpet as Perry froze on the spot. He knew, deep down, what he must do eventually, but was incapable of it today.

'I can't!' he shouted, sudden and furious; 'I can't, I can't, I can't!'

He stumbled away as Crank picked up a small dagger lying by his toes. With a harrowing flick of the wrist, he launched it at the creature. No sound escaped the animal's muffled lips, yet the white veil coating its body turned red. The bunny lay dead on the floor.

Perry squeaked. Kirito, meanwhile, hummed and juggled with the spider in his hand.

'If ya' can't kill a small thing like that, kiddo, ya' don't stand a chance in this forest.'

'It wasn't doing anything,' retorted Perry, dizzy and averting his eyes from the bloodied carcass. 'I had no reason to harm it.'

'Have ya' not been listenin', kiddo?' spat Crank. 'The tribes of Hades Forest don't need motivations. They kill ya' just 'cause they feel like it.'

'Now, then, lie down,' Saskat instructed.

'Do we really have to do this?' said Avanti, her eyebrows pointed.

'Yes, we do. Lie down, kiddo.'

Crank stroked his goatee as Perry shut his eyes. Any remaining training related to the Vemlin tribe, but he could not see how lying down linked to this. Nonetheless, resting would allow him to take the pressure off his legs…

He collapsed onto his mattress and his muscles morphed into the surface.

'Right then, kiddo. Just shut your eyes.'

Perry obliged, still thinking of the dead bunny lying metres away. The heated fragrance of flowers washed over him however, and the cave became silent and peaceful. Flames shimmered through the air, enveloping his skin. His body merged with the mattress.

A sharp pain split through his shoulder and brought the world crashing down. His flesh was shredded, torn apart. Agony surged through every vein, from the top of his forehead to the heel of his foot. He screeched and writhed, determined to rid the torture from his body, yet external hands bound him to the bed. A distant cackling assured him that his pain was terminal. He was going to die.

'I'll do anything!' he heard himself cry, 'Please stop! Please don't!'

His nails were clamped upwards, pushing away from his skin. Pain edged him closer to death.

A sizzling, crackling noise entered the chaos. His yelling was drowned into insignificance by a burning torch searing his tongue. It delved into the wet surface, steaming against the saliva and slicing through his mouth.

Then, as instantly as it started, the torch withdrew and the clamping stopped. The splitting rod departed his flesh. He lay in the unforgiving cave for minutes – or was it hours? – as his echoed cries faded into oblivion. All that existed was his own feeble panting.

Eventually, Perry opened his eyes, but his persecutors were nowhere to be seen. He shifted his torso with immense pain, his legs stretched ahead of him. He tried to produce a sound with his tongue, but winced with the scars of torment.

He had denounced Borea to evade its grasp, yet his new reality was far more grotesque. He would give anything to be free from the blinding pain in his tongue, shoulder and nails. He would give anything to be reunited with the insufferable loyalty of Mabel once more.

The state motto, with its three sticks of bamboo, shadowed him wherever he went.

Bamboo…

Bamboo…

Betrayal clogged his throat as vomit spilled onto the Juniper floor.

'Ooooh – not very sexy!' wheezed Saskat, who emerged from the darkness on the other side of the cave. Perry peered up, loathing himself and hating her. She held a bottle in her hand. 'But Cranky boy won't be happy. Best for 'chu to go get shum water from the stream.'

Shaking, Perry hauled open an exit door and stumbled outside into the Juniper clearing. The image of bamboo inhabited his brain, but was disrupted by an arrow flying past his head and hitting the cave with a loud clunk.

'What the hell do ya' think you're doin'!?'

'Are you insane!?'

'Kirito thinks that the fat man should not be outside.'

Perry tripped as four hazy shapes hounded him. Crank pushed him back into the tunnel, and within moments the cave warmth enveloped Perry again.

'What is he doin' out there?' stormed Crank, marching towards Saskat.

Perry tripped across the cave floor and tumbled onto his bed.

Shouts filled the cave all around, but it was unconnected and unimportant. He had been fooled. Hades Forest was not salvaging him from a better place; it was where his pitiful dreams of freedom went to die.

He rolled onto his side, trying to expose his bleeding shoulder to the heated cave air, and glanced a final look at Avanti. She stared at him, fretful and weak, as Perry's eyes rolled upwards and submitted him to a night of restless sleep.

# Chapter Eight

# Crocodile Tears

Nightmares filled Perry's slumber for the entire night as he lay in the Juniper cave. He spent the intermittent minutes of drowsiness between each one trying to mumble syllables over the top of his debilitated tongue. His mattress was stained by the blood leaking from his head.

'Are you all right?' sang a field of red tulips in his dreams. Was someone speaking to him? It mattered not. He had been betrayed, and the entire world laughed at his stupidity, cackled at his solitude.

'Get up.'

He would not get up.

'Get up.'

He wanted it to end.

'Get up or I'll slice ya' throat.'

*Do it, then*, said the voice in his head – or had he spoken aloud? The red tulip wanted his hand in marriage, but he would not do it. He wanted to be with Mabel, and would copulate, if necessary, one more time.

But he did not want to do that, either.

'Please excuse Kirito, mister fat man, but he should like to have some company on his trip.'

Perry squeezed open his eyes and saw Kirito's chubby cheeks leaning over him. He had a gapped, toothy look of anguish.

'If the fat man should like to shower first, then that would be a good idea.'

A small, square object was distinguishable in the figure's left hand. Was it food?

'Kirito is sorry about yesterevening, sir. The Leagros king scares him very much, and the king made Kirito promise that he would let the new man be tested in the same way that Vemlin would attack him.'

'Tested?' Perry murmured between gritted teeth. 'You call that testing? It was torture.'

'Kirito knows, sir, and he is deeply sorry. Testing is the word used by the king, sir. Kirito did not know that it would hurt the fat man so much, but he has some healing cream here, sir, to make the pained man feel better. The scary woman applied some to the pained areas of sir's body last night, to make the pain more tolerable.

If the fat man would permit Kirito, sir, he should like to have the pained man accompany him on a trip through the forest.'

Pained was the adjective Kirito used, yet Perry felt no resentment at this description. The world had persecuted him for twenty-seven years – there was no healing cream for that.

'I don't want to go anywhere.'

'Kirito understands, sir, and will leave the cream next to the fat man's mattress. Then, if the fat man showers, the skinny woman said she will change sir's mattress for a clean one.'

So, Avanti had said that, had she? It was a hollow gesture. He was foolish to think that she was his friend. He had never had friends, and never would. He wished that his denouncement of the state had ended in death.

Was he overreacting? Could he really blame Avanti for the pain he felt?

*You chose this*, said the voice in his head. *You denounced the state. You did this to yourself.*

A delicate thud signalled the shutting of a cave door. Kirito had left, and Perry was alone; alone as he had always been.

He swung one leg over his mattress, trudging to his feet. He did not know where the shower was, and dislodged one of the five stone entrances to step into the thickening mould.

Perry sniffed his upper torso. An amalgam of blood, sweat, dead insects and charred wood had taken to his body as a fortress.

'Boo!'

Perry recoiled as an unseen figure emerged from the darkness and poked him with a stick.

'Just Kirito's little joke, sir,' giggled Kirito. 'He deliberately did not tell the fat man where the shower is, so that sir would be intrigued and levitate from his bed.'

'Um, right,' gasped Perry, 'So, where is it?'

'Follow Kirito, sir! Follow Kirito!'

Kirito's fluorescent pink and turquoise spikes of hair danced down the slimy avenue. Perry followed, until they arrived in the light of a truly glorious day. The vine-strung bridges above swayed in a delicate breeze, and the palm and coconut trees surrounding Juniper were more flamboyant than any Perry had seen before. The sky was a soft, lazy blue, and multicoloured birds traced circles through the air, bathing in its serenity. Kirito led him to a small stream behind the cave where a network of eight wooden buckets were suspended in the trees above the water.

'Each bucket has a vine attached, mister fat man,' Kirito said, walking over to demonstrate. 'When Kirito pulls the long vine at the back, the bucket lowers into the stream and gathers water. When Kirito pulls the front vine, the bucket is lifted back into the branches again. Then, mister fat man, if Kirito tips the bucket with his hand, it pours the water over him. If sir likes, he can also detach the bucket and throw the water onto specific parts of his body. The fat man should take care when doing this, though, because if sir does not put the bucket back correctly, the scary woman will get mad.'

'The scary woman?' Perry asked.

'The king calls her Chintu, sir. Often, Kirito gets distracted during his shower, sir, and forgets to put some of the buckets back. The scary woman gets angry.'

'So, what do I wash myself with?'

'The paste, mister fat man,' answered Kirito, skipping and splashing through the stream to a small bucket on the other side. He threw it to Perry.

'What is this stuff?' Perry asked. The bucket was filled with a thick yellow substance. He dipped his hand into it and swirled it around. It was gooey and textured.

'Duck faeces, sir.' Perry yelped and threw the bucket

to the floor. 'Oh no, oh no, sir – the fat man need not worry! It has natural cleaning properties. The paste is good for the fat man, sir.'

At this, as though Perry was invisible and the pair hadn't been having a conversation, Kirito dropped to his knees and stuck his nose out. He was fascinated by a slug traipsing along the forest floor.

Besides the occasional previous outburst of rain, Perry had never felt clean water against his body before. Each drop from the buckets was heavy, giving an odd pattering sensation, but he was nonetheless pleased with his negotiation of the various contraptions alongside the stream.

The duck excrement dissolved in the presence of water. Although the smell could not be described as pleasant, he found that, after learning to keep the water away from his still-fragile shoulders and nails, he re-entered the cave twenty minutes later feeling cleansed.

'Grab the axe, then, mister fat man, and Kirito shall lead the way!'

The pair embarked into the flourishing forest. Kirito refused to account for their journey's purpose, which unnerved Perry, yet he was pleased to be amongst the natural world once again. Creatures hummed an invisible welcome from within the shrubbery, chirping and clicking their throats. Kirito, meanwhile, would repeatedly bound ahead of Perry, only to then remember that he had left his companion behind, and return once more.

'Sorry, mister fat man,' he would say each time, 'Kirito forgot that the fat man was here.'

'Why do you call me that?' said Perry.

'Because the fat man is very fat, sir.'

'So, what do you call Saskat?'

'The fat woman, sir.'

'But I'm nowhere near as fat as her!'

'That does not make the fat man skinny, sir.'

Perry walked with greater zeal for the next ten minutes. There was something about Kirito's uncompromising honesty that made him want to burn as many calories as possible on their journey.

'Where're the others, Kirito?' asked Perry.

'Scouting, sir.'

'What does that mean?'

'Gathering information on other tribes, sir. The king likes to know where they are, and what they are doing. The Leagros warriors also note where the different animals of the forest are. Different creatures hibernate in different seasons, fat man, while others change their habitat throughout the year. The king likes to know these patterns so that when Leagros battles in certain areas, the king knows which animals are nearby.'

'So, who does the hunting?'

'Mostly the king, mister fat man. Now, it is time for Kirito to teach the fat man how to use the axe. That way, sir can help Kirito with his task later in the day.'

He yanked the weapon from Perry's grasp and twisted it between his fingers.

'This is the sharp part of the axe,' said Kirito, pointing to the blade. 'The fat man should place his hands around the long wooden handle, and then move his arms at speed to drive the sharp point into his target. Try!'

Perry gawked at his companion.

'Swing, mister fat man, swing!' cried Kirito, handing over the axe. A lima in the tree above shrieked in protest.

'Swing?'

'Swing, sir, swing! The fat man should pull the handle behind his body, and then move it around in front.'

Perry did so, and –

'Ouch!'

His elbow bashed into an acacia tree.

'Check your surroundings, sir, and try again!' Kirito cheered, cartwheeling through a small opening.

Perry rubbed his bruised arm and repeated the movement. This time, the blunted handle slipped from his grasp and spiralled into the air, colliding with Kirito's cartwheeling backside.

'Crocodile calamity!' yelled Kirito.

'Oh my!' said Perry, 'I'm so, so sorry! Are you all right?'

'Never better, mister clumsy fat man, never better!' Kirito leapt to his feet, beaming at such an entertaining turn of events. 'Try again!'

Perry did so, wedging the blade into a tree.

'Much better, mister fat man,' said Kirito. 'Try again, and with more power!'

Perry aimed for an overhanging vine this time and sliced it in two.

'Excellent, sir, excellent! Once more!'

This time, as the pair passed a tree stump, Perry swung the weapon over his shoulder and lodged it into the surface.

'Crocodile conquest!' cried Kirito, jumping up and

down.

After ten more minutes of travelling, the crashing hub-bub of a river became audible. As it came into view, Perry saw that it was not particularly deep, and that an array of creatures were distinguishable beneath the surface.

Schools of fish drifted through the different currents, dazzling beneath the sunlight streaming through a canopy opening. Various mounds of rocks were piled onto the riverbed, holding under the river's pressure. Groups of cichlids – wide-mouthed creatures with scaled skin – glided alongside these. Some fish, darting between the weeds, were as small as five centimetres and barely noticeable. Others were over a metre in length.

Perry now realised, despite the noise, that the river was not as violent as first judged: the crashing sound was caused by the vast width and length of the river, rather than the strength of the water itself.

Arching across the surface farther downstream was a narrow and feeble-looking bridge. It appeared incapable of withholding more than one person at a time.

'The East River,' announced Kirito.

'What are we doing here, Kirito?'

'For the fat man to understand that, he must first know what Kirito's weapon is. He calls it his Zhua.' Kirito held up the long wooden pole he often carried. It had a sharp green claw on the end. 'Kirito attached a crocodile claw to the end, because the crocodile is a holy creature and it protects Kirito in battle. The five claws are sharper than any other animal's in the world, and will tear the skin of anyone Kirito strikes with it.'

He smiled, before thrusting himself forwards and shouting.

'Rawr!'

Perry leapt back as the claw swished centimetres from the end of his nose.

'Just Kirito's little joke, mister fat man,' Kirito tittered to himself. 'Kirito has brought the fat man out here because he wants to strengthen his arsenal. He wants to acquire a second Zhua, so that Kirito can fight with one weapon in each hand, rather than one in total.'

'Hang on,' said Perry, starting to suspect what was coming. 'But if that's made from a crocodile claw…'

'Yes, mister fat man, yes! Kirito shall enter the river and kill a crocodile.' He jumped to the floor and kissed the ground, muttering, before standing up again. 'The holy crocodile's claw will be used to guard Kirito's soul.'

'Soul?' said Perry in disbelief.

'Yes, sir.'

'Then, why am I here, Kirito?'

'The fat man is going to help!' yelled Kirito, hopping from leg to leg.

'But Kirito, I've never been in water before. I don't know how to swim.'

'Worry not, sir! Kirito's first mission is to teach the fat man how.'

'Kirito,' he pleaded, 'I really don't want to.'

But before Perry mustered another word, Kirito pushed him into the river. Water clogged his sinuses as his head sank below the cold surface. He opened his mouth, hoping to receive oxygen from the rushing water, but it did not work. He thrashed his neck to dispel the unwanted substance, and pushed up from the riverbed to gasp at clean air.

'What was that for?' he wheezed, as Kirito laughed on the riverbank.

'The fat man needs to learn, sir!'

'I couldn't breathe, Kirito,' Perry said, still panting and blowing water from his body.

'Very good, sir, very good! The fat man cannot breathe under the water, so he must bring his head to the surface whenever he needs air. He must also keep his mouth shut.' Perry struggled to maintain his stance; the riverbed was muddy and soft, making it difficult to dig his feet in. 'This time, fat man, keep your mouth closed beneath the water and move around a bit.'

Perry spat more water from his nose and glared at Kirito. Nonetheless, he obeyed.

Keeping his mouth closed was a useful strategy – the water pushed itself around his face rather than passing through his throat. He attempted swishing his body left and right, but found the water heavy and resistant against his movements. The liquid stung as he opened his eyes, and the swirling, faded outline of fish was increasingly vivid.

'What does the fat man think?' asked Kirito as Perry rose up again.

'It's bizarre,' said Perry. Kirito chuckled.

'As the fat man moved, did he feel the water pushing against him?'

'Yes.'

'The water has texture, sir, meaning that if the fat man

pushes it, it will resist. This is what humans use to swim: if a person stretches their hand in front of them, brings their fingers together and forces their arm backwards, the water is pushed behind them. This movement drives the human forwards in the water.'

Kirito demonstrated the movement.

'Is that it?' said Perry.

'The fat man must also kick his legs, sir, to help his body move.'

'Kick?'

Kirito jumped to the floor and displayed the motion.

'First, try swimming down the river, fat man. Then swim back up again.'

Although Kirito's demonstration seemed simple, Perry forgot to bring his head to the surface on his first attempt and subsequently couldn't breathe. On his second attempt he remembered to do so, but struggled to raise his head while still moving his body. Fortunately, any failed attempts were saved by Perry sinking his feet to the bottom of the shallow river and regathering himself.

He acclimatised as time went on. After nearly an hour of splashing and flapping in the water, he learned to move his arms and legs in synchrony, bring his head to the surface while swimming, and make the optimum arm movements.

'Excellent, sir, excellent! The fat man did very well. The Leagros king will be most pleased. And now, sir, you can help Kirito!' Kirito walked farther along the riverbank. Perry climbed out of the water and followed.

'Listen, about that,' said Perry, 'I really don't know

about this. I thought you loved crocodiles. Why do you want me to help you kill one?'

'By using the crocodile claw for his weapon, Kirito is protected in battle. The crocodiles are happy to sacrifice themselves for Kirito's protection, sir. That is what makes them so holy.'

'So, you want me to kill it?' asked Perry.

'Kirito will kill it, sir. But the fat man may have to save Kirito from dying.'

'But, but – we need a plan!' exhaled Perry.

'The plan is to kill the crocodile, sir.'

'But Kirito, how on earth are you going to wrestle a crocodile? It could take hours.'

'It won't, mister fat man,' said Kirito, patting him on the back. 'Kirito worships the crocodiles and they have spoken to him on previous visits, telling him where their weakest points are. The crocodiles want to help Kirito, sir.'

It was not unforeseen to Perry that his companion was slightly eccentric – but this, he decided, was taking it too far.

'Well, besides,' Perry said, trying to establish reason in the discussion, 'there's no crocodiles anywhere to be seen.'

But this was not true: a small, murky shape floated along the nearby riverbank.

The crocodile was both dull green and earthy black, at least four metres in length, and scaled all over. The end of its nose was elevated, and both eyes rolled above a long, beaked mouth of razor-sharp incisors. It seemed unaware and lazy.

'I'm sorry, Kirito,' said Perry, coming to a decision, 'but I'm not doing it.'

'Waaaaaaah!' Kirito sank to his knees and launched his head back, crying.

'No, Kirito, please be quiet!'

'Waaaaaaah!'

Kirito dug his fingernails into the dirt and kicked his legs out on either side.

'All right, fine!' Perry shouted over the noise. 'I'll do it! Just *please* be quiet.'

'Excellent, sir!'

Kirito sprang to his feet and beamed without a tear in his eye. He launched himself backwards into the water with an enormous crash. The crocodile seemed unbothered. Kirito raised his Zhua out of the water and waded towards the beast, as Perry's hands clung to his face. A clique of kingfishers hovering on a branch above the river scarpered.

The crocodile blinked, floating forwards yet blindsided by Kirito being behind it. The rushing water drowned out Kirito's movements. There was no indication of whether the beast had detected the predator. Kirito gestured to Perry across the river, signalling him to come forwards, and Perry trod over the wispy forest grass, holding his breath.

Kirito launched himself through the water and sunk the weapon into the crocodile's neck. A shattering crash uplifted the scene as the beast wriggled to escape, snapping its neck upwards and spinning its body. Water splashed everywhere as the forest shrieked in alarm. Kirito's grip faltered, and the crocodile darted away, only for the predator to dig the Zhua once more into the squirming creature.

Perry dragged back his axe and sprinted to save his companion. He threw the blade over his shoulder and leapt into the water, penetrating the neck of the beast.

The struggle continued, but with less zeal, and Kirito urged his partner to strike again as the crocodile weakened. Perry did so several more times, shutting his eyes with each hit, and the beast flapped its tail as the blood drained from its body. Perry's axe dug deeper and Kirito started to nod, signalling that Perry should not lessen his grip. A swishing noise sounded behind them both, however, and Kirito glanced to investigate the source.

'Kirito and the fat man must risk it, sir.'

'What?'

'More crocodiles are coming this way. Kirito is not sure that the crocodile is dead, but there is no other choice. Haul it with Kirito. One, two, three.'

They each placed their free arm on the creature's scaled underbelly, hoisting it out of the water and launching it over the riverbank. They climbed out, peeking back at the three crocodiles swimming to where they had just been.

'Waaaaaaah! Please forgive Kirito, mister crocodile Lord!' Kirito turned and rose to his feet, bowing to the three crocodiles floating in the middle of the river. He then faced Perry with a tearless grin once more.

'Excellent job, mister fat man, excellent! The Leagros king will be most pleased.'

Perry did not care whether Crank was pleased or not.

The fact that he had struck down several vines, walked in water, and killed an innocent crocodile in the same day shocked him. He had never done these things before.

An hour later, the pair arrived at Juniper with the crocodile lugged over their shoulders.

'Kirito and the fat man did it, Leagros tribe!'

Avanti smiled, and Chintu raised her eyebrows. Saskat and Crank, too, seemed shocked.

'Well?' said Crank, looking at Kirito as they placed the crocodile on the carpet.

'The fat man was excellent, Leagros king.' He smiled at Perry and dropped to his knees, using a sharp instrument from the corner of the cave to cut off one of the dead animal's claws. 'Kirito was struggling with the crocodile, and more of its friends approached, but the fat man jumped into the water and killed the crocodile and saved Kirito's life.'

All five Leagros warriors waited for Crank's reaction.

'Interestin'. Well, kiddo, that's just as well, 'cause now ya' can join in on tonight's attack.'

'An attack?' Perry said. 'Tonight?'

'Oh yeah,' Crank replied with a smirk, rolling his tongue over the beetle between his teeth. 'Tonight, we take on Taveron.'

— Chapter Nine —

# The Beat of the Drum

Standing in the Juniper cave, Crank outlined the plan to attack Taveron, but Perry did not understand a word of it. The rest of Leagros nodded along, so Perry joined in, while secretly longing for the Tambamba lifestyle he'd left behind.

'As ya' all know,' said the Leagros king, standing by a forest map drawn on the cave wall, 'Blackstream is the most fortified region of this island. Before ya' even get near the waterfall or cove, ya' have to avoid the booby traps. Taveron believes that only they know how to get through these traps, so we want to capitalise on that complacency. Saskat will guide the kid through the obstacles when we get there. As one of the traps is a concealed hole for intruders to fall into, Saskat will show ya' –' Crank poked Perry in the neck '– where it is.'

'Why?' asked Perry.

'Because ya' gonna climb into it.'

Perry's voice plummeted through his chest.

'Once the kid is in the hole, we'll proceed to Corinthian Cove, takin' five minutes. Kiddo, ya' count out five minutes and begin.'

'Begin?' grimaced Perry. Crank gestured to a small, hollowed drum adjacent to the cave wall.

''Ya' gonna be given this. When ya' beat the drum, Taveron will leave Corinthian Cove to investigate the noise, while we enter the cove to gather supplies. Then, Chintu will exit by an alternate path to retrieve ya'.'

At this, Crank made to exit the cave, but Avanti stopped him.

'We should introduce Perry to our weapons,' she said. Crank grunted, and Avanti held up hers. 'This is called a trident. It's what I fight with. As you can see,' she held the trident's sharp prongs into the firelight for Perry to inspect, 'it has three prongs, each of which is sharp and will impale any victim. I carved the prongs myself – it's made from rock, although the handle is wooden. It's useful in water because there isn't much water resistance against the prongs.' She smiled as Kirito spoke next.

'The fat man has seen Kirito's weapon already. Kirito calls it his Zhua.'

Chintu stepped forwards, with vines around her neck. 'I use these to destroy everything and everyone. Whipping, binding, strangling, tripping over – you name it, I will kill you with it.'

There was a deafening crack. Just like Kirito earlier that day, Chintu cast her weapon in Perry's direction. She snorted. Perry tried to keep his face passive – he did not want to show weakness to a tribe full of people who so obviously detested him.

Saskat held the largest weapon. It was an enormous gun that required both of her arms to hold it up. The main body was made from hollowed wooden sticks, and a strangely textured white box was attached to the front. Perry thought it looked somewhat familiar.

'This is a water gun. The tank stores all the water.'

'Is that –?'

'Plastic. Yes.' Perry only just recognised the material. He had destroyed it on many occasions during his time as an Eradict. Borea no longer used it, since it was harmful to the environment. 'It washed up on the shore, and Avanti recognised it since she used to work as an Eradict. The main gun is made from six water resistant sticks of wood. As you can see, each stick is hollowed out. The water is fired through each one at high speed.'

'How?'

'A pump. Avanti designed it.'

Next, Perry looked along to Crank's weapon, and was amazed by what he saw. The Leagros king held two small wooden handles – one in each hand – which both had five or six leather arms spinning off it.

'You can call this a Kraken,' said Crank. 'So named because of the sound it makes in the air. Attached to each handle are six leather whips. I made it myself from balata bark. I whip opponents in the eye, in the ear, in the crotch – wherever they are most vulnerable.'

After this final explanation, as Perry stared in disbelief at the lethal instruments surrounding him, Leagros embarked through the forest.

Perry's fingers felt numb as he spun the axe between them. He was entering the first battle of his life – a battle from which he might never return. After a few minutes of walking, Avanti shuffled towards him, holding an apple and speaking to him privately for the first time since the night before.

'I'm so sorry.'

'Forget about it,' shrugged Perry.

'No,' she said, placing the apple in his hand. 'I should've said something. I *was* going to say something, I just… but it's no excuse. I should've warned you, or said something to Crank, or volunteered to do it myself so it didn't cause you as much pain. I just… should've done better.'

Perry stared at a skunk plodding through the undergrowth ahead, and bit into the apple. It was sweet and nourishing.

'It's fine,' he shrugged, 'I was upset, but it was more from shock than anything else.'

'I understand,' Avanti said, plucking a leaf from a nearby branch and fiddling with it. Perry silently questioned whether Avanti, too, had suffered the same fate on her arrival in Leagros.

'I felt cheated, as well,' he went on. 'I don't know what caused it. I think I dressed up my denouncement as this great act of nobility. There were mindless idiots everywhere, but I was above them; only I was clever enough to identify the state's evil. But then I arrived here, and I'm the weakest and the newest, and –' he peered at Crank and Chintu '– they treat me like I'm nothing.'

Avanti nodded as Perry picked at the apple in his spare hand. At the front of the group, Crank halted.

'What's wrong, Leagros king?' said Kirito.

'I can't…' Crank stammered. 'Where are we?'

'The Trizone,' said Avanti, her eyebrows furrowed.

'Trizone?'

'The three-way border between Juniper, Arklow and Blackstream.'

'Right, yes. Of course. Lead on.'

Saskat proceeded, tapping the drum between her breasts and winking at Perry. Crank repeated 'Trizone… Trizone…' under his breath.

The group veered to the right, arriving in a section of forest radically different to Juniper. All flowers became suddenly bombarded by insects; every shoot and vine morphed a flourishing green. Perry battled against thickets, and a rhythmic pitter-patter sound rustled through the area as the forest opened up.

Visible between two olive trees ahead was a grand waterfall. On either side of the thundering curtain were thick layers of rock stretching back and forming the cove invisible beyond the water. The waterfall was wider than the Juniper cave, and the pristine circular pool at its base housed many shapes, colours and varieties of fish.

'Over here,' said Saskat, guiding Crank to a concealed square area beyond the olive trees. It was bordered by bushes and filled with an assortment of ropes, vines and wooden planks.

'Kirito knows that to the side of this garden, there is another one just the same,' said Kirito in Perry's ear. 'There are dozens of them, going the entire way around Corinthian Cove. Each is filled with booby-traps. Intruders can only access the cove by dodging all the obstacles in the square, then swimming across the pool. But the rape tribe thinks that no one knows how to get across.'

'How does it work?' said Perry.

'Look up, fat man,' Kirito whispered, pointing. Connected to each obstacle across the square, woven between the dozens of overhanging leaves, was an infinitesimal rope, barely noticeable beneath the sunlight. It ran out of the maze, dangling across the pool and vanishing through the crashing waterfall.

'If an intruder touches an obstacle, it will capture them. The rope attached to that obstacle then shakes, which alerts the rape tribe inside the cave to the intruder.'

'But couldn't an animal, or a falling branch, activate the rope?' said Perry.

'Yes, fat man, but Kirito suspects that the rope does not move so much when a branch or animal lands on it compared to an activated obstacle. On the occasions where a branch hits an obstacle, it is unlikely to trigger the trap, as the contact will be too light. Kirito suspects that it has been designed that way. However, when an animal is trapped by the obstacle, the rape tribe uses this to its advantage by retrieving the animal and eating it.'

'Wait here,' Saskat called back. She stepped forwards with the drum hoisted between her arms and swept her lop-sided auburn hair beneath her spectacles before springing into the air. She leapt, crawled and rolled across the square, borne with a newfound nimbleness now that her drinking container was absent. Perry marvelled at how her body fit between the obstacles. Occasionally, she steered herself away from an easier route and open space in favour of a more complicated path – she knew, it seemed, every hidden trap. After two painstaking minutes she reached the other side and turned back, eyeballing the maze. It took a moment for Perry to realise that Saskat had dropped small grains of wheat on the floor along her journey. A clear path was outlined across the square.

'Hey, sexy,' she cooed, 'step on each piece of wheat and stay on your toes. After the fifth grain, stop.'

'Stop?' he called across the maze.

Saskat pushed her bosoms together and nodded.

Perry could not understand why the two largest individuals must go first. He swiped back his fringe, inhaled, and leapt over a small wooden block to land on the first wheat crumb. He dug his toes into the dirt to prevent himself from continuing into a nearby swinging vine. He lodged the thinnest part of the axe handle between his teeth and ambled sideways to his second destination. For the third crumb, he wormed along the floor beneath a rope at knee-height. Reaching the fourth destination required a sideways shuffle between two adjacent planks of wood, and lastly, he ducked beneath an overhanging vine while hurdling a stick at ankle-height. Finally, he arrived at the centre of the maze.

'Put the axe down, sexy,' ordered Saskat.

'Are you sure it won't –?'

'Yes. Put it down and get ready to catch the drum.'

Perry felt suddenly gangly. One wrong move, and he would be left behind and raped by Taveron. Saskat launched the drum through the air, spiralling between two ropes and clanging to the floor just beyond Perry's reach.

No obstacles were struck, but an echo filled the area as Perry froze, gaping at the waterfall for figures that did not come.

'Put it to the left of your axe,' instructed Saskat. 'Now, crouch down, stick out your bum and claw at the ground with your nails.'

'Why do I have to stick out my bum?' said Perry. Saskat winked by way of response, and he squatted, keeping his buttocks tight to his body. He scraped his fingers through the earth but achieved nothing.

He was just about to stop and question why he was doing this when a wearied, square wooden door revealed itself beneath the earth. It was tattered and worn from months of concealment.

'Lift up the door, and climb in with the axe and drum,' said Saskat. 'Don't worry – we'll be celebrating this tonight.'

Under the door was a deep hole, tall and wide enough for someone far bigger than himself. He grabbed the axe and tugged the drum against his body, using his free arm to guide himself into the chasm. Only the forest canopy above provided comfort once he was inside.

He counted to five minutes. It was the one instruction he remembered. Each second seemed longer than the last, as his heart beat through his ribcage and into his throat. The shuffling sound of Leagros navigating the square passed overhead. Two minutes passed, and no longer heard his comrades. Three minutes, and his only company was the rustling of an animal nearby. Was it a snake? Four minutes passed, and still the world lay dormant. Was he one minute away from death? An owl hooted from a nearby tree and the sky above darkened. Fifteen seconds remaining. Ten seconds. Five seconds. Three… two… one…

His fingers drummed a macabre beat. The noise spilled from the hole into the black world above. A macaw chirped along with the sound as two birds joined in, and then a third.

The muffled shouting of a woman grew louder. One voice barked from the cove as others dispersed across the area. Perry's knuckles shook as he scraped against the drum's wooden surface. He lifted his body onto his toes and listened, but the bushes and olive trees bordering the maze made all outside noise unintelligible. The voices grew louder, until one penetrated the vacuum and screamed.

'It's over here!'

Voices surrounded the maze, growing louder and more frantic as two more women emerged through the treeline. He continued drumming, ready to die, as the footsteps and voices came nearer. Had it all been a trap? Was Leagros sacrificing him, leaving him to be raped and killed by Taveron? Three nearby bodies stepped closer, yet just as a woman's voice announced that she was going to look down the hole, a twang split through the air. An arrow shot into one of the wooden planks floating metres above Perry's hole. It stuck out from the timber, vibrating and threatening death.

'What the hell?' said one of the voices.

'Nearly took me' head off, that did.'

'Over here!' shouted a voice far away from the maze,

and with all memory of the mystery drummer forgotten, the three women danced away from the hole. High-pitched thuds signalled the connection of arrows, boomerangs and stones with the rock surrounding Corinthian Cove. Perry considered peaking up out of the hole, when a salvaging hand appeared from the inky blackness, reaching down into the pit.

'Come on!' urged Chintu, poking her head over the pit. Perry clasped the axe and drum against his body and took her hand, lugging himself up into the maze.

'Stick to the wheat,' said Chintu, weaving and rolling through the different obstacles. Perry followed, controlling his breath and peering through the streaks of blonde hair blocking his eyes. The axe and drum slipped as he moved along the crumbs, but he clutched them to his torso. He reached the final marker and launched himself over the rope.

His body smashed down into the earth. Dirt filled his mouth and nostrils as the rapid whooshing of three sharp instruments aimed for his head from an overhead tree. Instead of wedging into his skull, however, the darts lodged into the wooden base of the drum which fell and landed behind his head.

'Come *on*!'

Perry picked up his fallen items and raced away from the maze. He followed Chintu's path as she swiped away overhanging vines, her dazzling grey hair flicking behind her. Freedom beckoned as he sprinted, willing his exhausted body to move faster, when a deep thud shimmered through the wilderness. A rock, larger than both of his fists, slammed into the vines above his head.

'What are you doing?' shouted Chintu, looking over her shoulder. 'Drop the drum! Why are you carrying the drum?'

Perry did not know. The instrument slipped through his fingers as he clasped the axe, swinging to banish the vines and branches invading his path. More and more objects shot past his head as an unsuspecting, orange-spotted frog was impaled by an arrow. Perry's legs covered as much ground as possible, yet the taste of death swelled stronger in his throat.

Voices screamed through the forest some distance to Perry's right, but he maintained his focus. He ducked, jumped and weaved at random as he sprinted through the shrubbery, hoping to confuse his pursuers. The night became darker still as the labyrinth constricted around his helpless body. The forest suffocated him, and the creatures of the night guffawed as he ran, jeering as each arrow fired closer and closer to his head.

Where was Chintu? Moments earlier she had saved his life, yet his concentration at dodging the firing weapons distracted him from plotting her movements. There was no one in front of him.

*Please don't be dead,* he thought. *It's all my fault if she's dead.*

A razor-sharp boomerang flittered between the vines alongside his left shoulder, grazing his neck and spiralling into insignificance. Blood trickled down his chest, but still he moved as a second, sharper boomerang clipped his right ear. This time, blood spat everywhere, staining the earth and scarring the onlooking creatures. His entire face was drenched in red liquid, yet the adrenaline carried him on. He went to glance backwards at his attacker when his feet flew upwards from beneath him and his body was carried into a forthcoming tree.

'Go!' screamed Chintu as he landed. She was robed in green vines twisting throughout her skin, forming a human harness. She reached out and pushed him along the branches as his neck lurched forwards in fear.

'I've never been this high before!' he shouted back.

'Jump!' shouted Chintu. The branch drew to a sudden end and a gap appeared between himself and the nearest tree. Through sheer instinct, he flung himself from the surface and landed on the next branch, scrambling forwards.

'Keep going straight,' called Chintu, 'and then jump through the roof of the cave!'

'Where are you going?' he asked, hurdling onto another branch.

'To help the others!'

Unwilling to believe his ears, he gawked backwards, ready to testify that she was joking, when his face shattered into an unseen tree trunk. His body span through the air and landed on the earth. The howling pain in his shoulder, ear and neck was revitalised.

'Don't move!' barked a deep, throaty voice. Perry obeyed. The race was over. He was going to be raped.

'Stand up and face me.'

He did so, conscious of his seared body and the shouts echoing all around. It mattered not who they belonged to, nor whether Leagros was escaping. He faced his sole pursuer – the woman who would bring about his demise.

The woman glared at him, and he stared back. Her skin was unlike any Perry had seen before. It was both white and black – obscure, jagged patches of both colours were dotted across her body, unable to decide which ethnicity it most preferred. Long brown hair swayed far below her waist, and there were bronze patterns painted within each of the white splotches across her face. She rocked back and forth on her heels, almost about to fall over, studying him. She moved for the slingshot wrapped around her neck and kicked up a stone from the floor, fixing it in the holster. Perry shut his eyes, ready for death, as the woman prepared to crush his skull into the ground.

No contact came. He squeezed his eyes apart to find her staring at him, as though trying to decide something. A verdict glinted in her brown eyes, and she swung the slingshot over her shoulder and pointed it towards the distant sky. She fired the rock through the air, far above his head.

Perry blinked, gulped down the blood leaking across his face, and opened his mouth to speak. The woman hissed, and slid away from the scene, back towards the vicious shouts deeper in the forest.

He was alive. A pigeon clucked in the tree above, sharing his incredulity. The pain in his ear dampened, and the howling forest creatures were muted. Why was he alive? He climbed up onto the tree above, as instructed by Chintu, and trawled through the branches.

Perry regathered his senses as the branches sloped upwards some minutes later. The shouts of war returned to the forest as he neared Juniper. The cave revealed itself between the foliage and he dashed forwards with as much zeal as his wounded body permitted. The thick log beneath him moulded into a wooden bridge, and he sprinted along the wooden planks through the exposed forest air as arrows and stones whizzed up from below. An opening in the vines bonding the side of the bridge beckoned, and with a last look down at the open roof of the cave, he threw his body into the air. Two murderous arrows passed on either side of his face, but his body was quicker, as he landed on a mattress in a warm, heated cave.

Cheers erupted throughout the room as the rooftop slab slid shut above him. His vision was hazed, weakened by loss of blood, as a large figure stepped into the firelight and patted him on the back.

'Now *that*, kiddo, is much more like it.'

# Chapter Ten

# Rock, Claw and Vine

The Juniper cave held a tender glow that evening. Crank waded into the mound of food stolen from Corinthian Cove and handed it out, insisting that Perry eat enough to sustain him for the following day. Saskat heeded her king's lead, neglecting sexual provocations to join in asking questions about Perry's escape through the forest – he left out details of the mystery woman letting him go. Avanti smuggled assortments of food to Perry throughout the discussions, not eating any herself, and only when Kirito impersonated the Taveron queen, Tovia, wriggling and flailing as Leagros held her hostage and stole their supplies, did Perry excuse himself to bed.

Finally, his mind wandered back to the mysterious Taveron warrior, and her decision to let him live. Why did she look like that, and why did she save his life? The former question seemed less significant than the latter, yet the two were somehow connected in his mind. Her skin was both white and black, and it was not painted this way, as the pale patches had bronze, swirling patterns within. Equally as confusing was the woman's decision to hunt him down, trap him, and then release him uninjured. She seemed to debate some internal conflict upon seeing his face, but Perry could not understand it. He had broken through the Blackstream maze, and his tribe had stolen Taveron's supplies – why did she not kill him, or capture him at least?

Sleep was out of the question. Pleased to be safe and warm, he enjoyed the unfamiliar feeling of nourishment, as well as the aromas mingling with the back of his brain. None of this was enough to free his mind of that evening's events, however.

'The successful man is awake, sir,' whispered Kirito's voice from an adjacent mattress.

'Yes,' Perry confirmed; 'is that my new name, Kirito?'

'No, sir. Not until the fat man loses some weight.'

'Why are you awake?'

'Kirito rarely gets much sleep, sir. It is a busy place in Kirito's brain, and he often cannot push away the different thoughts.'

'What's on your mind?'

'Kirito's daughter, sir. Hazel. Kirito did not enjoy living in Borea very much, but his daughter was a good person.'

'You must've liked your wife, to have a child with her,' pointed out Perry.

'Not really,' Kirito admitted, 'but the leafy state wanted everyone to have a child by thirty, and Kirito was not sure he would denounce them at that point.'

'Do you miss your daughter?'

'Yes. Kirito concentrated better when he was with her. He hopes to get out of here, someday, and see her again.'

'You will, Kirito,' said a third voice, not belonging to Perry.

'Thank you, scary woman,' said Kirito, speaking to Chintu. 'Kirito showed the fat man how to use the shower this morning.'

'Did you tell him to put the buckets back in place after using it?'

'Yes. Kirito thought the fat man did very well today, but the scary woman did not seem pleased when he returned to the cave.'

Perry waited. There was no hint of accusation in Kirito's voice; it was his uncompromising candour, rather, that uneased Perry.

'I do not take his genius for granted,' tutted Chintu. 'Hesitancy kills in this forest, and that was pretty much all he was doing when we were in those trees.'

'But he made it back safely, nonetheless. Why did the scary woman not rejoice?'

'I was tired,' she responded. Perry waited a few minutes before speaking again.

'Kirito, can I ask you something?'

'The fat man certainly can.'

'The Taveron woman that chased me... her skin was both black and white. Do you know who that is?'

'The Leagros king calls her Miist, sir.'

'Why does she look like that?'

'The Leagros king does not know, sir, and nor does Kirito.'

Perry considered this obscurity for a moment, but Kirito was already breathing deeper towards sleep. Perry, too, closed his eyes and allowed the heated fumes to waft over him. Three days of extreme physical exertion absorbed him into his mattress.

The following morning, Avanti handed him some berries to eat.

'How did you sleep?' she asked.

'Best night so far, thank you. Everyone out scouting?'

'Yes. I've got to go too, but Crank said you should come with me.'

Neither Avanti's scraggy frame nor Perry's bulging stomach filled him with confidence as they marched into the forest that morning. Despite Kirito's eccentricities, Perry felt considerably safer travelling with him the previous day. This was hypocritical, of course, as his own pudginess could scarcely be used as a weapon. Nonetheless, he had not seen Avanti eat since his arrival in Hades Forest, and started to wonder the source of her energy.

'Which tribe are we scouting?' he said.

'We're not. Crank wants another attack tonight.'

'*What?*' exclaimed Perry. 'You can't be serious? But, what happened to driving all the other tribes towards one another? Why are we now going to all of them?'

'By stealing their supplies, we drive them towards one another,' said Avanti. 'Anyway, it might not happen, because he isn't sure which one to attack. You and I are scouting the animals in the south in case we take that path to attack Orynx in the east.'

It took the pair ten minutes to arrive on the south coast. The tangled grass bordering the beach reached up to Perry's crotch, scratching against his thighs as he looked out across the ocean for the first time in his life. The sky brightened above the morning sun as an exposed breeze pushed back Perry's sprawling hair.

He followed Avanti onto the sand, admiring the sparkling blue abyss, before spacing ten metres apart from her to scout for animals along the treeline. Perry took particular notice of the ocelots travelling in clutters of three or four. These were harmless and too intrigued by the forest insects to regard Perry. Each had a silken coat, beautifully mixed between cream and tawny, with white and black stripes lining their inner legs.

Yellow-throated martens were also numerous, dashing through shallow pools of water. Perry admired their mouse-like heads, but even more so their acrobatics, as they leaped between trees across different openings. Orangutans and chimpanzees were also sighted, but only once, as they were camouflaged in higher layers of the wood.

The first unexpected animal in the region was a blue-winged magpie.

'That shouldn't be down here,' said Avanti. 'The magpies live in the Halcyon pine trees.'

The next unexpected appearance was a panda. At this, Avanti's nose furrowed.

'What's wrong?' said Perry.

'They don't live anywhere near here. The magpies can fly, but…'

'What does it mean?'

'Vemlin has been torturing animals again. The pandas flee when they do that.'

Avanti diverted towards the ocean shoreline, gesturing for Perry to follow. She pointed at a drifting pineapple-yellow shape in the water.

'Sea snake.'

'I wonder what it's like to breathe underwater,' Perry thought aloud.

'Probably no different. Except, you'd have resistance against your body. Do you want to see something cool?'

Perry nodded, and Avanti waited for the snake to pass before stepping into the water and picking up a handful of flat rocks. She moved beside Perry and crouched down, turning back to face the ocean. Then, with a gust of breath, she launched one flat across the surface, dancing across the waves before finally sinking with a clunk. Perry was stunned.

'What about gravity?'

'The momentum cancels it out. I can teach you, if you like.'

Avanti demonstrated the movement required. Perry struggled to flick his wrist fast enough and keep his palm horizontal throughout the throw. He practiced while Avanti patrolled nearby waters and looked out for rival tribes.

After thirty minutes of inconsequential grunting, Perry achieved a second bounce.

'Yes! I did it! Did you see that?'

'Try again!' Avanti laughed.

Perry selected another rock, flicked it at the water, and whooped as it bounced three times.

'Amazing!' congratulated Avanti.

The pair exhausted their supply of rocks, taking turns to fling one across the ocean, before finally heading back to Juniper. Perry bid farewell to the sand and ocean, and admired the wildlife as they re-entered Hades Forest. He turned to ask Avanti about other unknown talents he could learn, when her bony hand clasped his shoulder and pushed him behind a tree.

'What the –?'

'Shhh!' She pointed through the leaves ahead.

Perry pushed back his fringe and peered through the foliage. Approximately twenty metres ahead stood a man. His dirtied, tanned skin blended into the surrounding wilderness. Hair spiralled from his nose, reaching below his chin, and he had long grey dreadlocks. He stamped on the floor, cursing under his breath, and pulled back his mane with one hand while battering his left eardrum with the other.

'It's you!' the man roared at a nearby tree. 'It's you plotting to kill me, plotting with everyone else! I know that it's you!'

He howled into the vacant forest and scratched his head. A sunbeam reflected off his clawing hands, and Perry choked down a gasp. Where there should have been hands, the man instead possessed animal claws. Each talon was arched: pearly-white at the base, but a burnt umber brown across the rest of the claw.

'You think you can kill me?' The man flexed up at the branches. 'You think you've got what it takes? Answer me!'

He charged forwards and connected with a dense,

screeching object. It fell to the ground with a thump. The orangutan looked up at its oppressor, as the man's claws sunk even deeper. He swished back and forth across the creature's face as it sprawled on the floor. Blood splashed through the orange fur and the man departed, sprinting deeper into the forest.

'You're all trying to kill me! All of you!'

The sky cracked with thunder and rain poured onto the leaves. The orangutan's blood drained towards where Perry and Avanti stood. They stared down at it when the collective grunting of more than twenty reddish dogs hounded towards them, yelping and spitting at the ground.

The animals clambered around the dead creature and feasted on its body. The forest was filled by gnawing teeth slobbering all over the carcass. Perry moved away, thrusting his fingers in his ears to hide the noise of the frenzied dogs. Avanti stepped ahead and led him through the flooding woodland, arriving at Juniper ten minutes later without another word between them.

'Status?' said Crank as they entered the cave. Avanti cleared her throat and shook the rain from her sleek black hair before speaking.

'Panda on the south side, likely due to Vemlin torturing animals. There was also a magpie there, but I don't know why that would be.'

'This confirms my theory,' Crank said to Chintu, Saskat and Kirito behind him. 'There must have been an incident in Halcyon last night. Two of their warriors fought.'

'Which ones?' said Avanti, coughing.

'Ryuga and Monosc,' said Crank. 'I don't know what

it was about, but it seems to have been pretty bad, as several animals have uprooted from there and relocated elsewhere in the forest.'

Chintu stood against the back wall, spinning a vine around her finger. Perry bit into a mango.

'They do not appear to have hurt one another, but tensions will be high and coordination low. Those in Feysal who dislike disagreement may volunteer to hunt elsewhere in the forest. We shall travel to Halcyon tonight.'

The next hour was spent in complete stillness, with the lightning and thunder outside breaking the silence. The Leagros warriors sharpened their weapons, fed themselves or rested. Even Saskat stopped drinking, despite maintaining a string of provocative glances at Perry from the edge of her mattress, with both legs spread apart. Finally, Crank called them together and posed next to the Juniper tree.

'Every evening at sunset,' he shouted above the crashing rain, 'Feysal retreats to Halcyon to sleep. This is because their large physique makes them easy to spot in the daytime, but less so at night. Sunset is in exactly forty-seven minutes, so we will be leavin' shortly. They will leave one vigil on alert while the rest of them sleeps.'

'Vigil?' said Perry.

'Someone who keeps a lookout,' said Crank, after a deep breath and flexing of the jaw. 'As today is the fourth day of the week, the vigil will be Malik. This is fortunate for us, because he has a weakness: food. Avanti will therefore gather all the fish in our supplies, start a fire, and stand upwind, so that the smell of cooking fish wafts towards Malik. If he doesn't know that anyone else is nearby, he will leave to investigate.'

'Idiot,' smirked Chintu.

'While this is going on,' Crank continued, 'Saskat will watch to make sure that the rest of Feysal remains asleep. Once she gives us the thumbs up, Kirito and I will use two vine harnesses, provided by Chintu, to lower herself and the kid down towards the supplies. They will then gather as many supplies as possible and place them into a wooden basket.'

With a final nod, the tribe followed Crank from the cave.

'Who was that man earlier?' Perry asked Avanti.

'Killua. He's in Vemlin. I don't know why he was so far away from Arklow.' She wiped away the snot running from her nose.

'What are you guys talking about?' said Chintu, overhearing and walking over.

'Just something we saw earlier,' muttered Perry.

'*Well then*,' said Chintu, 'I'm glad you went into detail, or else I wouldn't have understood.'

'We saw Killua,' said Avanti, and Chintu's nose wrinkled with a knowing look.

'What happened this time?'

'He kept talking about being betrayed,' said Perry, 'and then he killed an orangutan.'

'Honestly, that guy is crazy,' said Chintu. 'Remember that time we saw him in Broadfields a couple of months ago, Avanti, and he asked us why we were walking side-by-side with black and grey hair, and whether we were trying to tell him some secret message?' They both shared a nervous laugh.

'What's wrong with his hands?' asked Perry.

'It's like Avanti said: he's in Vemlin. He's tied coyote claws to replace his amputated hands.'

Despite the roaring rain, the air slumped with humidity as Leagros travelled. Thickets and branches drooped under the deluge, and Perry wondered how the downpour might hinder their attack. Fortunately, it did not matter: as the forest sloped upwards, the echoing thunder stopped. Trees were scarcer on the slope and the ground was muddy. More than once, Perry slipped and dunked his elbows into the muck.

Finally, Leagros reached the top of the hill. Feysal's base fell into a deep crater on the other side. It stretched for hundreds of metres, with thousands of trees packed into the area. The falling rain was trapped inside the trench, forming a grand lake filled with pine trees poking out. Birds of all shapes and sizes perched on these branches.

Scattered across the other side of the lake were five identical wooden huts. Beyond these was the ocean, stretching for all eternity yet partially blocked by a sixth, grander hut that undoubtedly belonged to the Feysal king. It was stationed at the foot of an enormous, abnormally contorted tree. Its trunk was thrice the size of the surrounding pines, and the upper branches twisted and spiralled upwards in dozens of different directions, forming a thirty-fingered claw reaching for the sky. The branches were bare and animal-less.

Crank handed Avanti a pile of fish, and she gave a parting grimace before walking eastwards around the top border of the crater. Crank brought the tribe to the west side of the lake, and martialled them into the trees.

'Saskat,' he whispered, 'go 'round the back of the king's hut and make yourself visible to us. Make sure the vigil can't see ya'.'

Saskat departed. Chintu handed Crank two vine harnesses.

'You two,' Crank said to Kirito and Chintu, 'get to the farthest tree over there. Make sure the vigil can't see ya', but ya' have a clear sight of Saskat. When she gives the signal and the vigil departs, climb forwards through the next four trees and do as instructed. Kiddo, come with me.'

Perry trailed the king eastwards towards the lake.

'We'll start at this one,' Crank said to Perry, pointing at a nearby tree submerged in water. 'I'll get higher and have a clear view of Malik. Once he moves away, I'll climb forwards through the trees for ya' to follow.'

Crank stroked his goatee and waded into the water. He hoisted his body around the tree like a sloth and dragged himself up into the canopy. Perry followed suit on a set of thick branches just below Crank's. If he leaned away from the bark, he could spot the back of Malik's blue hair, arranged in a bun. Sitting next to the Feysal warrior's feet were two handles of a wooden nun chuck, connected by a short vine. Beside him was a crackling fire, which sent smoke wafting across the distant ocean.

Perry smelled an ashy burning, and saw more smoke drift through the trees from the east. It floated into Malik's face and he lumbered to his feet, peering around. Finally, he moved away to investigate.

Crank pulled himself forwards onto the next tree and Perry did the same. The silhouettes of sleeping bodies shadowed Feysal's wooden huts – particularly that of the king's, which was vaster than the rest.

A firm vine dropped by Perry's side, and Crank signalled that he should tie it around his waist. After doing so, Chintu gestured from their left, and together Crank and Kirito passed a wooden bucket down to their harnessed partners. Perry grasped it and stepped out from the branch, dangling and lowering to the ground. The wooden huts vibrated with the snores of the Feysal warriors, but Perry focused on his goal. Piles of food, buckets of water and other supplies were littered across a colossal wooden table, and Crank directed his partner to a pile of mushrooms. Perry scooped them into the bucket and was lifted back up. Crank deposited the bucket's contents in a spare container, before handing it back.

Next, Perry retrieved a pail of water from the table and handed it to Crank. The snores from the huts grew louder as he went on, but Malik remained absent. Perry scraped a pile of lychee berries into his bucket on the third cycle and looked up, only to find the Leagros king examining the green vine in his palms.

'Psst! Lift me up,' hissed Perry.

Crank did so, before asking: 'What's this called?'

'What?' said Perry, distracted by emptying the lychees into another free bucket.

'What is this green thing?'

'It's a vine harness, Crank, but does this matter?'

'Vine…' Crank mumbled. 'Vine.'

'Um, Crank? Concentrate! Help me put the lychees in that bucket.'

'The what?'

'The lychees.'

'I thought these were called cowpeas.'

'Well – they're – so?' said Perry.

'I just thought… I can't remember.'

Perry cleared his throat and Crank came to his senses, grabbing the lychee bucket with his spare hand but tipping it as berries spilled out. The king released the vine harness and clasped onto the slipping bucket with all ten fingers – only to gape down as Perry racketed through the branches and landed in the earth with a resounding thud.

The snoring stopped. To Perry's left, Chintu was nowhere to be seen – until she, too, was plummeted to the floor by Kirito, who dropped her harness in shock. The two fallen warriors gawked at each other, petrified and bound by their vines, when the Feysal king burst from his den.

He was as giant-like as his shadow suggested: far taller than two metres and stocky enough to tackle three lions at once. Antlers were attached to his head, cushioned by the king's orange hair. He bounded past all five huts and straddled Chintu, who struggled to free herself from her harness. Perry attempted the same, but to no avail: the king rolled Chintu's helpless body towards his own and pounced on them both, roaring up at Crank and Kirito with a triumphant smirk.

'Treachery!'

Figures emerged through the fumes as Saskat darted into the tree line behind the king's hut. Perry twisted his neck to take one last look at Crank, knowing that all was lost. The Leagros king was suspended in the branches, mourning his mistake, when the trees started to shake – the Feysal warriors climbed up. Kirito and Crank gave a grieving glance backwards, and catapulted themselves through the trees and away from the clearing.

Chintu sobbed into the dirt. A centipede wriggled up her bridged nose and infiltrated her hair, but she had no way of shaking it off as the camp shook with uproarious laughter.

The Feysal king crouched down to inspect his prey.

— Chapter Eleven —

# Hogpits Bottom

Nearby birds flew away from Halcyon as the Feysal king berated the treachery of the two intruders. Four other Feysal warriors leered behind him, much taller and stronger than Perry but still dwarfed by their king.

'Rodents! Scum! Maggots!'

Perry and Chintu's vine harnesses were tied tighter around their bodies. Chintu no longer wept into the soil – once Leagros fled, she wiped her face in the dirt and scowled up at Feysal, defiant.

'Do you know who I am?' said the king. An enormous pair of antlers curved around his bright orange hair, pointing up to the sky as he leaned down to interrogate them.

'A pitiful leech,' snapped Chintu. The king stuck out his mammoth foot and kicked her across the dirt.

'What did you call me?'

'A leech, Yasha, that's what you are.' She spat dirt onto his toes. 'You're no different to the Demiurge – no different to Borea. Entertain me, your majesty! Make your pathetic subjects dance for you now, and let us all watch. Go now, do!'

Two of the Feysal warriors launched their spears at the

ground, landing centimetres from either side of Chintu's face.

'Tie the vermin to the huts,' said Yasha, facing his tribe. 'Fabe, go and find Malik. Now!'

A man with wooden shoes tied to his feet departed through the trees. The others hoisted three huts from the ground and carried them towards the two prisoners.

'Quickly, now!' shouted Yasha. 'That's better. Tie the insects to the huts and see if they won't seek to satisfy the Feysal king after a trip down to the pit. Quickly now – go, go, go!'

He clapped his hands, chivvying them into action as the man called Fabe arrived in the clearing with Malik, kicking and punching, hoisted over his shoulder.

'You'se is makin' a big mistake, you'se is!' shouted Malik. 'Me thinks the king –'

'I ordered it, you loathsome egg!' boomed Yasha. 'You *know* who I am. You *know* that I am invincible. But not for long, with pests like you running off at the first smell of fish. Are you a peasant mule? Ryuga, take him with the others.'

Feysal marched in single file through the trees and out of the crater. Perry was suspended in mid-air, his weapon taken from him and his body fixed to the hut. He scanned the surrounding trees in the hope of spotting a rescuing Leagros warrior. Chintu spat insults at Feysal.

The prisoners were paraded down the hill out of Halcyon. A ghastly smell burned through the forest but the captors trooped on, unblinking. The three hostages were carried around a collapsed tree to a long pit tunnelled in the ground. Animals wriggled along the trench, slurping nutrients from the earth.

With a nod, the man called Ryuga gestured towards Perry, and the four Feysal warriors lifted his hut over the pit. Perry did not see the intended destination until it was too late. Deep layers of pig excrement coated the pit, and his head was dunked into the centre.

Rotting mud slushed into his mouth. The substance suffocated him until he was returned to the damp forest air, covered from neck to scalp in pig faeces.

Malik was next, then Chintu, as Perry hurled the filth from his mouth. Feysal then turned around, waiting for something, as Perry longed for the clean, warm Juniper cave he had left behind. Finally, the Feysal king swaggered from the bottom of the hill towards the pit, and Chintu hacked faeces at him as he passed.

'Welcome to your natural habitat, my dear mongrels. You see, girl? I, too, can make stupid little jokes.'

'You'se is overreacting, king, me thinks,' grunted Malik. 'I'se di'n't do nothin'!'

'You disobeyed your king!' bellowed Yasha. 'I, the most ingenious, the strongest, the best warrior in the playground – well, you won't make that mistake again. Let the gnats go, and let's have some fun.'

Feysal untied Perry, Chintu and Malik, and encircled them with spears as they fell to the floor. The three prisoners huddled together, pronged on all four sides and unable to escape.

'Herd them into the pit!' roared Yasha, his antlers shaking on his head. 'Quickly, quickly! The worms must learn what happens when they enter Yasha's playground.'

Perry's body was lathered in pig dung as a spear pushed him into the muck. A squelching sound along the pit signalled the approach of six or seven animals: all pigs, with each one fascinated by the new arrivals.

'Welcome to Hogpits Bottom,' snarled Yasha. 'I'm sure you will find yourselves at home here. Now then!' He clapped his hands together. 'What shall we make our slaves do first? I think a nice bit of acting will do them well. What say you, my subjects?'

'Yes, my king!'

'A magnificent idea!'

'The more they suffer, the better!'

Yasha smirked at his tribe and stepped into the pit. He placed a gargantuan foot on the head of a pig. It froze, petrified.

'The pigs seem to take kindly to you. You are one of them, woman. But how about you really make yourselves at home? On your hands and knees, all three of you, and let's see your best pig impressions!'

'You're revolting,' scathed Chintu.

'No talking,' Yasha grinned, with a mock attempt at a girlish voice. 'You are pigs, remember – pigs do not talk.'

The stench absorbing Perry's skin was sickening. He could no longer remember what cleanliness felt like. With a meaningful glance at Chintu, he crawled, oinked, and sank his knees and elbows farther into the dung. Pigs rushed towards him, licking his hair and sniffing his buttocks. He shut his eyes and thought of a distant, happier place, but none came to mind. Perry heard Chintu and

Malik oinking, too, but dared not open his eyes to see how many pigs had now amassed in the pit.

'Hogpits Bottom is *my* playground!' bellowed Yasha. 'Mine! Crawl quicker, my livestock. Oink louder! Satisfy your Feysal king. Oink louder!'

Perry reached deep within his throat and snorted as loud as he could. Chintu and Malik did the same, and the surrounding pigs squealed – they nuzzled deeper into Perry's head, closer and closer to his anus, until not a single centimetre of his skin was free from the snout of a pig or the reek of its faeces.

'Lick your feet!' shouted Yasha. Perry tried, but they were too far away, and his neck could not reach that far. 'Lick your neck – shoulder – hands – lick your knees! Show your king how much you want to please him!'

Tears streamed down Perry's face as he carried out Yasha's every wish. The speared Feysal warriors surrounding the pit sniggered, shouted, and chanted.

'Hold the pig down and kiss it on the lips!' Yasha demanded, venturing into the pit and prodding them with his antlers. 'You will not attack Halcyon again, will you, my pigs? Oink to show me that you won't attack Halcyon again.'

Perry oinked.

'Stick your buttocks in the air if you bow to your Feysal king!'

Perry stuck his buttocks in the air.

'Kiss one another if you will do *anything* to satisfy your holy king.'

Perry kept his eyes shut, thrust his neck forwards, and

felt two pairs of dung-covered lips touch his own.

'Tie my pets to the ground,' instructed Yasha. The Feysal warriors did so with strongly knotted vines. 'Monosc, stay here and guard the dirty thieves.' A man with blue marks painted all over his body bowed. 'Everyone else, follow your king into his playground. Monosc, you need not worry about the filthy Feysal traitor – Malik is no match for you. And this fat one,' he removed the antlers from his head and poked Perry with it, 'seems useless, too. But *this* young lady is different. Keep an eye on her, for your king. I want her lovely and dirty when I return.'

He placed the antlers back on his head as three Feysal warriors trailed his shadow into the forest.

'Chop, chop!' said Monosc, placing one hand on his behind and rubbing the other through his hair, as though searching for antlers that did not exist. 'Off to bed. You've got a long day tomorrow.'

Monosc perched on a nearby stump, eyeing the three captives. Perry's eyelids fell under the weight of the manure, but he could not fall asleep. His brain was clogged by the mess covering his skin. No one spoke until, after a few hours, Monosc's head lulled backwards. The guard was sleeping.

'What should we do?' said Perry, looking at Chintu.

'Nothing. Not even I can undo this knot.'

'Leagros might come back for us?'

'Never. Feysal will hunt next to Juniper, so they can't pass. We're gonna be here for days.'

Chintu rolled her neck backwards, looked at the black sky above, and tears leaked down her face. With her hands tied she was unable to wipe them away, and more flooded down as she submitted to the grief that had revealed itself earlier that evening.

'What's wrong?' said Perry.

'*Oh,*' she snapped, 'what do you reckon, genius? Do you think it's the faeces or the squealing animals annoying me?'

Perry didn't speak for five minutes, as Chintu carried on crying.

'I'm really sorry,' he said.

'Shut up.'

'I'm sorry that you're crying.'

'I *said*, shut up.'

'But I just –'

'Stop apologising!'

'Why?'

''Cause it's all my fault!'

Chintu wept harder than ever. Perry did not move, wondering whether he was hallucinating. Of all the Leagros warriors, Chintu was the one that had always shown the least emotion.

'What is? What's your fault?'

'The vines,' she gulped. 'I should've added an extra harness, tying us to the trees in case anyone let go. I was too confident. I thought everything would be fine.'

'You weren't to know,' said Perry, startled to hear himself comforting Chintu. 'And anyway, we'll be out of here soon. We'll find a way to escape, and go back to Juniper, and it'll all be fine.'

'Whatever. Just forget it.'

'Forget what?'

'Nothing,' Chintu muttered. 'Stop talking to me.'

'No, really. What is it?'

'Nothing.'

'What's –?'

'I can't see the face anymore!' she sobbed. Perry glanced at Monosc, but he had not woken up. Malik, too, was asleep.

'The what?'

'The face,' she whispered, choking on tears and avoiding eye contact. 'There was a face painted on my fingernail, but I can't see it anymore 'cause of the mud.'

Perry was unsure why this was important. 'So?'

'My dad painted it for me,' said Chintu, her voice wavering.

'Did you... like your dad?' he asked. She nodded and swallowed some phlegm before speaking.

'I didn't at first. He was a bit strange. He'd pull these faces at me or do stupid impressions when my mum wasn't looking. One time he made a gesture at her. I never understood what he was doing. People in Borea didn't act like that.'

'Why was he doing it?' asked Perry.

'He knew,' said Chintu. 'He knew I wasn't loyal. I don't know *how* he knew; I guess he just saw it in my eyes or something. And that's when I understood that he wasn't loyal, either. I reckon he acted like that when I was kid to try and pry it out of me. Eventually, when I was older, we had this weird mutual understanding. I knew what he was thinking, and he knew what I was thinking, but neither of us said anything.'

A porcupine scurried past the other side of the pit, pursued by seven bobcats.

'But then, everything changed. I was in the state library on Recreation Day. The man's voice – you know the one – told the arena it was time to leave. I saw dozens of wheelchairs go down the middle aisle, but mine just stayed there. No one else was in my row, so I was stuck, and it was weird, but my brain just sort of went numb. I didn't call for help. I thought something was happening. Well, I was right.'

Chintu's dirtied silver hair sagged in front of her eyes, as her bandana fell into the mud.

'My wheelchair sank down into the ground. I started screaming but no one came. Everything went dark and then suddenly I was in this underground lair, surrounded by people wearing black clothes.'

'Demiurge?'

'Yeah. There were six men, and this one woman, shouting instructions. She told me to get off the wheelchair, so I did. She told me to lie on the floor, so I did. But then...' Chintu's voice broke. 'They... they jumped on me...' More tears fell. Her voice grew quieter. 'They held me down and...' Perry knew what was coming but did not want to hear it. 'They raped me.'

A nearby owl gave a mournful hoot. It flapped its wings and landed next to the pit, gazing down at Chintu.

'I'se is sorry, missus Chintu,' croaked Malik.

'The woman told me to get back on the wheelchair. It took me up to the library and carried me home. My dad knew straight away when I walked through the door that something was wrong. The rods took off my clothes and he saw the blood running down my leg. I didn't say anything, I just cried and cried. He hugged me and I knew that he knew what I was gonna do.

I went to go into the kitchen, but he reached out a hand and stopped me. He went upstairs, got a state leaflet, and cut his wrist open with the corner of it. He put his finger in the blood and drew a smiling face on one of my nails. I knew that he was with me – but I knew that I must do it alone. He held my hand, he kissed me, and he let me go.'

She sobbed and pressed her forehead into the dirt. Dampened tears rolled into her skin beneath the mud, and Perry knew that she had never admitted this before.

'You thought you were going to die, didn't you?' whispered Perry. Chintu nodded.

'The face was still on my nail when I woke up here. It fades every few days, but I trace over it with red paint. It reminds me of him. I would never forgive myself if I didn't see him again.' She sighed, and looked up at Perry. 'I hate this place. That's why I act like this.'

'Like what?' said Perry.

'The sarcasm; the jokes; the questions. It's why I'm always angry. I ask people why they are the way they are, so they don't ask those same questions about me. That's why I've been so horrible to you. You're intelligent and you ask questions, and I knew that you'd see right through me. I'm so sorry. It's just that there's nothing I wouldn't do to see my dad again, so when you were put in Leagros I thought, *typical, just my luck.*'

'Is that why you told the others that I should be killed?' scorned Perry, somewhere between pity and disdain.

'I put a rotting fish on your face, so you'd wake up. I knew that you could hear what I said. Well, I had to scare you into shape somehow, so you wouldn't get me killed and wouldn't ask me questions. But I didn't even need to. You're a good person, and a great warrior. You must've done some really impressive stuff to get away from Miist that night.'

'I didn't.' Perry hesitated for a moment, and decided to confess. 'I didn't do anything. I only lasted a few seconds without you before I fell. Miist trapped me with a slingshot and told me to stand up and face her. I did, but then something odd happened.'

Chintu stemmed her tears, her eyes now searching Perry.

'She looked at me, but didn't do anything. Something changed her mind. She fired a rock into the sky above me and ran away.'

'What?' Chintu muttered, choking on more tears and shaking her hair. 'Are you serious?'

'Yes.'

'I knew there was something going on.'

'What do you mean?'

'There's something wrong about this place,' Chintu said. 'There's definitely something wrong. I noticed it straight away.'

'Noticed what?'

'Didn't you listen to the story? Dolphin's story?' Chintu's nostrils flared beneath the pig dung. 'It made no sense. There's so many holes in it. *Why* didn't any Stitchers follow their escaping boat? *Why* has the state never found us on this island? *How* did Dolphin break back into the prison, again and again, without being caught or setting off an alarm?'

A flame struck in Perry's head. 'I didn't think…'

'But this is good news. Miist clearly agrees with me, or she wouldn't have let you live.'

'She might've just shown me mercy?'

'There's no point. Anyone who believes Dolphin's story is in here to kill. I just need to speak to her, and find out what she knows.'

Monosc's snores persisted for the following hour as Chintu and Perry lay distracted by their own thoughts.

'Methinks that you'se wills be made to dos more stuff soon,' said Malik, waking up. 'Methinks that Yasha should lemme go.'

'I'm not sure that *you thinks* very much at all, pea-brain,' said Chintu.

'Victory!' thundered a voice through the forest. 'Victory for the Feysal king! Bow to me, my subjects. Bow to me at the heart of my playground!'

The four Feysal warriors marched past, guffawing as Yasha spat in Chintu's hair.

'Set up camp here,' said Yasha, 'and bring the supplies down. Your king wants to keep an eye on his cattle.'

The tribe did so, and a small ember flamed about fifty metres away from the pit. A giant rat, about thirty centimetres long, burrowed into the soil next to Perry. It sniffed and chewed various parts of his skin, until being chased away by a tenrec.

'Oi!' whispered Chintu. Perry looked up as she jerked her head farther down the pit. 'Coyotes.'

Five or six dog-like creatures roamed through the dirt. One of them broke away to tread up to Perry, Chintu and Malik. It had a light grey coat of coarse fur and a pointed auburn nose. Both ears were raised, alert for the sound of prey elsewhere in the forest, yet it now seemed fixed on Chintu.

'Come on,' whispered Chintu to the coyote. 'Bite through the vine.'

She stared at the coyote. It gazed back at her. Chintu poked her head between the coyote and the vine strapping her arm down. Still the animal stood, separate from its peers, staring without expression.

'Please, please, please! Please just bite through the vine.'

Perry knew little about the intelligence of coyotes and was certain it had no idea what Chintu wanted it to do. So, he was shocked when it stepped closer and sank its head down towards the vine constricting his Leagros companion.

'Good boy,' ushered Chintu. 'Now, just bite through it.'

It sniffed at the vine for several seconds until, at last, it bared its teeth and nibbled.

'Good boy, good boy!' said Chintu, delighted and free. 'Look, Perry – I knew it!' Farther down the pit, the remaining coyotes urinated on the pigs below them. 'The coyotes are marking their territory. They're about to eat the pigs.'

She looked at Perry with a steely glint, inviting him to join her in a private joke.

'So?' he sighed.

'*Eurgh,*' she moaned, 'just get ready.'

Perry looked over at the five Feysal warriors, all of whom stood around the fire and mockingly waved Perry's axe at one another. Yasha clapped them on, as though it were a performance, and the antlers fell off his head as he laughed. Perry did not know what Chintu was about to do.

She picked up a stone from the ground and scanned upwards to search the tree above them. With a final, resolute nod to Perry, she pulled back her arm and launched the stone through the air, rocketing towards a dark shape in a branch above Feysal's camp. With a loud crack, the stone collided with the tree, knocking the dark shape through the air. The firelight revealed a birds' nest spiralling down at the Feysal tribe. Dozens of strangely coloured eggs rolled from the nest across the ground and each Feysal warrior jumped up to avoid them, distracted and vulnerable to what happened next.

Squeals erupted behind Perry and dozens of pigs scrambled out of the pit, racing to reach and devour the eggs. The coyotes, temporarily dumbstruck, regained their senses and chased after the pigs, who chased after the eggs, which threatened to bowl over the Feysal warriors.

Yasha and his subjects screamed. Pigs and coyotes bashed into them, knocking them onto their backsides. Chintu grabbed another rock from the pit and cut the second vine attached to her with it. Then, as Perry stared open-mouthed at her, she crawled across the pit and sliced away the two vines constricting him.

'Let's go!' she shouted. Perry looked back at the camp but Feysal seemed unaware what was going on. Yasha gaped, unable to account for the sudden onslaught of creatures racing through their midst. On the tree stump, Monosc woke and thrashed his spear through the air.

'Please don't,' begged Chintu, stepping backwards.

But Monosc halted, and Chintu stopped retreating. A dark shape sprang up from the pit, yapping at the Feysal warrior and herding him back into the tree.

'Good boy!' shouted Perry in disbelief at the barking coyote. 'Hey, Chintu – it's the same one from earlier!'

'Are you gonna stand there all day? Let's get out of here!'

The Feysal warriors stared at the escaping victims. Yasha jumped forwards, but the coyote attacking Monosc changed its path and backed him into the fire. Perry charged after Chintu, springing through the forest as Yasha's screams, and the shattering of an antler, echoed across Hogpits Bottom.

# Chapter Twelve

# Puppy

Chintu and Perry only stopped running through the forest when they felt certain that Feysal was not pursuing them. They gaped at each other, squinted from the morning sun now warming the leaves, mud and dung coating their bodies, and laughed.

They had escaped Feysal; they were still alive. The forest owls, whooping as they departed their nighttime shifts, seemed much more beautiful; the entire forest shone under a fluorescent pinkish hue. The pair walked the remainder of the journey until Juniper came into view, at which point a noise sounded behind them. A small coyote, equal in height to Perry's waist, leapt through the vines, licking the pig dung clean off their skin and barking.

'Good boy, good boy!' cheered Chintu, stroking the panting animal. 'You saved our lives, you little genius.'

'Thanks for saying goodbye,' Perry said, patting it on the head. They turned to walk into the cave, but the coyote did not leave. 'Really, we have to go,' Perry said to the animal.

The coyote's tongue was far out of its mouth, panting at what it clearly considered to be its new owners. Perry glanced at Chintu, who smiled.

'We should keep it.'

'What?'

'Come on! Why not?'

'Um, I dunno…' said Perry, pulling a mock thoughtful face. 'Because Crank will kill us?'

Chintu laughed. 'Oh, don't worry about that old idiot. He likes me. Come on!'

And without another word, Chintu marched the coyote into the cave.

'We're home!' she shouted, lighting several flames along the walls.

'Wha −?' was the collective noise throughout the room, as Leagros woke.

'Kirito is being licked!' shouted Kirito's high-pitched voice. 'Kirito is being licked! Crocodile calamity!'

It was true: the coyote wasted no time in greeting the cave's inhabitants, and was already fondly associated with Kirito's left cheek.

'What is *that* doing here?' demanded Crank, jumping to his feet. Perry stood at the back of the cave, hoping that he would not be shouted at.

'Geroff me!' said Saskat as the coyote jumped onto her body.

'Get it out! Now!' roared Crank.

'No,' snapped Chintu. She walked over to the coyote, whose neck was being nuzzled by Kirito. 'It saved our lives two hours ago, and it wants to stay, so it's staying. Thanks for caring so much about the fact that me and Perry just rose from the dead, by the way.'

Crank looked briefly ashamed of himself.

'What happened?' Avanti asked.

'What's that all over your bodies?'

'Did they take you down to that pit?' said Crank.

'Hogpits Bottom, yeah,' said Chintu. 'It's pig faeces. They made us roll around with them and touch them, but they saved the really bad stuff for tomorrow.'

Crank stopped listening and scowled at the coyote.

'We're not keepin' it,' Crank said.

'Well, at least let me finish my story!' said Chintu. 'We were in the pit and these coyotes showed up, trying to eat the pigs. So, I threw a rock at a bird's nest in the branches, and it dropped eggs everywhere. The pigs chased after the eggs, and the coyotes chased after the pigs – it was crazy. Monosc saw that we were escaping and stopped us, but that's when this little *champion,*' she pressed her nose against the coyote's, 'attacked Monosc and saved us both. So, he stays.'

'If that dog proves itself to be a liability in any way, we're getting rid of it,' warned Crank.

'Deal,' said Chintu. 'But if you keep calling it a dog rather than a coyote, we might have to get rid of you. Hey, we should make it the tribe mascot!'

Avanti gave a feeble cough, but did not speak. She smiled at Chintu and Perry across the room.

Perry looked at Chintu's body and recognised the stench coming from his own. He opened his mouth to suggest that they take a shower, but before he could speak, he was squeezed into a rib-shattering hug.

'Kirito missed you, mister fat man,' said Kirito, patting

him on the back and beaming.

'Oh,' said Perry, taken aback and suddenly emotional. 'Wow. Thanks, Kirito. But look, you've just got muck all over yourself.'

'Don't worry about Kirito. The scary woman and the fat man can go outside and shower, and when they come inside to sleep, Kirito will go outside and wash himself, too.'

'You should all go back to sleep,' said Perry.

'It's almost sunrise,' said Avanti. 'You two sleep, and we'll wake you up in a few hours.'

Both Chintu and Perry smiled thanks and left the cave when Kirito hollered after them.

'Wait! Come back, mister fat man!' He chased them down the entrance tunnel and turned Perry around to face him. 'Crocodile conquest... the fat man is not looking quite so fat anymore. Kirito must come up with a new name soon, sir!'

When Perry returned from his shower, Crank's look of distaste suggested that he already regretted his acceptance of the coyote into the tribe.

'I'm not feedin' it, and if you two aren't takin' it with ya' when you go out, then it's stayin' in the cave.'

'No worries,' said Chintu, launching herself onto her mattress as the rest of the tribe went hunting. When Perry was woken by Crank several hours later, a new axe was on the carpet next to his bed, replacing the one stolen by Feysal.

'Perry and Avanti, you two scout Arklow,' said the king. Perry's stomach squirmed as his eyes adjusted to the cave light; he had never entered Vemlin's region before.

'I want to be with Perry,' spoke up Chintu.

'What?' said Crank. 'Why?'

''Cause he's the only one that appreciates *this* handsome young man,' said Chintu, petting the coyote. 'Also, I'm taking it with me today and I want Perry's help naming it.'

'Fine,' said Crank. 'Kirito and Avanti, scout Broadfields, Blackstream and the Isle of Bees.'

'Kirito would like to do that on his own, Leagros king. That way, Kirito can worship the holy crocodiles.'

'*Fine,*' said Crank, spitting a beetle onto the floor. 'Avanti, go with Perry and Chintu. Saskat, come with me to… to…'

'Halcyon?' suggested Avanti.

'Yes,' confirmed Crank. 'Halcyon.'

Leagros diverged outside the cave and Avanti, Chintu and Perry set off into the deep forest.

'It's must've been horrible,' Avanti said to them. 'I'm so sorry you had to go through that.'

'It was fine,' Chintu shrugged, regaining her usual aura of nonchalance.

'Did we miss anything?' said Perry.

'The first kill. Sorowitz in Vemlin.'

'The hunchback?' said Chintu.

'Yeah,' said Avanti, sneezing. 'Feysal did it. We think she was hanging around Juniper, waiting to attack one of us if we came out of the cave.'

'Of course!' exclaimed Chintu. 'When Yasha came back, he shouted 'victory'. That must've been why.'

'What do you mean by 'hunchback'?' said Perry.

'Sorowitz looked really weird,' said Chintu. 'Vemlin is the tribe where they all look funny, and her neck came down lower than her stomach. She patted the coyote yapping at her heels. 'So, what should we name him?'

Avanti shivered.

'How do you know it's a boy?' said Perry.

'It stood above me outside the pit,' grimaced Chintu. 'Trust me, it's a boy.'

'We could name it after someone special to one of you?' suggested Perry, glancing at Chintu.

'No, I don't like the Borean names. Just make something up.'

The coyote yapped with greater enthusiasm at its new owners. It ran in circles chasing its tail, and then rose onto its hind legs to lean against a tree.

'Ruff!' shouted Perry at the barking animal. It barked back. 'Ruff, ruff, ruff!' Perry smiled at the other two.

'Let's call it that!' said Chintu.

'Call it what?'

'Ruff.'

'But – that's… an *amazing* idea!' exclaimed Perry.

'We'll add an 'e' on the end, though, so it's more sophisticated,' said Chintu. 'Nice to meet you, Ruffe.' She held out a hand which the coyote placed its paw into.

'I like that name,' shrugged Avanti. They each smiled at each other, and detoured around a collapsed tree in the woods.

'All hail, king Ruffe!' bellowed Chintu.

'Shhh! Keep your voice down!' urged Avanti, but

Chintu just laughed as Ruffe burrowed into the ground. The three of them halted and waited on many occasions along their journey as Ruffe climbed up trees to chase passing birds. Although it was early afternoon, the sun faded behind the forest woodland, which grew denser and taller as they travelled.

'Did you hear that?' said Chintu fifteen minutes later.

'Hear what?'

She pressed a finger to her lips and ushered them onwards. Millipedes scurried out of leaves scattered across the ground and departed into the wilderness.

'There's people there,' Chintu whispered. Avanti clutched her trident tighter, and Perry did the same with his axe while pushing down Ruffe's neck to lower him onto his belly. Chintu pointed into the darkness ahead.

'I shall only permit your nonsense for so long!' declared a deep female voice. Perry pushed back his hair and peered out from behind the tree.

The fat, auburn-haired form of Saskat was unmistakeable, but her voice was contrasted from its usual tone. Her words were not slurred, and there was nothing sexually suggestive about her voice. It was dark and foreboding.

'How pitiful you are being!' hissed another voice. It was Crank. He spoke differently: every syllable was meticulously pronounced, unlike his usual gruff manner. 'I see that your position of subservience has turned you into a babbling fool! I am fine. You'd do well to banish the matter from your mind.'

'How can I, when you act in such a way?' Saskat demanded. Perry pinned his body against the tree ahead of him as her voice grew quieter. 'If it happens again…'

'Keep your voice down!' warned Crank. His shadow reached out and dragged Saskat deeper into the trees. Avanti, Perry and Chintu did not pursue, instead gaping at one another as Perry released Ruffe's neck.

'What was that about?' said Avanti, tracing the outline of her ribs.

'Dunno,' said Chintu, although her eyes seemed ready to burst from their sockets. She kissed her teeth.

'We're not near Halcyon, are we?' asked Perry.

'No. We're at the south side of Arklow. Those two shouldn't be anywhere near here.'

'Should we catch up with them?' said Perry.

'No,' said Avanti and Chintu in unison.

Perry could sense Chintu's mind racing to comprehend what they had just heard. Crank and Saskat should not be in this part of the forest, and their discussion did not make any sense. Avanti sneezed and stepped out from her tree, when the heavy thud of a spear shimmered through the bark above her head.

'Get down!' screamed Chintu as Avanti spun and launched her trident through the air. There was a rocky clang and several kookaburras nesting nearby fled. Perry crouched down and stroked Ruffe, trying to stay calm even though his potential murderer stood only metres away.

'Through the woods –
And under the trees –
Puppy gets –
His foes on their knees!'

'Show yourself, you little brat!' challenged Chintu.

'You think you can kill me?' squeaked the high-pitched voice of a young boy. Perry poked his head out and saw the outline of a child no older than thirteen with shaggy black hair and very dirty skin. His hair was longer than Perry's – a thick mane dripping with sweat and falling to his shoulders – and he clutched a spear, ready to launch. Ruffe growled.

'Chintu, he's just a boy,' muttered Perry.

'Yeah, *Chintabelle* – I'm just a boy! You don't want the blood of an icky-wicky-wittle infant on your oversized nose.'

'You arrogant little…' she lashed the vine out between the trees, cracking at thin air but missing her opponent.

'Hey, Chintabelle,' said the boy. 'If you listen really closely, you'll hear all the animals saying you have pathetic aim!'

'I'm gonna kill you, Puppy!' Chintu roared.

'With those scary-wary leaves in your hand? Hey, Avantalina – want your trident back?'

The boy named Puppy pulled it out of the ground and hurled it back at her feet. Perry grabbed his axe tighter and was ready to run out through the vines when Puppy sang again.

> 'The fat man wants –
> To try and fight me –
> He's weak! He's mad! –
> I'll kill him with glee!'

All three of them hesitated, unsure what to do, when Chintu stepped into the open forest.

'Yippee!' shouted Puppy, his shadow jumping up and down on the forest floor. 'Three-on-one, and it took one minute for someone to grow a pair of testicles. I should've known it'd be *you,* Chintabelle.'

'Kill me, then,' Chintu said, her voice emotionless. Perry gasped. 'You always mouth off about doing it – well, now's your chance. Show Perry and Avanti what you've got. Kill me.'

'Oooooh!' squealed Puppy. 'Trying to act all tough, are you, Chintabelle?'

Perry could not stand listening to Puppy speak in this way. He stepped out from behind the tree as Avanti picked up her trident and did the same.

'Now I'm really scared,' mocked Puppy.

'Get on with it,' growled Chintu.

'Chintabelle thinks –
She's smarter than me –
She's dumb! She's dim! –
More thick than a tree!'

'Your songs are getting worse,' snorted Avanti.

'What was your king talking to fatty about?'

'None of your business,' snapped Chintu.

'You don't know, do you?' said Puppy. 'I'm disappointed in you, Chintabelle. Normally you're so omnipotent.'

'That's a big word for you,' said Chintu. Ruffe stepped between Perry's legs and barked.

'I'll kill that dog if you're not careful,' said Puppy, but he had gone too far. Chintu ran towards him, whipping her vine and bellowing a word on each crack.

'It's – not – a – dog – it's – a – coyote!'

She chased Puppy through the tangled vines, his glinting black hair bobbing as he darted and weaved away from the lashes, cackling. He hurled a spear back at Chintu, skimming between her torso and arm and skewering a lemur resting in the trees. Perry and Avanti pursued, taking care to avoid the spears now flinging in every direction.

Each weapon was concealed by the thickening vines, and the sunlight became even more evasive as they entered deeper into the forest. Kookaburras laughed all around and Ruffe yapped, running in circles between the trees but unknowing of what was going on. Perry raced ahead of Avanti and swiped his axe, banishing the vines from their path before throwing himself to the ground so that his partner would have a clear shot with her trident.

She threw the pronged weapon through the air, sailing far over Chintu's shouting head and between two trees to graze the top of Puppy's hair. He toppled to the floor, and Chintu placed her foot on his panting chin. He scowled up, his sweaty black hair now mingled with red.

'Oooooh, well done,' he said to Chintu. 'Three on one. Very impressive.'

'That's why you travel alone, isn't it, Puppy?' said Avanti. 'You like fighting against the odds, and still winning.'

'Well, you've lost,' Perry heard himself say, surprised that he was engaging in the joshing that he so often heard from other warriors.

'Or do you travel alone 'cause you haven't got any friends?' said Chintu. Puppy's face lost all its colour, and he gave Chintu a look of deepest loathing.

'You wouldn't be friends with those rag-tails either,' he murmured.

'So,' Chintu said, 'what's the deal here? What do we get for not killing you?'

Puppy giggled under his breath and chuntered.

> 'Chintabelle thinks –
> That she'll get a deal –
> She's wrong! Too bad! –
> She'll be my next meal!'

'No deal,' he said, his eyes regaining focus. 'You just haven't got the nerve to kill me, Chintabelle. That's all this is.' More and more thick red liquid dribbled through his hair. Metres to the right, in the corner of Perry's eye, Ruffe toyed with a rabbit he had caught.

'I don't need to lower myself to your standards,' said Chintu. 'We could carry you back to Juniper, right now, if we wanted. Crank would have no problem tasting your blood. Why shouldn't we do that, Puppy?'

'Because you three will look weak in front of your king if you don't kill me, and you don't want that. Then again, I don't want to look weak in front of my king, either. So, let's make a deal.'

'In case you didn't hear me the first time, you're currently –'

'Fight me properly,' Puppy cut across her. 'Like *real* warriors. Tonight. Lake Centurion at sunset. Leagros versus Orynx.'

The kookaburras cawed in the trees. Ruffe devoured the bunny, leg by leg.

'You think you're so clever, don't you?' scathed Chintu.

'Puppy knows –
That she can't resist –
She's proud! She's smug! –
And easy to twist!'

'That one doesn't even make any sense,' observed Avanti. She looked sideways at Chintu, and Perry did the same, a clear sense of desperation coming over them both. Surely Chintu would not agree to such a deal? She had been in the forest for a long time – she would know that it was a bad idea…

'Fine,' tutted Chintu. Avanti clasped her hands to her forehead and Perry let out a groan. 'We'll play your stupid game. You seriously think Orynx can win against us?'

'I know we can,' said Puppy, crawling backwards and jumping to his feet. 'Well, Chintabelle – this has been the pleasure of a lifetime. Avantalina.' He dropped into a deep bow in Avanti's direction. 'I would bow for you, Perry, but you wouldn't be able to see me over that fat belly!'

He danced away through the forest, singing at the top

of his voice.

> 'Puppy wins –
> He couldn't be stopped –
> His skill! His flair! –
> Will never be topped!'

'What – on – *earth* did you do that for?' said Perry once Puppy was out of sight.

'That was the wrong decision,' echoed Avanti.

'He needs to be taught a lesson,' said Chintu, facing them both.

'But why like *this?*' pleaded Perry. 'Why in a way that puts everyone else in danger as well?'

'Whatever,' muttered Chintu, turning away and kicking Ruffe's dead rabbit farther into the forest.

'You know the other tribes will hear about this, don't you?' said Perry, growing more and more impatient at her haughtiness. 'They'll come along too, to pick up the pieces.'

'Then let them!' said Chintu. 'I'll kill them all – just so long as I kill him first.'

Perry threw his arms up in the air, glanced at Avanti, and shook his head.

'Come on,' Avanti said to them both. 'Arklow.'

The trio trudged farther into the woodland. The trees got denser, and no one spoke for several minutes.

'It's strange,' said Perry, as they waited for Ruffe to catch up with them. His blood pressure returned to normal, and he turned to face Chintu. 'Puppy reminds me of you a bit.'

'He *what?*' she demanded, nostrils flaring and ears pointing out.

Avanti smirked. 'That's what I've always said.'

'I am nothing like him,' Chintu said, rolling her tongue as though trying to dispel dirt from her mouth.

'Headstrong,' said Avanti.

'Proud,' said Perry.

'Sarcastic.'

'You hate one another.'

Chintu let out a cry of rage and stormed back through the vines to locate Ruffe. Perry and Avanti laughed.

'How does he fight like that?' Perry asked. 'Where did all those spears come from?'

'He makes them each night,' Avanti explained. 'Then, when he goes into the forest the next day, he wedges them into the floor as he travels. It's kind of like what Saskat did with the crumbs in Blackstream. That way, if he's attacked, he retraces his steps and dislodges the spears from the ground.'

'Pretty clever,' Perry thought aloud.

'He's a good warrior and,' she lowered her voice, 'as you've noticed, he's quite like Chintu. I think that's why she doesn't like him.'

'Why wasn't he wearing a mask?'

'I don't think he likes it much.'

'Those songs are annoying.'

'Oh my – look!' interrupted Avanti. She pointed ahead into the darkness, but it took Perry a few moments to identify what she was looking at. Several metres ahead, twinkling a delicate silver in the darkness, was the largest spider's web he had ever seen.

'Hey, Chintu – over here!' Perry called. She bustled through the branches. Ruffe followed.

'Woah!' she exclaimed. 'That's gotta be –'

'Darwin bark spiders,' Perry finished. 'They create the largest webs in the world.'

And so it was. A shiny labyrinth of interwoven string stretched through multiple layers of trees. The web was angled up towards the sky, making the entire construction visible and revealing hundreds of tiny black spiders with white hairs spinning at the centre. The web was perhaps thirty metres in both length and width. It was thin yet artfully designed so that the entire creation moulded around nearby trees. A feast of insects were dotted across the surface, all paralysed by the masterful trap.

'I knew they lived in here, I just never knew they worked together,' said Avanti. She rapped a knuckle against her forehead in deepest disappointment, and sneezed.

'Sometimes it's better to approach things as a team,' said Chintu, catching both of their eye with a smile that referenced the deal she had just made with Puppy.

'Come on, let's keep going,' said Perry.

By now, the darkness meant that Perry could barely see his hand in front of his face. Only by holding out his arms did he decipher where the various vines, trees, thickets and branches were.

Every animal that he encountered had bright, shining eyes: lemurs, frogs, spiders and fossa. It seemed that few birds lived here. On one occasion, Perry's foot sunk into a shallow pool of water, and the fluorescent blue skin of a sea slug shone up at him. The splashing noise was eerie within the silent vacuum that the trio now entered. Chintu reached down and held Ruffe tight. None of them spoke, and Perry sensed that they were reaching the centre of the forest.

Laughter filled the wilderness. Kookaburras guffawed at him from all around and hundreds of tiny, flickering flames lit up the distant forest visible through the trees. Perry could not see who the flames belonged to, but Chintu placed a hand across his chest and he leaned up against a narrow tree to conceal his body from the flames ahead. Only then did he see it.

The entire forest constricted around his heart, which hammered against his ribs. The soft, hollow coating of a bamboo tree touched his skin and beat through his throat. The forest was suddenly lavished in heat, yet this hot air stemmed from his chest as his lungs squeezed together and made breathing impossible. Perry's legs collapsed as the bamboo grew, circling his body and tangling itself through his windpipe.

He lay, flat on the floor, unable to breathe amongst the venomous leaves.

— Chapter Thirteen —

# Lake Centurion

Perry woke up on his mattress in the Juniper cave, squinting at the five Leagros warriors standing over him. They all grimaced, except for Crank, who spat a beetle onto the floor.

'What just happened, kiddo?'

'I don't – I don't know,' Perry stuttered, still coming to his senses. Bamboo had always had inexplicable effects on him, but he saw no point in divulging on something he did not understand.

'Is there somethin' ya' want to tell me?'

'I have nightmares about it. About –' he willed himself to say the word, but could not do it; 'the plant. I don't know why. It's happened for years – even when I lived in Borea.'

'And why did ya' not tell your king about this, kiddo?' The veins running over Crank's bald head pulsed.

'It didn't seem relevant.'

'Not relevant?' Crank shouted. 'Kiddo, anythin' that risks the lives of the people in this cave is relevant. Did your king not make that clear enough to ya'?'

'You did. I'm sorry. I should've said something.'

'Go easy on him,' Avanti murmured.

'Go easy on him?' Crank bellowed. 'Go easy on him? Ya' better listen to ya' king right now, Avatron…'

'Avanti,' Chintu corrected.

'*Whatever!*' spat Crank. 'Ya' king needs full disclosure to protect the subjects in this cave.'

'Kirito thinks that the Leagros king shouldn't call the tribe his subjects.'

'No,' interjected Chintu, and the cave went still. 'Crank's right. Perry should've said something.'

Perry hung his head as the tribe dispersed to their different mattresses. Only Chintu remained behind. It was shameful enough that he could not understand his mystery fear of bamboo, but even worse to have put Leagros in danger. Avanti tossed him a well-cooked slab of meat across the cave, which he waited several minutes before picking up.

'Did you tell Crank about Puppy?' he asked Chintu as she sat down in an armchair next to him. Across the room, Saskat slid a tree root between her thighs.

'Yeah. He was actually kinda happy.'

'Happy?'

'He says that 'cause Orynx only has five warriors, five of us can fight them while a sixth person steals all their supplies.'

'Who's doing that?'

'Me,' Chintu said, flicking her hair back and curling her lip. 'He reckons that my dislike of Puppy might interfere with my fighting judgement. I mean, seriously, have you ever heard such nonsense?' She retied her bandana and kissed her teeth as Perry reflected that Crank had a fair point.

'Kirito thinks that the scary woman should not criticise the Leagros king,' said Kirito, walking past Perry's mattress.

'I'll give you something to be scared about in a minute, if you don't shut it,' Chintu said. Kirito did not seem to hear – he snapped his legs outward from his body in a strange sort of dance. Perry scratched the back of Ruffe's ear.

'What happens if I have to go back to Arklow?' he said to Chintu.

'Well, obviously, if you can avoid it then that'd be best. But, if you have to, then just shut your eyes when you walk through the trees.'

Perry made a mental note to try this next time.

Evening loomed, and thickening raindrops spattered against the Juniper roof. Saskat, after being shunned by Perry, instead invited him to play throw and catch with a wooden disc. Ruffe bounced avidly between them once Chintu joined the game.

'If ya' stupid game makes that dog knock over the tree, there'll be – ouch!'

Chintu span the frisbee into Crank's forehead. 'Ruffe is a coyote, not a dog.'

'Kirito does not understand the game,' said Kirito, watching from his mattress. 'What is the aim?'

'Not to drop it.'

'Kirito does not think that that counts as an aim. The crocodile Lord will be unhappy that the Leagros tribe is participating in such nonsense while living in the forest.'

'Do you speak to the crocodile Lord much, Kirito?' said Chintu, laughing as Ruffe chased his tail.

'Kirito knows that the scary woman is making fun of him, but he will answer anyway,' said Kirito, puffing his chest out. 'Kirito spoke to the crocodile Lord today, while he was on his scouting trip. Kirito asks whether it needs his help, and sometimes it tells him to hunt down the squirrels of the forest.'

'Ya' can shut it with that rubbish,' said Crank, rising to his feet and intercepting the frisbee. 'It's gettin' late. Everyone get ready for the lake.'

Avanti stepped into the firelight and traced the outline of her knees. Perry grasped his now slightly less rounded stomach and fell onto his mattress. What events waited for him in the next hour? One warrior had already been killed in Hades Forest. Would he be the next to die?

'Ya' better be ready to fight,' said Crank to the tribe after Perry spent ten minutes sharpening his axe. 'We'll approach Lake Centurion from the west, Orynx will get there from the east. If Feysal or Taveron has heard news of the battle and wants to pick off the pieces, then Feysal will arrive from the north and Taveron from the south.

'For those of ya' who don't know, there is a steep bank surroundin' the lake. Ya' have to jump down it to get any-where near the water. Under no circumstances should any of ya' do so. Goin' down the bank leaves ya' exposed, so stay above the bank, behind the trees. Also, if Taveron has heard about what's about to happen, they'll have gone to the lake earlier to place traps 'round the perimeter. Make sure ya' watch out for them.'

'What if one of the other tribes goes into the water?' said Perry.

'Do *not* engage,' said Crank. 'Orynx might send some-one into the water as a distraction. They'll want us to jump out and attack them, revealin' our hidin' place without re-vealin' theirs.'

'What about me?' said Chintu.

'I trust ya',' nodded Crank. 'Be precise and quick. The Isle of Bees is the easiest location to hijack, so ya' won't have much trouble as long as ya' avoid the beehives on the climb up and look out for the piranhas in the water. One last thing.' Crank looked up into the firelight, which illu-minated the scars across his face. 'This could be a trap. Orynx could be standin' outside this cave right now, waitin' to kill us. Stay alert. And Chintu, take care of ya'self.'

Leagros shuffled down the entrance tunnel with their weapons. Ruffe remained behind.

'Shouldn't we spread out, so it's harder to hit us?' said Perry as they approached the light.

'No,' said Crank. 'I'll step out first, to make sure it's clear.' He craned his neck forwards and peered across the opening through the pouring rain. Leagros waited with bated breath, until he marched forwards and nodded back at them.

'Good luck,' whispered Avanti as Chintu departed. Perry was too nervous to speak. The tribe walked back-to-back through the forest, each person looking in a different direction as the rain fell faster and heavier. Perry faced straight into the wind, which blew droplets now so thick into his face that he doubted his ability to spot a foe standing two metres away. The sky was sullied with ashy grey clouds, and the air grew heavier as they travelled, until Perry yelped in shock as a finger poked him in the back and instructed him to turn around. Leagros had arrived at Lake Centurion.

The lake was as large as the Juniper opening. It was shaded a mossy green, clouded by fragments of forgotten leaves and grass floating on the surface. Groups of lily pads clumped together made the water almost invisible. The bank was a couple of metres high around the edge of the lake, and Perry spotted a long vine hanging over the other side of the water.

A dense head bobbed through a lily pad to the surface, displacing an unsuspecting toad.

'Aaaah – pssst!' sprayed the gasping voice of Malik. He coughed water from his throat, blinking into the rain. 'I'se should practice breasts strokes, I'se should.'

Malik was barely audible beneath the deafening rain. Saskat's pudgy hand pulled Perry's shoulder back as Crank's talons did the same. Leagros stood crowded around an enormous redwood tree, hidden from the rest of the lake.

'Should I kill him?' said Saskat, readying her water gun.

'No,' Crank said, chewing a beetle between his teeth more passionately than ever. 'It could be a trap.'

'Kirito highly doubts it, Leagros king,' said Kirito. 'The stupid man from Feysal is very stupid.'

'Malik might be stupid, but Yasha ain't,' growled

Crank. Malik dipped his head below the surface and gasped back up again, spluttering water everywhere. An enormous white gown flew down from the canopy, flapping its gigantic wings and landing in the water. Perry could not believe that there was a pelican in the forest.

'What's you'se looking at?' Malik demanded of it. The pelican did not acknowledge that the man was even there, and Perry discovered an absurd inclination to laugh.

A sharp twang rung through the air.

Perry turned around, seeking reassurance from Kirito or Avanti, but both looked as petrified as himself. Saskat pointed a podgy finger at the sky. There was no evidence of what she saw, until an enormous splash echoed across the lake, followed by Malik's head crashing through another mossy lily pad.

Perry crouched farther behind the redwood bark.

'Who's there? I'se has a rights to know if you'se is spying on me.'

Avanti grasped both sides of Perry's head and span him towards the canopy. Falling between the rain was three wooden darts, barely longer than Perry's fist, which landed in perfect synchrony in the water.

'Saskat's not the only one with a gun in this forest,' muttered Avanti.

'Where did they come from?'

'Those darts can travel a long way. Orynx sent them up in the air to attack Malik without revealing their position.'

'Watch out for the trees,' whispered Crank, stroking his goatee. 'They could be up there.'

'You'se is causing trouble!' roared Malik, panting at the attacker he could not see. 'You'se can waits 'till Yasha 'ears about this.'

He swam through the murky liquid and scrambled out on the far side, using the overhanging vine to hoist himself onto the bank. Saskat's finger twitched towards her gun's trigger, but Malik disappeared northwards into the distant wilderness and she sighed. Perry's heart pounded against his neck. He peered at nearby branches, but the animal mask of an Orynx warrior did not reveal itself. Avanti traced her jaw when the indisputable neigh of a horse echoed across the lake.

'Paraskevas!' Saskat hissed. Crank's multi-whipped weapon trembled as he slapped his bald head. 'Taveron is here!'

Perry's mind flitted to the woman with multicoloured skin, but an echoing whizz, followed by three loud clunks, brought him back to his senses. A boomerang, spear and dart had flown eastwards across the lake, but were diverted by three arrows from the opposite direction. The horse neighed louder as Orynx and Taveron emerged from the bordering trees. The opening was filled by the futile clunks of artillery missing their targets and lodging into trees. A spear launched by Puppy skidded off an overhanging branch across the lake, and a rope netting fell from the tree. The Taveron horse shrilled as it sprinted away, being cut by razor boomerangs as the grunts, thumps and whizzes of combat echoed all around.

Paraskevas shouted obscenities from her horse's back and reared it around the lake, nearing the Leagros tribe she could not see. The beast kicked through a mound of leaves and its rider was thrown off as the horse's leg fell down a hole. It screamed but clung to the earth with its front two legs, pulling itself out and allowing Paraskevas to remount. Crank's wrist quivered along the handle of his weapon when, with a shuddering groan, Saskat's gun drowned the beast with water.

'Blimey!' screeched Paraskevas from beneath the flood, and both Orynx and Taveron blasted weapons at Leagros while still pursuing their initial targets. Perry crouched behind the tree, resenting his axe's futility before darting along the bank towards Orynx. Saskat followed, but was knocked over by the tail of a shooting arrow. Her gun clanged to the ground and Perry lifted it up, pulling the pump and sending waves across at Taveron. He avoided hitting Miist, who battled Bunny. Saskat winked at Perry and grabbed the gun as Perry retrieved his axe.

A young girl wearing a hamster mask was hidden behind a tree. Her long hair fell down the back of the mask. She faced away from Perry and launched razor-sharp machetes at Taveron. Perry span the axe over his shoulder and aimed for the girl, but the wet wooden handle slipped from his grasp. It clunked against the tree far higher than he had aimed. Hamster heard the noise above and sprang away to re-join her tribe. Perry groaned and waited until Saskat recommenced firing across the lake to step forwards and retrieve his weapon.

Yet his axe was not alone. Hamster had left the machetes at the foot of the tree. Perry stifled an amazed laugh and picked up the nearest one. He launched it at Hamster, who had since recognised her mistake and crept through the branches above to retrieve her weapons. The Orynx warrior dived from the tree, rolling onto the floor and returning to her tribe.

An arrow clattered across the lake, skimming Hamster's right elbow, followed by a second, which skimmed her left. The child stumbled back as a third arrow pierced her foot. She tumbled over into a hole dug in the forest floor, before climbing out and returning to her tribe.

'Medium-sized man!' shouted Kirito's high-pitched rattle from behind him. 'Send more sharp objects at the murder tribe so that they take cover, and Kirito can get closer to use his Zhua!'

Perry hurled machetes at the masks of Kitten, Bunny and Chick. All three figures climbed into the tree branches, but Perry pursued them as Kirito curved around to attack from the right. There was only one layer of drenched trees between Kirito and Orynx now, yet the masked figures had not spotted him. An arrow skimmed Perry's wrist and he jumped back to hide from Taveron, as Orynx arched their arms through the trees to send more sharpened weapons his way. Kirito, poised behind an adjacent trunk, lurched forwards and swiped his clawed Zhua up at Chick's feet, splitting the child's toes as a muffled shriek cut across the lake. Chick fell to the ground and Kirito stepped forwards to kill his victim, when Taveron's arrows sent him, too, ducking to the floor. Kitten and Bunny jumped down to attack Kirito, but Perry broke their path with two machetes. Kirito crawled behind a tree, and then raced back to join Perry, who huffed in relief.

The battle appeared to be at a stalemate, until Avanti soared down from a high branch. She lashed her trident back and forth at two scurrying Taveron women. Leagros pushed Orynx farther around Lake Centurion towards Taveron on one side, while Taveron retreated towards Orynx on the other. Perry crouched behind a redwood and glanced back as Crank seized Saskat's water gun and drenched Paraskevas's horse.

> 'The fat man thinks –
> That no one's nearby –
> Look up! Watch out! –
> He's going to die!'

'Get down!' screamed Avanti, pushing Perry across the dirt and dodging the spear Puppy launched at his head.

'Hey, mister fat man!' called down the masked figure of Puppy, running through the branches above. 'Where's Chintabelle? Was she too scared to risk her neck?'

'None of your business!'

Beside him, Avanti ducked to avoid an arrow fired by Taveron and span one of Perry's machetes back in return. Above, Puppy lodged his spears into the trunk and used them as ladders, jumping from platform to platform until finally retrieving one from the bark and launching it at his victim. Perry dodged it, arcing round the tree and flinging a machete in return. Puppy jumped onto another spear and cackled as Perry's weapon tangled itself in the branches, and fell back down. For a moment, it appeared that the boy had not noticed – until he plucked the machete's handle and slung it at Perry in one swift movement. Perry dived across the floor as Puppy's laughter echoed through the trees, skipping away to re-join Orynx.

'Watch your back, *Periwinkle!*'

The pile of machetes dwindled. Farther around the lake, Crank darted through the trees above Taveron, whipping his Kraken onto unsuspecting heads as they collapsed to the floor, screaming and flailing. His accuracy was unrivalled. A brown and green haired woman was lashed, exposing that she did not have any hair, but rather a combination of twigs and leaves. Her now bald head crawled away as Miist and a dumpy older woman did the same.

'Get back!' screamed another voice farther around the lake. Bunny waved his arms to recall the Orynx warriors. 'Forces retreat! Forces retr –'

But the Orynx king did not finish his final breath. A razor-sharp boomerang soared through the rain, swerving between two trees and lodging itself in his neck. Blood spirted everywhere, coating the bunny's white mask. The fragile body of an eighteen-year-old boy collapsed through the rain, the fatal weapon immovable from his neck. Blood streamed down the bank, merging with the murky water. He was rinsed by the torrential rain, unknowing of the battle that ceased around him.

Taveron crawled back. Paraskevas reared her horse and fled. Tovia's fuzzy peach afro was the brightest thing across the lake, yet even that was now dirtied by the rain. She lowered her head into a solemn bow as a boomerang glinted in her hand. The rape tribe stepped away from Lake Centurion.

Storm clouds cracked lightning onto the howling ocean. Perry tore his eyes away from the trickling blood as Crank stood tall and saluted. Perry did the same, as did Avanti, Kirito and Saskat. The now-kingless Orynx tribe stepped forwards, interpreting Crank's gesture as one of good faith, and picked up their fallen king.

The vast lake did not notice the presence of blood. Its colour did not change. The fallen victim disappeared behind the trees, and Perry mourned a boy that he would never meet, and whom, due to the callousness of Borea's rule, might never have died at all.

— Chapter Fourteen —

# Beyond the Bamboo

It was cruel that Bunny's parents would never learn of their child's death. It was cruel that they would not care even if they knew. The inexplicable grief for a boy that Perry never met made him retire to his mattress in silence when Leagros arrived at Juniper.

'Suck it, Orynx!' shouted Chintu, dancing into the cave twenty minutes later with a huge vine-constructed sack over her shoulder. 'I got out just as they came back. It rained heavier at the Isle of Bees, though, so I don't think they noticed me. Plus, they were carrying something. I hoped it was Puppy's body, but then –'

'Don't say that,' Perry heard himself say.

'What?' said Chintu, only just noticing the solemn atmosphere in the cave. 'What's the matter? Look!' She pointed at the far side of the room. 'Look how much stuff I got!'

Three sacks of supplies – four, once she lugged the latest across the room – were lined up along the wall.

'Seriously,' she laughed, looking disconcerted that Leagros was not as excited as she was; 'who died?'

Her face sunk at the sight of three crying warriors.

Avanti's good nature clearly made the sight of Bunny's murder unbearable to witness, and Kirito, too, was struck by the immensity of what he had just seen.

Unsuspected to Perry however, and leaving him ashamed of how numb he felt, was the sight of Crank, crouched down on the edge of his mattress, weeping pools onto the floor.

'It was Bunny, wasn't it?' said Chintu. 'Bunny died.' Saskat readjusted the spectacles on her forehead, took a swig from her bottle, and nodded.

'But that's good, right?' Chintu stammered. 'One more down, one more step towards –'

'You didn't see it,' Crank croaked.

'It was horrible,' Perry said. 'Even the rain couldn't...'

Chintu lowered onto her mattress as Crank extinguished the torches around Juniper. Nighttime arrived, but there was a distinct absence of snoring in the ensuing hours. Only the occasional grunt from Saskat broke up the night, and after what felt like an eternity, the distant tweeting of birds indicated that morning had come.

Crank relit the torches and spoke to the cave.

'No scoutin' on the east side of the forest today. No killin' an Orynx warrior. If one of them attacks ya', you defend yourself only. No attackin'.'

Saskat tilted her floppy auburn hair to the side and eyed the Leagros king. Perry selected a small fish from Chintu's stolen supplies, but frowned. It felt wrong to eat food gathered by a dead child.

'Um, excuse me,' Avanti spoke up. 'I wondered if Perry and I could go to Arklow today?'

'Fine,' said Crank, still hoarse. 'Chintu, go with Saskat to Halcyon. Kirito, come with me to Blackstream.'

Perry and Chintu shared a meaningful look. Crank and Saskat normally scouted together. Was Crank avoiding her because of their unexplained argument yesterday?

'You can have Ruffe,' shrugged Chintu, 'I don't feel up to the stress today.'

Perry gathered his axe and trudged from the cave. He wished for an uninterrupted, peaceful day. The rain had ceased during the night, but grey clouds fogged the sky above. Perry felt that he would very much like to float into the sky and join the cloud – to fade into the grey.

'See you all later,' Chintu muttered as each pair parted ways. Avanti led him down the same path they took the day before, when it dawned on Perry: they were going back to Arklow.

'Hold on, I shouldn't be going here. I'll faint again. I'll put you at risk.'

'That's why I asked you to come. I think you should face your fears,' said Avanti.

'Not today. I'm not ready for it today.'

'I'm sorry, but you'll never feel ready. And the longer you're vulnerable to the bamboo, the longer you're in danger. The longer we're all in danger.'

'But we don't even know what the problem is,' said Perry.

'We don't really need to know *what* it is – just how you can overcome it. You don't have to do it if you really don't want to, but you'll need to hang back while I scout on the other side of the trees.'

Perry quivered and looked down at Ruffe, who walked between his legs.

'You'll protect me, won't you?'

Ruffe yapped and jumped around on the spot.

'How are you feeling?' asked Avanti some minutes later.

'Horrible,' he replied.

'Me too.'

'I don't even know what he looked like. I could hardly even eat this morning – just a small slab of meat.'

'Yeah, me too,' said Avanti, running her hand along her spine and staring at the floor. Perry noticed a blueberry bush nearby.

'You've always given me food,' he thought aloud.

'I try to be kind,' Avanti muttered.

'Even on the first night, when we walked to Juniper, you gave me some fish. That feels like forever ago.'

'Yeah,' Avanti agreed, wiping her nose. 'You were much bigger back then.'

'Is that what happened with you?' asked Perry. 'Were you fatter before you came here?'

'No, I've always looked like this. Everyone's always been bigger than me.'

'How come?'

'I just hate eating,' said Avanti. She glanced at Ruffe, who ran through the thickets ahead. 'It makes me feel weird and anxious.'

'Why?'

'I don't know. When I do eat, I usually just throw it up.'

'I've never seen you throw up,' pointed out Perry.

'I normally leave the cave or take a detour so others don't see.'

'You can throw up in front of me.'

'My body doesn't need to,' shrugged Avanti. 'I haven't eaten. Whenever someone gives me food, I just give it to someone else. It's weird because… I don't know.'

'What's wrong?'

Avanti grimaced.

'It's hard to explain. It's just – I know that I'm not very big, but whenever someone gives me food, I can't help thinking about how fat I'll be if I eat it. And it makes me anxious.'

'But that's ridiculous!' exclaimed Perry. Avanti dropped her head even lower towards the floor. 'Of course you won't be fat. How can you say that?'

Avanti flapped her arms out at her sides and bounced on the spot. 'I know it doesn't make any sense. I shouldn't have said anything, I just thought you might – never mind.'

Perry realised that he had reacted poorly to Avanti's confession.

'Well, you shouldn't force yourself to eat if you don't want to. But food gives you energy, for running and fighting and stuff.'

'But that's the thing – I don't like any of that, either. Whenever Crank tells us to go scouting, I just feel ill again.'

'Maybe eating will make you feel better?' Perry suggested.

'I *don't want* to eat food!' Avanti shrilled, losing her

temper and flapping her arms by her side. 'You sound just like my parents.'

'Well,' fired up Perry, thinking of his own parents and growing frustrated now, 'maybe if you explained a bit better…'

'I've told you – I feel like I'll become fat if I eat! Why do you have to be so horrible about it? I thought you'd be different from my parents.'

'Well maybe the problem is that you're acting like a child!' retorted Perry.

'That's so unfair!' yelled Avanti. 'You don't know what it's like. It's no wonder you get on so well with Chintu.'

'What's that supposed to mean?'

'You're just like her – so inconsiderate of others. You make no effort to put yourself in someone else's position.'

'Chintu's not inconsiderate,' said Perry. 'You don't know the half of what she's been through.'

'And what if I did?' said Avanti, her thinned nostrils flaring between coughs. 'Would that suddenly make her a hero? Would that make it all right that she makes fun of everyone she speaks to – *all* the time?'

'You don't know what you're talking about,' said Perry.

'Neither do you,' snapped Avanti.

They turned away from each other as Avanti sneezed. Perry crossed his arms, deplored at her cutting words. He was nothing like his parents – he was not inconsiderate. Was it not him who forgave Avanti for allowing him to be tortured on his second night in the forest?

As they walked on, Perry knew that the bamboo approached, but was in no mood to ask for Avanti's help.

'Do you want my help or not?' she said.

'No.'

'Don't be ridiculous.'

'*You're* being ridiculous.'

Perry thought he could smell it now – the pungent aroma of past panic attacks and fainting. He squinted down at the floor and dared not look up.

'Shut your eyes,' said Avanti, looking at him.

'What are you going to do?'

'Guide you. I'll lead you through the bamboo.'

Perry flinched at the word.

'Fine,' said Avanti. 'I'll lead you through the *trees*, then. You'll be on the other side before you know it.'

'But it's still wet,' said Perry. 'I can smell them, and feel them.' His heart rate accelerated as the forest's humidity pushed up.

'Hold your nose then.'

'Fine.'

Perry did so and shut his eyes, stationary on the spot as Avanti's sallow, scaly hand grabbed his elbow and guided him forwards, pinching him harder than she might otherwise have done. With his eyes closed, Perry's other senses intensified. Every step over the rutted forest floor was accompanied by the sickening sound, smell, taste, and mental image of bamboo. Perry breathed, thinking of a white, open space where his mind could be at rest. For a few moments, he was free: twigs crackled beneath his heel, insects crawled over his toes. *Focus on the insects,* he urged himself. *Focus on the insects.*

'Open your eyes.'

'I can't,' said Perry.

'You can.'

'I can't.'

'Don't be ridiculous.'

His throat closed up and his ears shrunk; every limb, vein and muscle tensed. Avanti was tricking him – he was about to die. But the distant hope that he was far, far away from the bamboo gave him the faith to squeeze apart his eyes. Light shined in the distance, illuminating the surrounding forest. Perry squatted to the ground but cringed at a tree root next to his foot; it was thick, matted and ran for metres around the tree. This was not bamboo. He was not looking at bamboo.

'I did it?' he said, turning to Avanti. 'Did I do it?'

'You did it. Well done.'

'But, this is unbelievable,' he stuttered. 'I've never been able to even look at it before.'

'Well, you just walked past it. Did you clear your head?' asked Avanti.

'Yeah. I kept thinking about all the stuff under my feet.'

'Good. Now, we should go back in.'

'*What?*'

'It'll be fine,' reassured Avanti. 'It'd just be better if you touched it.'

'No way!' shouted Perry.

'Shhh! Keep your voice down – we're in Arklow, remember.'

'I can't do it, Avanti. I just can't.'

'I'm sorry, but you have to. You can keep your eyes shut, and I won't tell you when it's about to happen – it just will.'

Perry glanced back at the light illuminating the distant forest and decided that he did not want to know what caused it. With a loathing shudder, he shut his eyes and nodded as Avanti led him through the bamboo once more. The humid air got hotter, he choked, and his dry throat tightened.

Avanti mumbled some words, but his echoed breaths filled his ears and he did not care what she had to say. His arm reached out, dragged by Avanti towards the bamboo. He screamed, petrified of the darkness that engulfed and suffocated him as it always did. The peeling, sandy surface of the bamboo met his fingertips for the very first time and he recoiled in terror. Avanti pressed her hands against his chest as he fell to the ground. He flailed and squirmed across the leaves, his forehead butting into a hard surface. He squealed again and curled his feet and arms beneath his body, forming a shell to expel his nightmares.

Two hands hauled him into the air. They carried him through the screeching forest as he sobbed, moaned and gasped. He was lowered again as he whimpered on the cold, sodden floor of the wilderness.

'You're all right,' said Avanti. 'Just keep your voice down. You're going to be all right.'

Whimpering sighs spilled between Perry's closed lips. The noises died in his throat as Avanti, between sneezes, maintained waves of encouragement.

'You're all right. Just keep breathing. You're going to be all right.'

'I'm broken,' he admitted in a hopeless whisper. 'I can't survive here. I don't want to live here anymore. I don't want to live.'

'Perry, you're going to be all right,' Avanti said. 'You're just in shock.'

'But I don't want to live anymore.'

'Yes, you do.'

'No, I don't.'

'There's so much more to fight for, Perry,' said Avanti. 'Once Leagros wins –'

'We won't win. Not with me in the tribe. I'm fat and I'm useless and I can't even touch a tree.'

Avanti waited several moments before speaking. 'You're not useless. You're not fat. And you just *did* touch a tree. So, once Leagros wins, you'll get away from this place –'

'*We'll* get away from this place,' corrected Perry.

'Yeah,' murmured Avanti. 'Both of us. And we'll take on Borea.'

'Which will bring even more trouble,' said Perry. 'Why can't I just die?'

'Because…' said Avanti, and Perry could tell that she was thinking hard. 'Because Ruffe will be upset. He loves you and it's his job to protect you, so if you die you'll be taking away his job.'

The excited wetness of a coyote's tongue flooded Perry's ear with saliva. The buzzing in his brain quietened down and his body stopped shaking. He allowed himself a small smile as a soft chirping broke through the surrounding woodland. He reminded himself that Vemlin was nearby, and stood up to face Avanti, resolute.

'Are we on the north or south side of the trees?'

'North,' frowned Avanti. 'It was closest.'

Perry nodded, looked over his shoulder to make sure the coast was clear, and rested on a stump, sighing and petting Ruffe. The coyote danced on its hind legs, before bounding into deeper layers of the forest.

'For my entire life, I've always had nightmares about bamboo,' said Perry. 'I always knew something was wrong with me.'

Ruffe was out of sight now. Perry peered around a row of trees but could not see into the darkness. He stepped away from the tree trunk, crunching over broken leaves and looking ahead. With a glance over his shoulder, he saw Avanti step towards him without much conviction.

'Ruffe?' whispered Perry, turning into the darkness. 'Ruffe? Here, boy. Where did you go?'

Perry passed through more layers of trees and gripped his axe. Avanti was nowhere to be seen behind him, but he knew that she would be searching the trees he missed. More lights flashed to his left, but Perry fixed his eyes onwards. He crouched down and pushed away some vines.

'Ruffe?'

There was a soft, gulping noise ahead. A dark mass shadowed the floor, wrapped around a central focal point. Ruffe's whines were intelligible, but only just, as the enormous olive and black stripes of the anaconda ensnared the coyote into its trap.

'Avanti!' bellowed Perry, leaping back in terror despite knowing that he must attack.

The snake constricted its pray, hissing as the coyote vibrated.

Perry stepped closer, but the two animals were inseparably one. Where the anaconda twisted, Ruffe's furry skin was only a centimetre away. Perry pulled back his axe but did not strike, creeping forwards as he tried to line up the blade with the black and olive scales. The anaconda hissed. Ruffe was going to be killed, and Perry swung with all his might at the undulating back end of the serpent's tail.

'Aaaaahhh!'

He split the blade through the serpentine skin. The snake recoiled, not loosening its grip on the coyote yet halted in its progress. The two creatures continued to breathe as one, but a loud hiss emanated from the snake as its neck twisted to locate its attacker. Ruffe moaned louder and Perry knew that he must strike again. He hacked at the tail once more and the serpent's long head twisted around, extending beyond its prey and facing Perry. He brought the axe down, roaring as the creature's eyes parted between a devastating blade.

Blood-red liquid oozed everywhere, bursting between the separated head like a blooming flower. It carpeted the forest floor as the beast softened its grip on the victim. Still Ruffe whimpered, and Perry panted and glanced around, aware that Vemlin was nearby.

'It's all right,' he reassured Ruffe, comforting himself just as much as the coyote. It whined as Perry slid the axe blade through the snakeskin entangling Ruffe's neck.

Blood dripped onto Ruffe's skin but Perry squinted and ignored it. He dipped his fingers into the gruesome slit and pulled the snake's neck free of his pet. He edged farther along the snake, halving it with precision while ignoring the spirting blood.

'I'm sorry,' he said each time; 'I'm so sorry.'

Finally, the anaconda was dissected, and Ruffe hobbled towards his owner. Perry patted him, blood staining his hands.

'Avanti!' he called back through the trees. 'Avanti?'

No one responded, but Perry did not fret. Avanti was right behind him only minutes earlier.

'Come on, boy,' he said as Ruffe limped at his side. Perry balanced the axe between his chin and chest and hoisted Ruffe into his arms, carrying him through the trees.

'Avanti!' he called, arriving at the point where they had conversed minutes prior. He was stunned to find the surrounding forest empty. The sharp laughter of kookaburras burst from the trees as Perry called his tribemate's name.

*She wouldn't leave me like this,* he thought. *She wouldn't just leave. Which must mean...*

He hurtled back through the trees, breathless and jaded but carrying Ruffe on his shoulder. He faced the floor as he approached the bamboo.

His mind filled with images of Avanti – where she had gone, who had taken her, and whether she was already dead. He bumped into trees left and right, almost dropping Ruffe on several occasions, but kept his eyelids shut. After several minutes, he glimpsed an opening.

'Come on, boy,' he gasped at the snivelling coyote. 'Stay with me. Not you as well.'

His legs travelled as fast as possible. The forest grew lighter as he emerged from the dense wilderness, shooting down the Juniper tunnel into the cave and explaining the danger. Leagros left immediately, Crank lashing his Kraken at nearby trees as he led them back to Arklow.

'Tell me what happened, again,' he demanded of Perry.

'Ruffe got attacked by an anaconda. I went for the snake and shouted for Avanti to help me, but when I looked back she was gone.'

'Did you hear anyone take her?'

'No, nobody!'

'Crank,' Chintu whispered as the king slowed down to a walk. 'Diablo.'

'You think I don't know that?' he bellowed at Chintu. 'You think I don't know what he'll do to her?'

Perry jumped backwards, terrified at the king's outburst. Saskat, meanwhile, swayed, bottle in one hand and water gun in the other. The pace of Crank's running meant that they were already approaching the bamboo.

'Stick with me,' said Chintu, taking his hand. Perry nodded thanks and cleared his mind of the damage he had caused. He allowed his hand to be soothed by Chintu's as they walked. Finally, she squeezed and let go as they reached the other side.

''Dat cotey ish more trouble 'den is worth,' slurred Saskat, rubbing her hand along Perry's back.

'Now is not the time, fat woman,' said Kirito.

'You were pretty happy to play with it yesterday,' hissed Chintu at Saskat, who slurped more liquid and nearly dropped her gun. A raised hand from Crank brought them to a halt as he turned to face them. He spoke between bites of a beetle.

'We are, if I'm not mistaken, about to witness something deeply disturbin'. It is crucial that ya' control your emotions. We are enterin' the belly of the beast.'

# Chapter Fifteen

# The Belly of the Beast

Crank led his troops onwards through the Arklow region of Hades Forest as Chintu placed a small wooden container in Perry's hands.

'Water,' she whispered, 'for your hands.'

Amidst the chaos, Perry had forgotten that his hands were covered in anaconda blood. He frowned at Chintu, as hers were tainted with the same liquid.

'It's all right,' she said, understanding his expression and flicking back her silver hair to look him in the eyes. 'Thanks for saving Ruffe.'

'*King* Ruffe,' Perry corrected with a faint smile, before falling silent. His last conversation with Avanti was an argument. He regretted not dragging her with him to rescue Ruffe. It was his fault that she was missing.

'Now,' whispered Crank as the distant yellow lights grew brighter. 'Ya' king doesn't know what animals are in this part of the forest. Ya' king also doesn't know what Diablo is gonna be doin' to her. Just stay calm, stick to different trees, and wait for my signal.'

Leagros nodded.

'Kirito, 'round the back. Perry, on the right. Chintu,

stay here. Saskat, on the left. I'll be up in the trees.'

Each warrior avoided one another's eye as they dispersed. Perry followed Kirito, dropping Chintu's wooden container to the floor.

'Is mister shaggy man feeling all right?'

'Fine,' muttered Perry.

'Stay calm, sir. It is not the shaggy man's fault. Try to stay calm.'

Perry gulped as the incandescent yellow light drew closer. Leagros positioned around it. There were thousands of different tiny lights, flickering on and off and floating through the air between different branches.

'Kirito will be seeing the shaggy man on the battlefield, sir,' said Kirito. He gripped Perry's shoulder to indicate that he should halt, before walking farther into the light.

Perry could not see the layer of trees in front of him. How was he supposed to see Crank's signal through the glow? How was he supposed to find Avanti? He leaned against a nearby trunk when he noticed that the trees were formed differently in this part of the forest. Sticking out from each one were dozens of long wooden cuboids, providing a thick staircase upon which he could climb. The planks were embedded in the bark, built and solidified over more than two years. Each was so large that Perry did not doubt that it could hold his weight. He could find no other way to see beyond the yellow mass, so he stepped onto the lowest plank of an outlying tree and climbed upwards.

He was lifted above the fiery fog. Finally, with a birdseye view over the scene, he could comprehend the mystery light.

The forest was filled with fireflies. They flashed as they clung to the barks, buzzing between different trees. The rest of Leagros, too, had climbed up the wooden planks. Each warrior stood in the canopy, looking down at the opening.

Vemlin prowled the forest below. Avanti's frail body was pinned to the ground by two men, one of whom Perry recognised as the man with claw-hands named Killua.

The second man was deformedly tall. He was over two and a half metres in height, and had a stretched appearance, as though his limbs had been pulled outward from his body on either side.

A man stood between them, and two women prowled the perimeter of the opening. They glared up at the trees and held something indistinguishable in their arms. One woman had a light purple mohawk and showed no evidence of existing physical deformity. The other woman had a deep groove in the middle of her stomach, giving the appearance of a crater pressing against her gut.

Avanti whimpered on the floor, her body discoloured. The skin on her face had been seared by something. It was blurred between nose and cheek. All her hair was singed away, and she gasped through her barely open mouth as she blinked at the forest canopy.

The leading man turned and looked up to the light. Avanti made no attempt to break away from her captors, and the man relished his triumph by shutting his eyes and holding out his arms, as though accepting an invisible gift. His skin was dark and dirtied, not unlike Puppy's, and his face was engulfed by a dark shape stretching from the top corners of his forehead to the bottom of his nose. Perry had observed a birth mark before, but never one that so polluted an individual's face. His hair was a deep black, absent from the sides of his head but pushed back into a long arc over the top. His eyes were black, too, as were his lips, which were shrouded by a black goatee. For a brief moment, it seemed that the man opened his eyes, until Perry uncovered a façade: blood red eyes were painted onto each eyelid, scanning the wilderness even when its master was unseeing. The man was coated in luxurious coats of fur across his body, and as he lifted his arms up to the trees and gazed into the light, Perry saw that both armpits were covered in the hair of animals the man undoubtedly slayed.

'Give me the torch, disgusting woman!' demanded the man.

'It will do better to leave the skin searing for some time longer, Lord Diablo,' said the woman with a groove in her chest. She bowed to her leader, her periwinkle blue quiff sparkling in the light.

'Silence!' roared Diablo. 'Do not address me with those infernal lips. You judge that I care for your nonsensical spew?'

The woman bowed and placed a lit torch in Diablo's arms. The flame sizzled. It was greater and more frenzied than the gentle torches of Juniper, and Diablo lifted it up as a beacon of strength.

'Thou art at my mercy! I speak to you, pathetic woman. Do you confess thyself worthier than a man?'

Avanti did not speak. She gaped at the Vemlin king.

Her charred skin quivered as the torch neared. Diablo withdrew his neck and spat into the flames, adding to the hissing noise. Crank studied the scene from a tree opposite Perry's, but remained in place, slowly chewing a beetle.

'Do something!' Perry muttered to himself, burning into Crank's eyes across the trees. 'Do something now!' He looked sideways at Chintu, who stared bewilderedly back at him. What was Crank waiting for?

Killua and the stretched man cackled as Diablo lowered to his knees and spoke to Avanti. It seemed that she was about to reply, when the torch burned into her right arm.

Screams echoed through the clearing. The fireflies buzzed at the sound of burning flesh. Vemlin's laughter was dark and rasping, and the smouldering skin cracked louder.

A rustling to Perry's left stole his attention. Chintu launched herself to the ground, landing on a dark purple mohawk and clawing at the exposed skin of the woman's head.

'Flo!' screamed the second Vemlin woman, racing across as Perry dropped down and faced her, axe pointed. Avanti's screams stopped and Perry charged, ready to split his axe through the second woman's body, when a dark shape tackled her to the ground. Kirito stood up, eyes wide, as Diablo stepped forwards and swished the flamed torch at Kirito's skin. The light extinguished in a burst of blue, however; Saskat's water gun shot across and snuffed the flame. Shadows sprinted through the yellow gloom, locked in ferocious battle.

'Florius, pathetic woman, use this!' bellowed Diablo, tossing the mohawked woman a dagger. He picked one up himself and thrashed at Chintu, who was now outnumbered two-to-one.

'Take this, weird-haired woman!' wheezed Kirito, spearing his Zhua at the woman with the blue quiff. 'The Leagros king may call the weird-haired woman Aruba, but she is nothing more than a squirrel ancestor to Kirito!'

A jet of water blasted Florius to the ground. Perry hurtled through it, shaking back his dripping hair and swinging his axe at Diablo. The Vemlin king parried, knocking the weapon from Perry's grasp and turning to launch a kick at Chintu. She blocked the attack but was knocked over by its force.

Diablo stepped back, teeth bared, and departed through the mist of fireflies. Perry heaved Chintu to her feet and pushed her across the square as they both hurdled Avanti's helpless body. Chintu resumed battle with Florius, while Crank and Saskat attacked Killua and his lanky companion. Perry sprinted to Kirito, who stood over Aruba with his foot on her chest.

'Crocodile conquest!' Kirito shouted.

'Kirito,' panted Perry, exhausted and checking his shoulder for Diablo.

'Yes, shaggy man?'

'Help Avanti!' he panted. 'Carry her back to Juniper.'

'Is the shaggy man sure?'

'Yes!' gasped Perry. 'Go!'

Kirito lifted Avanti over his shoulder and disappeared into the yellow mist. Perry pressed his axe against Aruba's neck. She stirred on the floor, reaching out for a dagger that fell from her grip, but Perry thrust his heel into her nose. With a clean snap, it broke, and Aruba fell unconscious. Only three Vemlin warriors remained.

'Get outaffit, Hexen-boy!' bellowed Saskat from the tree above, drowning the abnormally tall man with her water gun. Hexen collapsed as Crank snapped his Kraken at Killua, who dodged and weaved, avoiding spats of water and the flailing whip. His streaming silver locks flowed as he dived to the floor, rolling onto his front and using his crouched legs as a launch pad from which to leap at Crank. The Leagros king fell as claws sunk into his scalp. Killua was ready to rip him apart as Chintu's cries echoed behind Perry.

'Help! Hexen – help!'

Saskat drenched both Hexen and Florius, who cornered Chintu, so Perry focused on Killua. He leapt and swung his axe. The blade connected with a claw swishing towards Crank's chest: Killua's nail was dislodged from his hand and sent flying into the yellow mist. Killua yowled in pain as the axe followed through and slit his cheek.

Crank jumped up, unharmed, and struck Killua in the eye. He fell, shouting, as Perry once more cracked his heel down against the victim's nose. Crank nodded thanks and spat a beetle onto Killua's unconscious face.

Crank and Perry faced the last two Vemlin warriors: Hexen and Florius. Saskat's water gun had greater impact on the former than the latter – Hexen's thinned body was pushed back by the forceful water. Chintu, meanwhile, abandoned hand-to-hand combat and mounted branches on the outside of the opening, plucking overhanging vines from the trees and lashing them at Florius. The Vemlin warrior stood open-mouthed as a deafening crack sounded, but not from the intended target.

A razor-sharp disc the length of Perry's arm was spun off course by collision with Chintu's vine. A deep roar rumbled from within the yellow light and Diablo's dark figure emerged, silhouetted by the buzzing fireflies and the kookaburras laughing in the canopy. He unstacked the discs piled in his arms and tossed them at Leagros, who all leapt to the ground as Hexen and Florius regathered themselves. Crank and Chintu ducked beneath a disc and charged at Diablo while Perry engaged with Florius, who picked up the knife from Aruba's body and pointed it at him.

Saskat's water gun hindered Hexen. He yelled a muffled cry from beneath the torrent as he fell back into Perry's path. Florius was momentarily distracted, and Perry took the opportunity to swing the axe at Hexen's leg, slashing into his thigh and knocking him to the floor. Hexen squirmed, looking up with venomous eyes but unable to rise to his feet as blood streamed from his leg. Florius was pressed down under a torrent of water as Chintu appeared, diving backwards to avoid a flying disc and whipping Florius in the face with a vine. Florius stumbled, scratching at her blinded eyes until eventually disappearing into the yellow swarm of fireflies.

Only Diablo remained. Perry took Chintu's place and swiped his axe as he dodged the flying discs. Diablo roared, veins running over the outline of his birth mark as one of his discs sliced through Crank's Kraken, leaving the Leagros king defenceless. Saskat shot another stream of water, but Diablo dodged it, and the blast drenched Perry instead, knocking him onto his back. Saskat stopped shooting, realising her mistake, as Diablo turned and launched a disc at Chintu. She dived to the ground but it skimmed the top of her silver head, travelling onwards and arrowing towards the floor until sticking with a silent thud.

Leagros did not move, and even Diablo's arms stopped swinging. The kookaburras cackled at the sliced body, spattering blood all around. Diablo had not killed the female foe – he killed Hexen, instead.

Diablo shrieked and turned towards the yellow light. As his body retreated however, a second higher-pitched shout broke across the clearing. Kirito's stocky silhouette burst through the light, swiping both Zhuas at Diablo's head and knocking him to the ground. The claws grazed Diablo's birthmarked face and Kirito rotated the weapon, thrusting the wooden handle into the Vemlin king's left ear. Diablo, too, was unconscious on the floor.

'Kirito!' screamed Crank. 'What are ya' doin' here?'

'Kirito came back, Leagros king,' he beamed, puffing his chest out.

'Where's Avanti?' said Chintu.

'In a tree.'

'A tree?' repeated Crank. 'What did ya' leave her in a tree for?'

'The skinny woman is quite safe,' said Kirito, frowning in bewilderment at Crank's reaction.

'Take your king to her!' demanded Crank. 'Now!'

Kirito skipped into the yellow mist, excited to show-case his brilliance. Saskat jumped down from her tree and followed, as did Perry and Chintu. They exchanged furtive glances but did not speak, each trying not to look at Hexen's mangled body on the floor.

As Leagros passed the bamboo, Perry shut his eyes and was once again guided by Chintu. Then, five minutes later, Kirito used a collapsed tree as a platform upon which to launch himself onto a branch high above.

'How on earth did he get Avanti up there?' muttered Chintu, half laughing, half despaired. Perry shook his head in disbelief, feeling his scratches and wounds. Kirito flung himself up the branches and disappeared behind a sheaf of leaves, before emerging several moments later with the limp form of Avanti in his arms. She breathed sighs of pain but did not speak.

'Is Kirito allowed to throw her down, Leagros king?'

'Fine,' said Crank, holding out his arms to catch Avanti's light body.

Kirito jumped down and Leagros walked on, fatigued and silent. Crank shook his head for the rest of the journey, while Perry and Crank shared glances of mild amusement. That was, until Avanti recommenced her moaning, and they grew solemn at her condition.

She was almost unrecognisable. Her skin was burned and stretched over the sallow bones poking out from her skin. Her hair was completely seared off. Her lips were thick and swollen. Only a cold, bumpy skull remained where her hair once was, giving her a bald, ghoulish appearance. The pink glow of sunset radiating over the forest only further revealed Avanti's scarred flesh.

Once Leagros entered the cave, each person took it in turns to shower while Avanti lay on her mattress. Eventually, she started moaning again, and widened her lips to produce words over the top of a tongue which, fortunately, remained untouched.

'I'm sorry,' she mumbled.

'No,' spoke up Perry, 'I am. This is all my fault, Avanti. I shouldn't have let you go. I shouldn't have let you out of my sight. I can't believe what's happened – and I did it to you and – I understand if you never want to speak to me again.'

He looked at her weak frame, her eyes blinking up at him, and wept. Tears flooded his cheeks and he fell back onto his mattress, submitting to the grief. Avanti would be weak for the rest of her life.

'*Honestly*, Perry – the poor girl just had all her skin burned off, and *you're* the one crying?' said Chintu.

'It's not your fault,' mumbled Avanti, wincing. Perry sat up on his mattress.

'What does the burned woman mean?' said Kirito.

'Don't call her that,' snapped Chintu.

'I did it on purpose,' said Avanti. The words echoed around the cave. 'I just couldn't stand it anymore. When Perry wasn't looking, I threw a stick for Ruffe to chase. Then I waited for him to go after the dog, and I walked into Arklow. I wanted Vemlin to kill me. I asked them to.'

'But why?' said Chintu. 'Why would you do that?'

'I hate myself,' said Avanti. 'I always have. I wanted

to die when I denounced the state. I don't want to be alive. When Perry talked about how much he hated himself, it just reminded me how much I feel the same way. I want it to be over. I wish I didn't look the way I did. I wish I didn't care so much about other people's feelings, when I can't even look after myself. I wish I were dead.'

Perry gaped, open-mouthed, unsure what to say. Avanti's nose wrinkled as she stared at the Juniper celing.

'The skinny woman is loved,' said Kirito. 'Kirito cares about her very much.'

'Me too,' said Chintu. 'That's why we saved you, Avanti. Nothing would be the same without you.'

'All of us love you, Avanti,' said Perry.

'But I don't love myself.'

'There's five of us to make up for that,' said Chintu, leaning down to kiss her on the forehead. 'You're the kindest person I've ever met. You really, actually care about people's feelings. It's amazing.'

'The skinny woman is kind to Kirito. She makes him feel like less of a freak.'

'You give me food,' said Perry, 'which is important because, in case you haven't noticed, I'm very fat.'

The tribe laughed.

'And you're an amazin' warrior,' said Crank, finally. 'I'm proud to have you in my tribe.'

Avanti's head shifted at this admission. She murmured a reluctant acknowledgement, traced a finger along her collar bone and winced in pain. Under the Juniper firelight, she looked worse than ever – discoloured, gaunt and frail. Her entire face was no longer outlined at each feature, but blurred between each one, scarred into a face unrecognisable from the one they all knew and loved.

'Can I please just be alone?' she mumbled. 'I won't go anywhere. I can't, anyway. Maybe you could just sit outside or something?'

'It's still only sunset,' said Crank. 'We'll be back in a couple of hours, Avatron. Everyone, scouting, please.'

'Kirito shall go alone,' said Kirito, walking towards the stone slab blocking the entrance tunnel. 'Kirito shall search for the holy crocodiles of Lake Centurion!'

'There's no crocodiles in the –' began Chintu, before being silenced by a nudge in the ribs from Perry. Kirito's fluorescent hair disappeared down the tunnel, captivated by his own imagination.

'Kiddo, go with Chintu to the Isle of Bees,' instructed Crank. Perry nodded, ruffled Ruffe's hair to signal that he should come along with them, and left Juniper.

'What do you think's gonna happen to her?' said Chintu as they left. Ruffe jumped into the stream behind Juniper to wash the anaconda blood off his skin.

'What do you mean?'

'Well, she won't be able to fight again.'

'She might not need to,' replied Perry. 'Not for a while, anyway. Ruffe can take her place.'

He smiled down at the coyote, who rubbed along the bark of a fallen-down tree.

The forest darkened as Perry and Chintu walked, and they did not speak much. Ruffe chased after various butterflies drifting across his path, which they both laughed at, but were otherwise lost in their own solemn thoughts for Avanti. After some time, the gushing East River sounded ahead.

'Is it weird that I feel sad, even when I see another tribe's warrior die?' asked Perry.

Chintu shrugged. 'We're all humans. It's just best not to think like that in battle. Feel sorry for them afterwards, not during.'

Perry nodded.

'Let's go over the bridge,' said Chintu, leading the way. 'It's probably better to approach from Broadfields, as there's more trees to cover us on that side.'

Perry waited for her to step ahead over the creaky bridge, then followed behind, eventually continuing through the trees and coming out in the long, scratchy grass of Broadfields. It reached up to his torso as a thin cloud emerged in the sky and showered rain across the field.

They waded through the grass, when Chintu's body lurched forwards and she fell onto her face. Perry hooted, clutching his stomach in aching joy as Chintu retied her bandana and stuck her tongue out at him.

'Stupid tripwire,' she mumbled, kissing her teeth. 'Stupid Taveron.'

With Perry still smirking, they moved through the tree line to the river and, for the first time, Perry arrived at the Isle of Bees. The island was larger than he had expected. It took up much of the currently visible length of the river. Three tall, narrow trees were stationed within reasonable distance from one another on the isle, each disappearing up towards the sky. On top of two of these trees, just beneath a huge box constructed of vines that was filled with overflowing supplies, was a buzzing beehive. It was swarmed with yellow and black dotted creatures flying around it. The beehive on the third tree, however, sat beneath an enormous wooden carving of a dolphin's head.

The rushing water combined with the fins, noses and tails poking out of the river made the isle an alarming sight. Yet, above the crashing river, something else grabbed Perry's attention. A rapturous cheering swarmed the Isle of Bees as Puppy, Kitten, Chick and Hamster chanted. Each prowled the perimeter of the island and prodded their weapons at two figures at the centre.

Both Taveron warriors were stationary.

'That's Shix!' gasped Chintu, 'Shix and –'

But Perry did not need to be told who the second woman was. While Shix span a long wooden pole between her arms, Miist darted her eyes across the isle in search of objects to fix inside her slingshot.

The stage was set. A Taveron warrior was going to die. Miist and Shix faced each other, ready to fight to the death.

— Chapter Sixteen —

# Sleepers Den

Miist and Shix stood on the Isle of Bees, unmoving. Orynx circled them, screaming with glee.

'I don't want to watch this,' said Perry.

'We've got to. That's why we're here – to tell Crank what's going on in the forest. We need to know who wins.'

'But what if Shix wins?'

'So what if she does?' said Chintu, temporarily confused. Realisation struck, however, when she recalled that Miist had saved Perry's life – a decision they did not yet know the reason for. 'We'll get to her before she dies.'

Perry nodded, without really meaning it, and stared closer at Shix's weapon. It was a long wooden pole about one metre in length, with a spiked circle at the end wide and long enough to fit a human head inside. The spikes poking along the outside threatened to impale anyone who came near.

'What is that?' whispered Perry.

'A Halo. It has spikes on the inside, too. She jumps down from trees and places it around your head. Then she twists a knob on the handle, and the spikes inside the wooden circle impale the victim's neck. If she manages to get it around your neck, you're already dead.'

Shix and Miist stepped towards each other. The former span the Halo between her knuckles, the latter flicked away her long hair. Metres away, Puppy tossed a wooden stick at one of the three beehives in the trees above. The impact wasn't strong, but several insects buzzed down towards the ground. The warriors leapt into action.

Miist backed away, collecting stones and twigs from the floor as Shix stepped towards her. She yanked the snakeskin from her neck and whipped at exposed parts of her enemy's skin. Miist jumped back and neared the isle's edge. Orynx shifted around the perimeter, blocking the combatants from outnumbering them and escaping into the river.

'Should we do something?' said Perry as Shix avoided a rock fired by Miist. 'Should we save them?'

'Too dangerous,' said Chintu.

'She saved my life…' muttered Perry. Ruffe whined at his feet. Water crashed against the island's edge as Shix swished her pole back and forth. The handle was thick, batting away rocks fired by Miist into the river with a loud clunk. The fight was relatively tame thus far and Hamster, Kitten and Chick stepped closer to their victims. Puppy sprinted back and forth, singing and poking each warrior with a spear.

Miist thrust four rocks into her slingshot and threw herself to the floor to avoid a lashing from Shix's snakeskin. Rolling over, she shot all four rocks at her opponent, who flipped up into the air, spinning above the bullets and landing with a triumphant smile. The snakeskin whipped again, followed by a swinging Halo, as Shix cackled and Orynx cheered. Miist struggled to her feet, dislodging the hair trapped beneath her buttocks and scrunching her face together.

The situation seemed hopeless. Miist's slingshot was empty and Shix's two weapons were ready to strike again. Miist jumped up and raced across the isle, whishing her enormous hair round her body and smacking it against her opponent's face. Shix was buffered, tripping backwards as her opponent followed up with a punch to the face, kick to the knee and elbow to the crotch.

Shix collapsed and Miist crouched beside her, pulling her opponent's neck into a headlock and winging her hands sideways, appearing to loosen something. Chintu gasped as Miist's bold strategy paid off. The vine holding the leaves and twigs atop Shix's head came loose, and the foliage fell to the floor.

Shix's bald head glimmered in the sunlight. Miist picked up the vine and whipped it at her foe. Shix gathered her snakeskin and did the same until both warriors faced each other, throwing occasional cracks across the isle. Orynx screamed with delight.

> 'Miist and Shix –
> Will fight to the death –
> Oh no! Too bad! –
> They'll take their last breath!'

The Halo sat at Shix's feet, yet she showed no intention of using it. Miist's vine was longer than the snakeskin, and she capitalised on this by jumping backwards and connecting a crack against her opponent's upper arm. Shix howled in furious pain and reached down for the Halo, swinging it at her enemy who approached too closely.

Miist fell back with a scream and Shix swished the spikes of the Halo through the victim's skin. She faced the tree beside her prey and hoisted her body around it like a sloth, slithering up the trunk as Miist cringed on the floor. Shix looked down at the flinching body and launched herself on top of the opponent, splitting the spikes deeper into Miist's leg. Blood decorated the grass as the pair fought, scrambling back and forth.

The Orynx warriors ran forwards to kick the rolling bodies. Eventually, Miist's wounds weakened her, and Shix pushed on top, clasping her hands around the victim's neck and pushing her to the ground. Miist collapsed, limp, as Shix picked up the Halo and thrust it around the neck of her prey.

The strangled eyes of Perry's saviour widened as Shix sniggered. She turned the handle, and dozens of spikes pressed into Miist's skin.

No one moved. Orynx screamed with glee. One spike pierced through Miist's neck, and blood spirted onto the grass. Shix stood up, roaring in triumph. She smeared a bloodied finger along her forehead, and then into her mouth.

'No!' exhaled Perry.

Shix leapt into the river, dipping beneath the surface and emerging moments later cleaned of all blood. She sprinted into the distant forest. Several bees swarmed the leaves and twigs on the isle while other insects buzzed around Miist's defeated body. Puppy swatted them away with his spear and used the blunted handle to lift her up. She was alive, but only just. Puppy hoisted her into the air as Hamster, Kitten and Chick danced, shrieked and bowed towards the dolphin mask at the top of the central tree.

Finally, the Orynx warriors muttered between themselves. Chick pointed between the dolphin mask and Miist's stirring body.

'Surely not...' said Chintu.

'What's happening?'

'I think they're going to – but surely not?'

Perry rolled his eyes and looked down at Ruffe. 'Do *you* have any idea what she's on about?'

'I think they're taking her to Dolphin.'

Perry stared at the island. Orynx bandaged Miist's neck with leaves and carried her towards the river. The fallen Taveron warrior still blinked into the rain.

'Come on!' hissed Chintu, darting back towards Broadfields.

'We're not going to... Chintu, we're *not* following them!'

'We've got to! This could be our last chance to find out why she saved you.'

'But –'

'Go back to Juniper if you like, but I'm taking Ruffe.'

The coyote simpered, stepping towards Chintu. Perry sighed as he followed his companion, who ran along the grass and crept back towards the riverbank. On the other side of the isle, Orynx carried Miist through the river.

Chintu lay down in a bush and Perry fixed himself behind a tree. Then, once Orynx disappeared into the distant forest, Chintu ushered him forwards.

'Let's go!' she said, jumping into the river.

'One tiny problem,' said Perry, following her. He lofted Ruffe above the river with one arm, and held his axe in the other. 'How are we supposed to question someone that's being sacrificed to Dolphin?'

'We'll deal with that later.'

Perry splashed through the water and clambered onto the Isle of Bees. By this time, Chintu reached the other bank, and threw stones at him to hurry him along.

'You'll hurt Ruffe!' he protested.

'I'll hurt *you* in a minute, if you don't hurry up.'

He reached the other side and all three of them set off at a brisk jog after Orynx's vanishing figures.

> 'Shixalocks killed –
> A Taveron friend –
> Bye-bye! Farewell! –
> Her body won't mend!'

'She's not dead yet,' muttered Chintu. The four animal masks were faceless and dark from behind. Fortunately, with Puppy singing so loudly, Orynx was not difficult to track.

'Shut it, poo brain!' teased Hamster. Chick cackled.

'Agreed!' shouted Kitten. 'And, honestly, go and wash yourself. You smell disgusting.'

It was true that Puppy's body was even more dirt-ridden than usual. To Perry's surprise however, Chintu snatched insects from nearby leaves upon hearing this remark and flicked them away, muttering.

Eventually, Orynx approached a darkened section of the forest and Puppy subsided. Any purplish remnants of sunset had long since faded, and only now did Perry realise that he did not know where they were going.

'I don't actually know where Dolphin lives.'

'Yes, you do, it's in Arklow. We told you that.'

'I'm not sure you did.'

'Well, now you know.'

The rain stopped and the forest darkened. Chintu dropped her gruff tone and whispered: 'Just stay calm.'

Perry thrust his hand into hers, shut his eyes, and was led into the looming black. The all-too-familiar laughter of kookaburras shivered through his eardrums. He channelled his nerves onto squeezing Chintu's hands. He could not see the bamboo, yet it continued to press into his throat and chest. The familiar sensation of breathlessness pushed him towards breaking point, and his heart beat through every limb. Before too long however, they emerged on the other side. Perry opened his eyes and confronted the dark forest.

He rejoiced in his success and looked down to pump his fist, but suddenly did not want to let go of Chintu's hand. The bamboo was far behind them now, yet Chintu held on and stepped a little bit closer towards him. She stared ahead, distant in the eyes, as though waiting for something. Perry's heart raced unrelatedly to the bamboo, and he took the terrifying leap of squeezing her hand in his own. She squeezed back, a vulnerable smile flitting across her cheeks, and they each walked on in silence.

Perry was filled with an extraordinary sense of elation. He was certain that something was happening, although he was not sure what. This, somehow, felt different to Mabel. He wanted to step even closer towards Chintu. The hand connecting them, it seemed, was not binding enough. Yet Orynx moved farther into the darkness, and the dazed companions focused on remaining silent and unnoticed. After a few minutes, Chintu dragged Perry's hand back.

'Um, well, we should probably… um, y'know…' She looked down at their conjoined hands and cleared her throat. Perry felt her fingers hook onto his, as though battling against what she just said, but he took the hint and let go. They each leaned down to pat Ruffe, blushed as they collided, and stood up straight again.

Eventually the forest lightened with shimmering orange flames. Chintu and Perry arrived at a grand wooden fortress.

The building glowed a deep auburn. It reached high into the trees, with towers and turrets spiralling across the palace's four floors. Enormous fire-lit torches were dotted around the structure, billowing smoke into the world above. A magnificent, rock-carved staircase travelled up to the centre of the second floor from the ground. It had a marvellous, violet-painted door at its pinnacle. Triangular windows were spaced across the four levels of wood, two of which had a figure clouded by the smoke positioned within. At first, these shapes appeared to be more flames, but two pairs of blinking eyes alerted Perry to his mistake. He was not staring at pockets of flame. He was staring at two gargantuan tigers.

He stepped back, horrified, and leaned against a tree. Ruffe whimpered beside him. Ahead, Orynx stepped up to the grand staircase and climbed. Perry, however, felt much less enthusiastic.

'What now?' he asked Chintu.

'I don't know.' She looked at Ruffe, who lay sideways at her feet, and sighed. 'I think we're gonna have to leave you back there. Is that all right, buddy?'

Ruffe showed no reluctance at being left behind. Chintu led him farther back into the darkness and used a vine to tie him to a tree. The coyote lay down and Chintu and Perry watched as Orynx rapped a spear on the violet door, still carrying Miist between them.

'Do you think she's dead?' said Chintu.

'I hope not.'

An unseen figure opened the door and Orynx stepped inside. Both tigers left their windows, distracted, and Chintu took Perry's hand as she ran forwards and mounted the staircase. The deep rumble of tigers was audible beyond the door, but Chintu went along to the farthest window on the right.

'Lift me up,' she said to Perry. He did so, all too aware of how exposed they were in the clearing and that the tigers might be on the other side of the window frame. Chintu sat on the ledge, checked either side, and dropped down. She reached out an arm to loft Perry into the vacant window. Once in, they huddled behind a potted plant in the corner, listening to distant voices in the next room.

The inside of the fortress was just as remarkable as its

outside. Even more lavish than the Juniper cave, the building was thoroughly decorated. Illustrious carpets made from animal fur coated the floor. Sitting atop the carpet were smooth wooden tables, washing tubs made from rock, and bowls of food for the two resident tigers.

'What is this place?' whispered Perry.

'Sleepers Den. Dolphin's fortress.'

Through an empty doorway in the next room, several voices spoke. Chintu pulled Perry out from behind the plant. They stepped through the doorway to get a look, before Chintu pushed Perry back. The backsides of five masked figures, and two tigers, climbed up a staircase. Chintu and Perry crawled up the carpeted stairs, near enough to hear Dolphin's words.

'Welcome to Sleepers Den. I see that you have brought your liege a gift.'

Perry and Chintu glanced at each other. Something was different about Dolphin's voice. Although it was muffled beneath the mask, it seemed different to the deep tone Perry had heard on the boat journey from the state prison.

'Yes, our liege,' said the girlish voice of Kitten. The shadows along the back wall revealed that she had displaced her mask and bowed it forth towards Dolphin, who sat in a throne.

'Very well,' said Dolphin. 'Your liege trusts that you are on-course to be victorious in Hades Forest.'

'Yes, our liege,' said Puppy, who also removed his mask.

'Do you need your liege's help with anything?'

'No, our liege,' said the tribe in unison.

'Then drop her body into the pit.'

The four shadows lifted Miist over a central point in the floor. The body was dropped down a hole, and a booming thump in a floor below indicated Miist hitting the bottom.

'Be gone,' said Dolphin, waving a staff at them.

Orynx ambled down the stairs and Perry and Chintu jumped off, hiding beneath its thankfully hollow underside. Chick, Hamster and Kitten, with Puppy trailing, turned into the next room. Puppy glanced sideways as he passed through, angling his mask towards the staircase. Chintu's hand pulled Perry farther back into hiding.

'I'll go out the back,' said a voice in the next room. 'Time for some hunting.'

'Whatever,' said another voice.

'No one cares,' said a third.

Perry waited with bated breath as an out-of-sight figure stepped back into the room. It remained still for a minute, before poking an enormous, glooming head beneath the staircase. Chintu clasped her hand to her mouth in a petrified squeak.

'Oooooh! Don't scare the toddler, Chintabelle,' said Puppy, taking off his mask and shaking his shaggy black hair. 'I should tell my *daddy-waddy,* really, if there's bad guys walking around his home.'

'Get out of it, pea-brain!' hissed Chintu.

'Not very friendly, Chintabelle. Hey, Periwinkle – have you toughened up a bit yet?'

Chintu opened her mouth to repeat ill-sentiment when a slow plodding vibrated through the floor above. The tigers approached the staircase. Puppy jumped down and huddled beside Chintu and Perry as the tigers stepped down the stairs, which seemed liable to collapse under their weight. Perry pressed himself against the staircase as the tigers sniffed, hacked spit onto the floor, but otherwise trod into the next room.

Puppy, Chintu and Perry glanced at each other as the spitting noise continued. This noise, however, was not reverberating from the next room. It was a very human noise, coming from the floor above.

'Truce?' said Puppy, looking at them both.

'Truce,' they said together, stepping out and creeping up the stairs. They peaked over the flooring. Standing between two amber flames, looking down over a circular hole in the floor, was a bald, thin woman.

She faced away from them, vomiting into the pit. The dolphin mask lay neglected on the floor, as the woman lifted her face back up and turned away from the hole.

Perry held back a gasp as the floorboards creaked beneath his feet. He blinked sideways to see that Chintu was shaking. She recoiled her neck backwards and cringed behind her hands, stepping down several steps. Her eyes glazed over and became scarily wide. Puppy and Chintu grabbed hold of her.

'It's her,' she muttered. 'It's her…'

'It's who?' said Puppy.

'Her,' she growled, looking at Perry. He blinked, refusing to believe what Chintu was saying.

'The woman?'

'The woman,' she confirmed, forcing out the words in

pain.

The woman that raped Chintu stood only metres away.

'Don't do anything,' said Perry, but too late. Chintu jumped up the final step and roared in fury, picking up Puppy's spear and launching it straight into Dolphin's chest. The woman was thrown over the hole, pinned against the farthest wall. The movement of tigers sounded on the floor below, but Chintu was immune to it. She pressed forwards onto the blood-soaked woman as Perry and Puppy followed, petrified.

'It was you!' she screamed. 'You! You did it to me! Why did you – arghhh!' She looked up to the ceiling and yelled again. The imposter looked petrified, her eyes wide and unbelieving. She was already dead; the spear had killed her, and all that remained were her final seconds of consciousness.

'How are you here?' shouted Chintu. 'How? You are not the real Dolphin. How are you standing in this room?'

The woman did not speak. Blood dribbled from her mouth and both lips vibrated as though trying to form words. Slowly her neck and eyes drooped, pinned against the wall by the spear of her victim.

Chintu punched the lifeless body in the face. She raced over to the Dolphin mask and stamped it beneath her feet. It would not break. She stamped again and again, but it was unyielding. She screamed, raced back over to the woman, and punched her in the face again. Her hands were smothered in blood.

The roars of tigers vibrated through the floor below. A loud bang sounded as Puppy tried to work a contraption attached to the wall. He pulled a lever and the staircase folded up into the ceiling, blocking entrance from the floor below. He was marginally too late, however. One tiger already stood on the staircase, and as the structure folded into the roof, the creature was flung through the air into the room. The gigantic orange beast turned, growling, and charged at the blood covered Chintu. It leapt over the hole and headbutted her to the ground, sinking its claws into the floor on either side of her.

Perry lunged forwards, but Puppy got there first. With three bounding leaps, the Orynx warrior dislodged the spear from the woman's body and flung it with incredible accuracy through the heart of the tiger. The beast was speared across the room as Chintu curled on the floor, sobbing.

Perry fought away the shackles of fear. He stepped over the central hole and saw a ladder running down the side. It was a deep pit, falling through both layers of the fortress into a tunnelled-off section of the forest below. He climbed down as fast as he could, clambering to the bottom. Miraculously, Miist was still alive, but only just. Her face was pale and emaciated, bloodied by the battle with Shix, and covered in the imposter's vomit. She seemed unaware of the man standing before her.

'What happened?' shouted Perry, tilting Miist's face upwards and urging her to stay alive. 'What is it you know? Why didn't you kill me?'

Miist blinked in miscomprehension, conveying no secret message.

'Come on!' urged Perry. 'Tell me! They're in here,

aren't they? The Demiurge?' The dying body looked as though it wanted to speak, but Miist's muscles could not manage it. 'I can save you,' Perry said, deciding; 'we can take you with us and keep you alive. You can tell us then.'

But Miist, showing her first real sign of life, shook her head.

'Let – me – die. Leave – island.' Blood poured from her nostrils, coating the long hair falling over her shoulders and resting on her chest. She coughed, unable to speak.

'Nod your head or shake it. Are the Demiurge in here?'

'Don't – know,' she stuttered.

'Then why did you save my life?' yelled Perry. 'Why?'

Miist's shoulders lifted, and then fell back down, as the inevitability of death engulfed her. She, too, lay against the blood-stained hole, covered in vomit and no longer breathing.

Chintu cried with rage from the floor above, as all explanation of the forest's existence petered into nothingness.

# Chapter Seventeen

# Crank's Confession

Miist's dead body slumped into the corner of the Sleepers Den pit as Perry collapsed against the ladder behind him.

'No... no, no, no. How? Why? Stay with me, please.'

He shook Miist's head, but she did not respond.

'I need to get out of here,' said Puppy from atop the hole. 'Orynx will wonder where I am.' Crashing objects upstairs signalled that Chintu was tearing the place apart. Perry glanced up at Puppy, who looked scared, and decided to climb the ladder.

Chintu was red in the face, her spotted bandana thrown on the floor as she destroyed everything in reach. A wooden table flew across the room; the violet throne followed close behind. She sprinted into one of the four walls and bashed her fists against it, screaming, before picking up a firelit torch and launching it at Perry's head.

'You...' she muttered. 'You. You!' She charged head-first at Perry, but Puppy intervened and pushed her back.

'Calm down!' the boy shouted.

'No! I will not calm down! I trusted you and – and – you let her die!'

'Let her?' Perry demanded, nose flaring. 'I *let* her die,

did I? You think I benefitted from what just happened? You think I wanted that woman to be dead – Miist to be dead?'

'That woman was my *rapist!*' shrieked Chintu. The words echoed through the room as she ran back over to the dead body and punched her in the face several more times. Puppy took two steps down the ladder into the pit, with only his head poking over the top.

'What's going on?' whispered Puppy. 'Did – did you know her?'

Chintu's fists stopped flailing at the dead body and she buckled, sobbing into the wooden floor, surrounded by the destroyed objects that could not make up for her pain. Perry raced to her side, picking her from the floor and stroking her hair.

'It's all right,' he said, 'it's going to be all right.'

Their two bodies morphed into one as Chintu wept into Perry's neck. She spat snot and tears all over him with howling, shaking sobs.

'I – just – I don't – you're not – but why – it's not – your fault.'

'Don't apologise. It's all right. It's going to be all right.'

A finger tapped Perry on the head as Puppy pointed to the window. Perry nodded, and the boy jumped through the triangular opening, landing with a distant thud in the forest below. Chintu shook in Perry's arms, as the grief consumed her for hours on end.

Chintu's deep wails made way for occasional jerks, which were replaced by determined deep breaths. Finally, after what seemed like an eternity, she looked up at him, wiping away the tears from her crinkled eyes.

'You are *not* weak,' said Perry. 'You are strong. No one in here can possibly imagine what you've been through, and that makes you a far more impressive person than all of us. You're allowed to feel like this. You're allowed to feel cheated. You thought this place was going to save you, and it ended up being more of the same. You just found out that the person who drove you to denounce the state is in here, too. You're allowed to feel like this.'

'But *how*, Perry? How can she be in here? What happened to the real Dolphin – the Dolphin we both knew?'

'I don't know,' he admitted. They locked eyes and he stroked the hair from her face. Together, they lifted each other up and Chintu retrieved her vine. They used it as a harness with which to abseil down out of the fortress.

Perry led the way through the forest this time. The pair did not speak until they reached Juniper. Five ocelot crowded around the entrance to the cave, licking the floor, and Perry walked over to see a layer of blood caked over the grass. As he stepped back and looked at the entire scene, he saw a clear message spelt out on the floor.

*Leagros Will Die*

'Pig blood,' muttered Chintu. They ignored the message and walked around the animals into the cave.

'Everything all right?' said Avanti, who sat up in her bed.

'Fine,' said Perry. Surprisingly, Crank, who lay on his

mattress, did not demand more information. 'How are you?'

'Terrible,' said Avanti, prodding her bald head, 'but I don't want to cause a fuss. Hopefully tomorrow will be better.'

'Hopefully,' said Perry. Chintu went outside to shower, after which he did the same. Despite the images of blood now seared into his brain, the overwhelming fatigue of such an eventful day permitted him immediate sleep when he returned to his mattress. It seemed that he had only just shut his eyes in the heated, aromatic cave when he was poked in the chest.

'Pssst!' hissed a noise above Perry's head. He ignored it and went back to sleep. 'Wake up,' the voice said again. The speaker had a recognisably deep growl, and Perry opened half an eye. It was Crank.

'Get up, kiddo,' the Leagros king whispered.

'What's going on?'

'Keep your voice down,' said Chintu, standing behind Crank. With both eyes now open, Perry saw that his king looked wearied and scared.

'Please,' begged Crank, his voice desperate, and different. '*Please* just come with me, kiddo. I need to tell you something.'

Perry got up, picked up his axe and followed them out of the cave. Crank continued to fidget.

'I'm sorry to wake you up, kiddo,' he said as they stepped into the entrance tunnel. 'I just need to tell someone. I have to.'

The king was pronouncing words more clearly and

checking his shoulders. He spoke in the same uncharacteristic manner as he had to Saskat in an overheard argument in Arklow several days prior.

They emerged into the black night. Chintu whipped a vine at the ocelot still clambering around the blood on the floor.

'Is everything all right, Crank?'

The Leagros king pulled hairs along his goatee without answering. He led them towards the stream behind the cave, veering left onto the walkway and taking them up to the bridges above the cave. As they reached the top, the beautifully glistening ocean was visible all around, reflecting the moonlight. Perry was too concerned by Crank's strange behaviour, however, to take much notice. The king continued to twitch and squirm, staring at his fingernails. There was no beetle between his teeth tonight.

'Crank, I heard Saskat leave the cave a few minutes ago,' said Chintu. 'Where has she gone?'

Still the Leagros king shook. Exposed to the chilling air, he managed to croak an intelligible word.

'Gone.'

'Gone?' said Perry. 'Gone where?'

'Beach.'

'Why?'

Crank's legs vibrated over the wooden planks of the bridge. The nighttime animals of Hades Forest cooed into the darkness.

'Come on, Chintu, let's go,' said Perry, dragging her down the bridge without any real intention to depart.

'No,' she said, shaking him off. 'Now we're here, I

want to get something off my chest. Something I don't think is quite right. Today, Crank, when we all waited in Arklow for your signal to save Avanti... why did you wait so long? We could've gone in straight away, but you held back. Why? Why did you do that?'

'I don't... I had to...' Crank said. Chintu kissed her teeth and narrowed her eyes.

'Is this to do with the Demiurge?'

Crank nodded, and Chintu stepped backwards.

'They're in here, aren't they?'

Crank nodded and steadied. He seemed relieved that Chintu had reached the crux of the discussion without his instigation. 'It's a lie. The story Dolphin told you, about saving everyone from prison, is a lie. Dolphin isn't even a Crolax – he's a Demiurge. But I don't remember every-thing.'

'Tell us what you do know, then,' tutted Chintu, rolling her eyes. 'The tough exterior has clearly been an act. I'm sure the forgetfulness is, too.'

Crank shook his head. Comprehension dawned across Chintu's face and she moved forwards, pushing Crank in the chest so hard that he fell onto his back.

'What are you doing?' shouted Perry.

'It's *you,*' she said, crouching down and staring into Crank's eyes. 'You are one of them. You're a Demiurge.'

Crank nodded and grew flustered: 'B – b – but, you have to believe what I tell you – *please!*'

'Why should we?' said Chintu, gripping the whip tighter.

'Because I'm not like them. I'm different. The memory

loss isn't fake.'

Perry did not know what to believe, as Chintu said: 'Get talking.'

'You're born into it, you see,' Crank began, rising to his feet. 'You don't have a choice. You're raised in these mind palaces and brought up by Stitchers.'

'Mind palaces?' said Chintu.

'Yes. The Demiurge live on islands around the world. I can't remember how many, I just remember lots of Stitchers. They train you in complete obedience. Obedience to the Demiurge mentality, and the Demiurge mission.'

'Mission?'

'To purge the world of the Crolax. The Demiurge mentality is that we are divine beings with the born right to rule. But the Crolax think differently to the rest of society, and that's what makes them dangerous.'

'Because they have mental or physical disabilities?' said Perry.

'Yes. Once a Crolax discovers that they are different to the people around them, they feel isolated. That's what makes all Crolax despise the regime.'

'But why do these people have disabilities?' asked Chintu.

'It's genetic,' said Crank, rubbing his skull. 'They are born with it. People with disabilities existed during the time before, but in much greater numbers. Having a disability wasn't something to be ashamed of back then. It was accepted.'

'What does any of this have to do with Hades Forest?'

'When a Crolax is discovered, they are put in prison.

But some are selected to be taken here.'

'Why?'

Crank shuddered and bit his nails before responding. 'To be studied.'

Perry and Chintu gaped at each other. 'But then,' she said, 'that's why – that's why the Demiurge are in here, too?'

'Yes,' said Crank. 'Everyone on this island that isn't a Demiurge is a Crolax. The Demiurge still doesn't understand certain aspects about the Crolax. So, they gather small groups of them on islands like this, and study them.'

'We're – we're not being recorded, are we? We're not still being tracked?'

'No. The recording device and tracker were removed from your bodies before you arrived in prison. There are dozens of islands like this across the world. The Demiurge report their findings after a week or two on each one. They manipulate different circumstances to see how it affects the behaviour of the Crolax – giving certain tribes masks; giving them a king or queen; changing the number of warriors in each tribe, and that sort of thing. Understanding how the Crolax react in different scenarios helps the Demiurge to get a more complete profile of how they work, and therefore better identify Crolax in daily Borean society.'

'So that's all this is?' said Perry. 'One big experiment? We're on this island... to be studied?'

'Yes.'

'But why put all the Demiurge in the forest with us?' said Chintu. 'Why risk the Demiurge dying?'

'The Demiurge don't view it as a risk. They don't think

that a Crolax could ever better a Demiurge. And, if they do, then that Demiurge doesn't deserve to live anyway.'

'How many Demiurge are in here?'

'Ten, including myself and Dolphin.'

'*Ten?*' exclaimed Perry.

'And what decides which Demiurge gets selected for each island?' Chintu continued, absent-mindedly retying her bandana and glaring at Crank.

'Each Demiurge is chosen randomly.'

'But are there rotations or something? We just saw Dolphin, earlier tonight, but it wasn't the same man we met when we arrived here. Instead, it was a woman – the same woman who raped me twelve months ago'

'Rotations are made, to relay information on the island's events.'

'How do they rotate?' said Perry.

'They switch out Dolphin.'

'When?'

'In the middle of the night. A boat arrives and swaps one of the old, masked Demiurge for a new one.'

'Why don't they just record us?' said Chintu. Perry was amazed at her alertness to flaws in Crank's argument. He, personally, was dumbfounded. 'It'd be so much easier to keep recording us, rather than take the risk of swapping out an inhabitant in the forest.'

'Perhaps,' nodded Crank, 'but the Demiurge believe that doing so would tarnish their results. For one thing, a flashing red light in each warrior's neck would influence the action in the forest – other warriors could see them coming from a long way away.'

'They could definitely just switch the flashing light off,' said Chintu.

'And secondly,' Crank went on, looking at her, 'the Demiurge technology is not as proficient as they would have you believe. The voice recorder, for example, is made from a specific set of compounds. Some substances react poorly with them. If the Crolax ate certain things, they could die – but the Demiurge needs them alive for a set period of time, to be studied. This is why citizens in Borea only have a limited menu of food.

'The Demiurge think about all of these different things. They monitor and plan for every possibility. While they do not view the testing process as a risk, they also do not take its success for granted.'

'But why are you telling us this, Crank?' said Perry. 'How do we know that this isn't part of the state's experiment? That we're not being studied, right now, to test for our reactions?'

'Because I'm like you.'

'How?'

'I don't remember.'

'You don't remember what?' said Perry.

'That's how I'm like you. I don't remember things. It's been getting worse for years now. I'm only thirty-nine years old, but there's so much that I can't remember. I don't know why, or what caused it – I only know that I'm not like them. It's been so difficult to admit it to myself. When you're surrounded by purist Demiurge, it's suffocating. But this evening, I got back to the cave early, and Avanti told me all about her past, and I just broke down.'

'Some people just have difficulty remembering things.'

'It's not like that,' said Crank. 'It hasn't always been this way. It's grown worse over time. Everything just started to fade somehow. I knew the memory existed somewhere in my past, but I could never reach out and grab it. So, I found methods of making it easier to ignore. Noticed how I've always called you kiddo?' Crank looked at Perry. 'Tricks like that makes it easier to ignore my loss of memory.'

'Why are you speaking differently now?' said Chintu.

'Borea encourages the Demiurge to speak and act differently while on the island. It helps us get into character, and see how different mannerisms affect the Crolax's behaviour. Saskat did it by acting deliberately sexual.'

'What?' blurted Chintu.

'Saskat? Saskat's a Demiurge?' said Perry.

'Yes. I've just told you, there's ten of us in here.'

Perry leaned against the bridge railing. His time in the forest was spent living with two members of the state that he so despised. How could he not have known? Shame and fury overcame him, but he remained alert in the conversation so as not to miss a single detail.

'Hang on,' said Chintu, 'is that why Saskat's been flirting with him? As part of the study?'

'One of the things the Demiurge are interested in is how the Crolax react to sexual advances.'

Chintu puffed and clenched her fists even tighter.

'We overheard you arguing with Saskat in Arklow,' said Perry. 'Was that what this was about?'

'Yes. She's noticed that I keep forgetting things. She thinks that I'm a liability. She wanted me to prove that everything was fine – that I was not going to let the secret out, betray the Demiurge, or accidentally give myself away.' He winced. 'That's why I waited so long in Arklow. I'm so, *so* sorry. It broke my heart to see Avatron get burned like that, but I didn't have a choice. If I'd rushed in before Diablo burned her a second time, he would've known something was wrong.'

'Diablo is a Demiurge, too?'

'Yes.'

'Who else in here is a Demiurge?'

'Yasha, Shix, Diablo, Hamster – I can't remember all of them, but they're all waiting on the beach right now.'

'*What?*' cried Perry and Chintu in unison.

'I told you, we have to be quick,' said Crank.

'Then why did you just tell us all that stuff?'

'Because otherwise you won't understand what's going on,' Crank pleaded. 'The Demiurge are all meeting on the beach, now. The *Leagros Will Die* message was the signal. That's why Saskat isn't in the cave: the Demiurge are leaving Hades Forest.'

'What?'

'No!'

'They won't leave until all the Demiurge are there. Saskat will tell them that I'm not dead, so they'll wait for me.'

'What about Dolphin?' said Perry.

'What do you mean?'

'She's dead,' said Chintu. 'I killed her.'

'Then they won't be leaving for a while,' said Crank. 'But be quick. They won't hang around all night.'

'Be quick about what?' said Perry.

'Stopping them!' shouted Crank, losing control now. He pulled his fingernails away from his head and stared at them both. 'You have to stop them! You must do something! They're just going to leave you here to die.'

'How are we supposed to stop them? They are trained killers!' said Perry.

'Gather all the tribes,' said Crank. 'Bring them all together and fight the Demiurge. I'll join you. You'll outnumber them two-to-one.'

'That's impossible. The others will never believe us.'

'You have no choice,' said Crank.

'Most of these tribes just follow their king or queen,' said Perry. 'If we can convince the leader of the truth, then we'll convince the tribe – and it'll be even easier if the leader is one of the Demiurge, and therefore not present.'

'Kirito thinks that it sounds risky,' said a voice farther along the bridge. All three of them jumped. Kirito's pink and turquoise hair glowed in the blackness.

'How much have you heard?' said Perry.

'The whole thing, shaggy man. Not intentionally, of course,' he bowed, 'but Kirito couldn't sleep, sir, and he heard three Leagros warriors leave the cave, so he followed them and listened to the lying bald man's story. Only the skinny woman is in the cave, now.'

'Kirito, we need your help,' said Chintu.

'Kirito isn't sure. It sounds risky.'

'Of course it's risky, but what other choice do we

have?'

'Kirito, please,' pleaded Perry. Kirito chuckled.

'Just Kirito's little joke, scary woman and shaggy man! Kirito will help!'

'Excellent,' said Chintu. She looked at Perry with a hardened resolve, submitting herself to the awaiting danger. 'Let's do this.'

'Right then,' stuttered Crank. 'I'll see you on the battlefield.'

Perry did not move as Kirito and Chintu walked away. The pair looked back at him, confused.

'You shouldn't fight,' Perry said to Crank. 'It's too dangerous. You've done well to tell us this, but if the Demiurge see you fighting against them – and you lose – then you'll die. If you stay here, and say that you got lost or captured or something... well, that way you can spread the truth to other Crolax in the world.'

'But I can't take it anymore!' Crank shouted, stamping his feet on the planks of the bridge, clenching his fists and looking up at the moon. 'I can't! It's too much! I can't handle it – I hate them! I hate the stupid Demiurge and everything they stand for. I hate all the stupid purity and the superiority and the treatment of citizens as vermin – making them think in certain ways, act in certain ways, like a bunch of mindless robots. I can't do it anymore! I am different. I think differently. I do not think that what the Demiurge does is right. I do not think that Borea is governed in the right way. The citizens are stripped of all their freedoms. The humanoids were better than this!'

Chintu glanced towards the ocean while Perry stepped

forwards and placed a hand on each of Crank's shoulders.

'It's all right,' said Perry. 'It's all right. I understand. You're not alone.'

Crank shook and fell back against the bridge railing. Perry lifted him to his feet. Kirito stared at one of his knuckles, seemingly bored by the Leagros king's admission of despair.

'This is why we need you to stay here,' said Perry. 'We can't do it without you. You say you want to take Borea down – well, we feel the same way. But we can't rely on the fact that we're going to win this battle. We might lose. And if we do, we need you to carry the torch; to take your message to other islands and tell other Crolax the truth so they can fight back. Let us be the martyrs. You need to be the beacon.'

Crank sniffled and looked up at him, as though seeing him for the very first time.

'Let's go,' said Chintu. Herself, Kirito and Perry ran down the bridge, following the arched walkway to the forest floor and facing each other.

'I'll do Orynx and Vemlin,' said Chintu. 'They should be the easiest since they've both lost their kings. Plus, Orynx has Puppy, and he'll believe me.' A note of pride entered her voice. 'Kirito, do Feysal. Perry, do Taveron. They're gonna need the most persuading 'cause their queen, Tovia, might still be with them. Crank didn't say whether she was a Demiurge. If she's there, focus on her.'

Chintu's determined aura faltered. She took Perry's hand and interlocked her fingers between his, giving a soft squeeze. Perry smiled.

'It's going to be all right.'

'Thank you,' she said, tears forming in her eyes.

'Kirito and his friends must be successful,' said Kirito, taking both of their hands. 'For Avanti.'

'For Avanti.'

'For Avanti.'

Chintu let go of Perry's hand and gave a small nod. They each entered the forest in different directions, focusing on the path that lay ahead. Perry's mind raced, considering ways to convince the Taveron queen to join the cause.

'Perry – wait!'

A sound rustled through the wilderness behind him, and he turned around as a long streak of silver hair suffocated him. Perry dropped his axe as Chintu hoisted herself onto his body and, with an enveloping curl of her legs, pressed her lips against his. She gripped the back of his neck and pushed in even closer, until they were the same being, intertwined around one another's skin and absorbing every second of passion. Perry's mind was free. He did not wish to ever leave her lips, to ever separate himself from the fire stoked in his heart. She was his partner in this journey, and even as he placed her to the floor and smiled, he knew that he must never let her go.

'I'll see you soon,' he said, brushing her cheek and leaning in for one final kiss. And then, with the taste of Chintu's lips still fresh, Perry turned away from the light and condemned himself to the inevitable darkness.

— Chapter Eighteen —

# Taveron

Bounding through Hades Forest, confused by the elation of kissing Chintu and the dread of facing Taveron, Perry forced his mind to the task ahead. He was going to enter Corinthian Cove, unaccompanied, and persuade Taveron to join him in battling the state. *Surely*, he thought as he waved his axe through thickets and vines, *this mission was impossible.*

Perry had no idea where he was going. He veered to the right, spotted the ocean and knew that he was not far from Blackstream. He kept running as the crashing East River revealed itself. He travelled downstream until the freshwater dropped off into an enormous pool far beneath. Trees arced over the waterfall covering Corinthian Cove. On both sides of the river was a regrettably familiar maze.

Perry braced himself for what he must do. A vine hung down from one of the trees, but it was on the other side of the maze. He did not know the secret route through the maze, but he would have to guess. He must do as Saskat – Saskat the traitor – had done.

Perry boxed each eardrum and launched sideways into the maze. He landed on his hands and knees between four separate contraptions. Each was a snare of some degree, and he rose to his feet and plotted a route ahead. A lark chirped from a rope above, and although Perry knew that it would not set off a trap, he was somewhat distracted. He made a strange, feeble, cawing sound, hoping to frighten the bird away, but it only jiggled its way farther along the rope towards him.

The designated path was uncertain. He wriggled along the floor below a loosely hanging rope with his axe held out ahead of him. He approached a long wooden plank, but there was not enough space between the two obstacles to stand up. His arms could not lift from the floor without knocking the wooden plank, so he instead jerked his body onwards like a caterpillar, his arms stationary by his side.

The silence broke with a clank. Perry's shirking head knocked into the wooden plank above him. It fell from its perch, revealing a dart pointing upwards from the floor which twanged into the air and connected with the over-hanging rope. The entire material shook, displacing the guffawing lark and creating a soft jingling from the water-fall.

'Move!' barked a throaty voice as an enormous wooden cage dropped from the tree above. It landed over Perry's body, trapping him. Filled with dread, he looked up and saw an overhanging vine trembling, along with a second one next to it. Two women climbed up the vines, gritting their teeth down at him.

'Victory,' said one of them.

'Tovia!' called back the other. 'We got one!'

'No, no, no,' Perry mumbled. 'You don't understand.'

'Oh, we understand *perfectly*,' jeered Paraskevas, sneering down at him. 'You saw Shix and Kallias go out for a nighttime hunt and thought you'd take the chance to attack us. Where are you friends, eh? Can you see them, Yozora? Where's Cranky-pants?'

'Tovia, stay alert!' called the woman named Yozora, whose appearance was almost as bizarre as Kirito's. A decapitated crocodile head was fixed above her head, suspending by two elongated vines. Her face was hidden by a lily pad, with holes cut for her eye sockets. On her left shoulder perched a red fody bird, humming.

'The planets told me that this would happen tonight,' said Yozora, slapping her hand against her left ear.

'I've come alone,' said Perry. 'Please take me into the cove. I have an urgent message.'

'What about now, Yozora? What are the planets telling you?' Paraskevas looked up at her partner's tall form, still sneering.

'Jupiter is telling me to trust him, but Venus is not sure,' said Yozora. 'Wait, never mind. Venus agrees with Jupiter now.'

'Fine, we'll take you in,' grumbled Paraskevas. She walked to the edge of the maze and came back with four connected wooden bars which she used to seal the box shut beneath Perry's legs. Then, both her and Yozora remounted their vines and shuffled back down.

Perry's box was transported by a thin rope which he had not seen, shuffling him closer to the waterfall. He could not move as the box edged off the cliff. Perry screamed as it swung down. The box crashed through the waterfall and was caught by a third person in the middle of a damp, smelly, dark cove.

'Welcome to Corinthian Cove,' said Tovia, her mellow voice echoing between the cave walls. She stroked her chin and studied Perry.

'I have a message!' spat Perry between mouthfuls of water. Tovia stepped forwards into a dim candlelight. A slimy salamander scaled the wall behind her peach afro.

'Where's Leagros?'

'Alerting the other tribes,' said Perry. 'Except for Saskat, who's – but that's what I'm here to tell you!'

'Such nonsense,' Paraskevas said, rolling her eyes. Tovia turned back towards her tribe member, and went silent for a few moments. Then, finally, she said: 'Everyone strap on. Let's do it.'

'The Demiurge is in Hades Forest!'

A stunned silence filled the cove. A clip-clop echoed from the back of the chamber.

'What did you just say?' whispered Tovia.

'The Demiurge. They're in here. Shix and Kallias haven't gone for a nighttime stroll. They've gone to leave this island, with the rest of the Demiurge!'

'How *dare* you,' stuttered Tovia, flushing crimson with rage. 'How you dare – how you – Yozora!'

'Yes?'

'What are the planets telling you?'

Yozora shut her eyes, flicked her left ear and faced up towards the dingy ceiling.

'The planets say that there is no harm in letting him speak.' The fody squeaked on her shoulder and flew into a darkened corner of the cave.

'You were left a message today, weren't you?' said Perry. '*Taveron will die.* It was written outside this cave in blood. Well, so did we. There was one outside Juniper, and I didn't think anything of it, but Crank woke me up earlier and told me the truth. There's a reason we're all on this island, and it isn't because Dolphin saved us from the state prison.'

'Dolphin –' started Paraskevas.

'Is gone,' finished Perry. 'He fled from this island, to report his findings back to the Demiurge. And Chintu killed his replacement. Why would I tell you that unless I was telling the truth?'

'So, what are you saying?' asked Tovia.

'The Demiurge took twenty of us to this forest to be studied. They want to improve their identification of Crolax in daily Borean life – and by better understanding how we think, they will be able to. But now they've done their testing. They've got what they need to know about us, and they're meeting, right now, on the beach.'

'How does Crank know this?'

'He's one of them. And so is Saskat – she went for a *nighttime stroll*, too, earlier this evening. But she's not coming back. The Demiurge are leaving Hades Forest, and we have to stop them!'

Perry panted against the freezing, damp floor of Corinthian Cove. A swarm of beetles scurried past, just outside the cage.

'What a load of rubbish,' said Paraskevas, wrinkling her nose. 'Absolutely ridiculous. Tovia, *he* could have drawn the message in blood earlier today. That's how he knows! The rest of it is absolute rubbish. Cranky-pants is probably waiting outside this cave, right now, ready to kill us.'

'Yozora?' said Tovia, turning her neck towards her leaf-covered friend.

'I'm not sure,' she said. The crocodile head above her moved into the candlelight. 'I don't think the planets can help us this time.'

'Fine,' said Tovia, staring between her fingers down at Perry. 'I agree with Paris. Everyone strap on.'

Perry went to mutter his indignation, but his voice was swallowed by a pressing horror. Paraskevas licked her thin lips, and all three women disappeared into far corners of the cove. They stepped back into view two minutes later, each with a long block of wood attached to their crotch.

Taveron lowered to their knees in a line behind Perry. The wooden box was lifted from above him. Paraskevas and Yozora stepped forwards to hold down his wrists – he did not struggle, so immense was his shock – and Tovia shuffled closer behind him, pressing a long wooden object against his buttocks…

'Miist saved my life!'

Perry did not know what made him say it, but it worked. The wooden log did not enter, and even Yozora and Paraskevas let go. He looked up at them both, desperate.

'What are you on about?' snarled Paraskevas.

'She – I – I don't know why.'

'When was this?' demanded Tovia, standing up behind

him as her eyes widened.

'When…' he felt embarrassed saying it; 'when Leagros raided Corinthian Cove. I was the one playing the drum, and she chased me away. I fell off a tree and she trapped me, stared at me, but didn't kill me.'

'Why?' said Tovia.

'I don't know.'

Perry's head hung at the lameness of these words. He shuffled forwards away from Tovia.

'I do,' said Yozora.

'The planets?' said Paraskevas and Tovia together.

'No. The Demiurge. Miist told me that something was wrong about Hades Forest. She was always saying it. She said that Dolphin's story was flimsy and that there must be another explanation. She always said that she thought the Demiurge were in here, but…' a tear trickled from Yozora's eye; 'but I asked the planets and they said it couldn't be true. So, I dismissed it.'

'What's that got to do with Miist saving his life?' said Paraskevas.

'I was the last one to enter the forest,' said Perry, speaking as his brain tumbled towards the conclusion. 'She knew I wasn't a Demiurge. If she thought they were in here, they would be in here from the beginning. She would've known that as many rebels had to stay alive as possible to fight. That's why she didn't kill me.'

'She was wrong,' muttered Tovia, stroking her chin. 'If the Demiurge are in here, they could've brought in more and more warriors at any point. You being last in here doesn't mean that you're not a Demiurge.'

'Miist clearly disagreed,' said Perry.

'She was willing to take her chances, anyway,' said Yozora, who resumed hitting her left ear. 'Plus, Miist always avoided hurting people if she could help it.'

The Taveron queen and Paraskevas glanced at each other, both frowning in concentration.

'Paris?' said Tovia. Paraskevas curled her lip, gave a reluctant shrug, and nodded. 'Fine. We'll go with you. But you're going out first. If Leagros is waiting out there, then you're the one getting killed.'

All three women unstrapped their blocks of wood as Perry stumbled to his feet. He could not believe that he had convinced them. They all gathered their weapons and formed a suffocating triangle around him. Tovia shot an arrow through the waterfall and waited, expecting weapons to return from outside. They did not.

'You're telling me that you have no idea which side of the island they're on?'

Perry shook his head as Yozora extinguished all the candles in the cove and retrieved a large wooden object from one of the walls. It was a canoe. They each sat in it, Perry at the front, and the three Taveron warriors scraped along the damp cove floor.

They pushed through the waterfall and were drenched as they landed with a plop in the pool beneath. It was still pitch-black all around, but the moon revealed a sky devoid of cloud. Tovia and Paraskevas pointed their weapons, alert to any lurking Leagros warriors.

'Did she say anything?' sniffled Yozora. Perry shook his head and she looked away. Tovia placed an oar in

Perry's lap, and the three of them, excluding Yozora, pushed through the water and out of the pool.

A small stream carried them away from Blackstream. The luminous eyes of forest creatures batted at them from either side of the water. Perry rowed until the trees opened and the crashing ocean came into view. He clutched his axe as Paraskevas and Tovia moored the canoe onto the sandy beach. All four of them got out, Yozora wiped away her tears, and the three women turned to face Perry.

'What now?' demanded Paraskevas, staring up at him.

He stared around into the darkness. The beach was dimly visible beneath the fading moonlight. Nobody stood along the coast in either direction. 'Let's go this way,' he said, leading them down the beach to the left. All three Taveron warriors shared sceptical glances, but obeyed.

'So, where are the other tribes?' called Yozora as Perry broke into a run.

'Chintu is talking to Orynx and Vemlin. Kirito is talking to Feysal.'

'What about Crank?'

'He's staying behind. We don't want him to get killed fighting the Demiurge, because then he won't be able to spread the truth to other rebels if we lose.'

Perry slowed to a walk as he led them around the end of the beach. The coast opened up again, and a group of people appeared several hundred metres along the sand. Perry reached back and pushed Yozora, Tovia and Paraskevas into the treeline.

'Get off me!' grunted Paraskevas. 'What was that for?'

'Look!' implored Perry, pointing at the figures. There

was eight people in the group. 'It's the Demiurge.'

'Wait, that's them?' said Yozora, twisting her neck. 'Then what are we standing here for? They killed Miist – so I'll kill *them!*'

'No,' said Perry. 'We need to wait for –'

But Yozora was already gone. She charged along the beach, defenceless, and punched both her ears in a furious war cry.

'She's left her bow and arrow here,' hissed Tovia, panicking as the fody from Yozora's shoulder hovered in a branch above. Paraskevas tutted, reached down for Yozora's weapon, placed a small dome-shaped cover over the tip of an arrow, and prepared to strike her fellow tribe warrior. Before she could do so however, a boomerang flung out from a tree along the beach and struck Yozora on the ankle. An absence of blood indicated that the boomerang, too, was blunted.

Perry stared along the sand towards the Demiurge, but none of them had spotted Yozora. Instead, they each stared at the blinding sunrise along the horizon.

Two Feysal warriors darted out from the trees to retrieve Yozora's sand-covered body. Her muffled shouts of protest remained unnoticed by the Demiurge, and Perry led Taveron along the trees between thickets and vines.

'Fabe?' called out Tovia. 'Jonas?'

The two Feysal warriors stood above Yozora, who thumped against the ground. Kirito held her down.

'The crying woman must be rational,' said Kirito. 'Kirito respects the decorative crocodile on her head, but that does not mean that he will let the crying woman instigate a crocodile calamity.'

'There's nothing to be rational about. They killed Miist, so I'll –'

'We *will* kill them, Yozora,' said Paraskevas, hunching her shoulders. 'That's the whole point. But we've got to find the right time. And we've got to find Orynx and Vemlin.'

'I'm not fighting with Vemlin,' muttered Jonas, as Fabe crouched down and pulled Yozora to her feet. He whispered something in her ear. It was inaudible to the rest of the group, but the Taveron warrior subsided. She stared up at Fabe with a mixture of bewilderment and understanding.

'Oh, hello, shaggy man!' beamed Kirito, grinning at Perry. It seemed, despite Paraskevas having spoken moments earlier, Kirito only just noticed the new arrivals.

'Hi, Kirito,' Perry said; 'how was it talking to Feysal?'

'Oh, quite fine, shaggy man. Once the slavery tribe saw that Kirito was alone, they believed him straight away.'

'Um, excuse me?' snapped Paraskevas. 'Is this really the time to discuss this? Come on!'

She pulled Yozora from the floor, and they ran farther through the trees. Perry followed with Kirito, Tovia, Jonas and Fabe.

'What did you say to her?' Perry asked Fabe as they ran.

'Not much,' replied the Feysal warrior, staring at the ground. 'I can't really remember.'

Kirito burst into immense laughter.

'It is an epidemic, shaggy man! First the Leagros king, now the whispering Feysal man. No one remembers a thing!'

Perry pushed back his fringe as he considered Jonas's strange behaviour. Moments later, Paraskevas held out her arms for them to stop.

'What took you so long?' said Chintu, staring at each of them before throwing her arms around Perry's neck.

'You all right?' he said.

'Yeah. Let's go.'

She took his hand and led on the group, which now included Puppy, Kitten, Aruba, Florius and Killua. They arrived at the edge of the treeline and peered at the Demiurge, who still stared at the horizon.

'What are they looking at?' said Perry, stepping onto the sand. Only then did he see ten driverless boats speeding across the waves towards the island.

Beside him, Chintu stared at the arrows in Tovia's hands. The boats zoomed closer until finally mooring on the beach. Each Demiurge stepped towards a different one as Perry turned to his partner – who was suddenly gone. He glanced around the tree line, but could not see Chintu anywhere.

'We can't just stand here, we need to do something,' said Yozora.

'Agreed,' said Tovia, but still none of them moved. Perry could not find Chintu. It was almost too late.

Arrows flew over his head. Paraskevas ambushed the Demiurge, and Yozora and Tovia joined in. The Demiurge span around, crouching to identify their attackers. The group of Crolax remained hidden, until Kitten span a boomerang out. Puppy sprinted onto the beach and launched a spear. Fabe followed, as did Kirito, until the entire group formed a line along the sand, ready for battle. Silence followed as both groups waited for the other to strike.

A shooting flame soared across the beach, high above all the warriors, and landed with perfect accuracy in one of the ten boats. It exploded and the Demiurge dispersed, crouching in the ocean and searching for the unseen attacker. Perry already knew who it was – and her victory call confirmed it.

'That's right! That's right! I killed Dolphin, and I'll kill all of you, too!'

# Chapter Nineteen

# The Hidden Warriors

The Demiurge retreated along the beach. The firelit boat fizzled out some moments later, and the vehicle was destroyed. Perry stared at Chintu, now huffing alongside him, when a disc glided across the beach and sliced Tovia's cheek.

Perry pulled back his axe, ready to bat away any flying weapons, as Killua, Fabe, Jonas and Kirito charged forwards. Arrows soared over the group's head as the Demiurge retaliated. They each wore a grim smile at the damage they were about to inflict upon their lowly challengers. Chintu whipped her vine at an enemy as Kirito swiped his Zhuas at Yasha.

'The Feysal king took the shabby man and his scary lover to the pit of pigs!' roared Kirito, spinning both weapons into Yasha's legs. 'The Feysal king will pay!'

Perry jumped in. He and Kirito were dwarfed by Yasha, but worked in synchrony to expose both sides of his body. Unfortunately, the Feysal king had two weapons: a rock-carven sword was fastened in each of his hands, glinting in the morning sun. He parried Perry on one side and Kirito on the other.

Perry threw the axe over his shoulder and swung at Yasha's head. The foe swerved and Perry's weapon instead collided with Kirito's Zhua, knocking it from his hand. The axe, too, slipped from Perry's grasp, and Kirito's single Zhua was helpless to prevent Yasha from swinging one of his swords round into Perry's body.

It missed. Instead of feeling a deadly stabbing, a clang signalled Fabe's arrival as he parried Yasha's advance with his own spiked wooden club. The two giants faced each other, king against servant, until Yasha was drowned by Jonas's water bucket. Fabe pushed his former king to the floor, and continued the assault.

Perry spotted Chintu cracking her whip at Diablo's discs as they danced between the attacks of other warriors across the beach. Perry turned back to Kirito, but took a few moments to find him, as he now lay across the sand, moving his arms left and right.

'Kirito!' shouted Perry; 'what are you – you need to help the others!'

'Quite right, shaggy man!' beamed Kirito. He jumped up and raced to support Aruba, who fought Shix.

> 'The Demiurge thinks –
> That they can't be stopped –
> Not true! Quite false! –
> Their mask has now dropped!'

Puppy jigged across the sand, launching spears at Hamster as Perry wove between them to support Chintu. He willed her to avoid just one more disc, when a water jet blasted her from her feet and sent her spiralling across the sand. Diablo moved away as Saskat cackled. An evil mania occupied every centimetre of her now sexless body, but Perry capitalised on her glee by spinning his axe at her, landing at the right angle to lodge between two rolls of fat.

The malevolent grin flickered from her face. She looked down at the axe and then back up at its thrower. Perry jumped across the sand when a boomerang span in front of him and penetrated Saskat's skin. She fell back into the sand like a marooned beach whale. To Perry's right, Kitten raced forwards, her childish face delighted.

'Well, that was my best shot yet! Wouldn't you agree?'

'I – I don't...' stammered Perry, retrieving his weapon. He shut his eyes and grabbed the handle sticking out from Saskat's body.

'No, no, no. That is inopportune!' said Kitten. 'Abandon the axe, Perry. Master the dead lady's weapon as your own!'

Kitten danced away and flung her boomerang at Ryuga and Kallias. Killua, meanwhile, was mid-battle with Chick. Perry used Saskat's water gun to shoot a jet at Chick's body, but missed. Ryuga raced past, charging at Paraskevas. Chick avoided Killua's claws and shot lethal darts back at him, but Perry sent another deluge to knock one of these darts from its trajectory.

'You're plotting to kill me! You've all been plotting to kill me!' bellowed Killua as he swiped at Chick's body.

Perry, meanwhile, aimed the gun at Chick's red hair. She flipped her body backwards to avoid the water and landed on her feet, shooting darts high into the sky which veered before spinning back down towards Killua's head. The Vemlin warrior gaped upwards, unsuccessfully clawing at the sky to knock the artillery from its trajectory. The first two darts missed, but the third weaved between two claws and landed in Killua's bicep. An oozing, unknown purple liquid spilled from the weapon, sinking into his veins as the tortured man howled in agony.

Chick roared with glee, but Perry blasted water at the girl once more. She fell, head-first, at Killua's feet. The pair lay tangled in one united knot. Killua's eyes drooped, but he still managed to swing an arm into the little girl lying on top of him. His claws split through Chick's arm and she howled as blood spat everywhere and mixed with her red hair. A tired exchange of blows between the two warriors occurred, before both dropped into the sand, clearly dead.

Farther along the beach, Yasha kicked Jonas's feebly stirring body along the sand as Fabe struggled to his feet. A spear landed only centimetres from Jonas's body and Yasha, interpreting this as the action of an ally, looked to locate his companion – but Puppy's trick fooled him. The boy ran past Perry and launched a spear at Yasha's face.

The Feysal king plucked it from mid-air and laughed at his pathetic challenger. He spun the spear around and launched it back at Puppy, but Perry projected the water gun's blast into the path of the spear and knocked it to safety. Puppy grinned across at him and aimed at Kallias, who stepped towards Fabe. A roar behind Perry indicated that another foe was nearby, and he ducked beneath a wayward arrow before turning around to shoot Ryuga square in the chest. The Feysal warrior was prevented from getting to his feet, until a final pump of Perry's gun yielded no results. There was no water left in the tank.

Ryuga rose as Perry sprinted across to Saskat's fallen body, trying to retrieve his bloodstained axe from her chest. Ryuga charged at Perry, but was jumped on by Chintu, who appeared from nowhere and used one of the sticks forming Saskat's powerless gun to push her foe over. Ryuga collapsed and Chintu, standing over him, jerked the hollowed stick through his eye socket. With a harrowing squelch, Ryuga lay dead in the sand. Chintu dropped the stick and ran to Perry, pulling him across the beach.

'Don't leave me!' she shouted.

Florius fled from Hamster, the latter of whom Perry aimed a failed swing at with his axe. Hamster changed direction towards Perry and Chintu, thrashing her machete. Florius charged from behind and stuck a long, daggered knife into the little girl's neck. The life drained from Hamster's body and she fell to her knees, dropping face-first into the sand.

'Flora!' screamed a voice. 'Flora!'

Florius turned around and chased after Aruba. Perry yanked Chintu to her feet as a grunt behind them signalled Kallias's presence. She shot an arrow at Perry, who dived out of the way and in front of Chintu to protect her. Kallias, meanwhile, took an arrow from her bow and wielded it as a knife, but Chintu lashed her vine to displace it. Perry's body ached as Kallias aimed another arrow at him, but it did not launch. Tovia arrived and shot an arrow at Kallias. The Taveron warriors sparred as mortal enemies.

Kallias grunted louder as her athletic frame gained the advantage over her former queen. Perry and Chintu circled the action, determined to launch an attack on Kallias, when a wayward disc from Diablo knocked one of Tovia's arrows off-path. Kallias used her bettered position to strike her own artillery straight into Tovia's heart. The Taveron queen fell back, the arrow lodged in her chest. She gazed up at the sky, and Kallias returned her attention to Perry and Chintu. Kallias fired at Chintu but Perry swiped his axe upwards to connect with the dart and knock it farther along the beach.

'The evil woman shall not harm the scary woman and the shabby man!' bellowed the furious figure of Kirito as he thrust his Zhua at Kallias's body. Chintu and Perry pressed in, too. Kallias stumbled backwards as Perry's axe swiped against her chest, before Kirito knocked the bow from her hands.

'Mine!' shouted a child's voice. 'Mine, mine, mine!'

Puppy skewered Kallias to the ground with a spear. The life left her body as Puppy danced across the sand and collected his spear, giving Chintu a wry wink before launching it at Shix. Of the Demiurge, only she and Yasha were left on the beach now, but this made no sense to Perry.

'Where's Diablo?' Perry said, turning to Chintu.

'I'll go find out. Stay alive!' she bellowed, turning away from the action and sprinting into the treeline.

'But you just told me to stay close!'

On one side of the beach, Shix thrashed her Halo back and forth to keep her pursuers at bay. On the other side, Yasha battled with his two swords. Nine warriors closed in on the pair of them, herding them together, as Yasha roared louder with every blow aimed at him. Perry allowed himself the flickering hope of victory.

'You killed her! You killed her!' screamed Yozora. She picked up a spear lying on the beach and launched it at Shix. The Demiurge warrior batted it away, knocking it to Yasha's feet who flicked it up into his hands and threw it back into the densely packed crowd.

A short, stumpy body fell to the ground, and Yozora shrieked even louder. Paraskevas was dead, the spear sticking high from her chest. Perry moved forwards, knowing that he must join the fight, when a yapping sounded from the treeline to his left. Ruffe bounded across the sand, zigzagging into the fray.

'No,' Perry muttered; 'no, please, no.'

Kirito's stocky frame intercepted the coyote, lifting it up and running back into the forest with it. The fighting continued, but another body emerged from the trees too quickly to belong to Kirito. The scarred, hairless form of Avanti sprinted across the sand, her trident spinning through her wearied hands as she ran towards the Demiurge. She harnessed all her force behind the trident and thrust it deep into Shix's neck. The Demiurge warrior collapsed in the sand, and Avanti posed over her dead body.

Yasha edged backwards towards one of the remaining boats. Puppy threw a spear at the back of his head, but missed, and it seemed that the final living Demiurge was going to escape.

Metallic rods emerged from inside the boat and strapped themselves to Yasha's limbs. The vehicle stirred, ready for take-off, when another roar came from the treeline. Once more, an unknown figure ran across the sand, barrelling into the boat and capsizing it in the sea. Yasha's head bobbed up into the interior of the boat, which now lay upside down in the water, and he pushed it from his head, gasping at the salty air. His unknown attacker bobbed to the surface, too, and Crank's scarred head and black goatee revealed itself.

The Kraken remained in his grip and he yanked the weapon from the water, cracking it down on Yasha's head. The Demiurge warrior squealed, spitting water before pummelling both fists down onto Crank's head. The pair splashed in the water, seeking for the upper hand.

'No!' shouted Perry, distraught at the idea of losing Crank. He ran across the sand with the rest of the warriors, but none of them dared launch a weapon into the fray. An enormous beige fist reached up through the water and smacked Yasha's head, and another movement below the surface signalled that Crank connected with Yasha's crotch. Crank hauled his flailing victim over his shoulder and launched him onto the sand, roaring with fury as Yasha lay, facing the rising sun in disbelief.

'You?' whispered Yasha. 'You? It – it can't be?'

'Thought we were all perfect, just like you?' snarled Crank. 'Well, you thought wrong. Good riddance, Yasha.'

And with one final blow, Crank picked up a spear lying on the sand and thrust it through Yasha's heart, killing him.

'I'm so sorry,' said Crank, turning to face the rebels. 'I'm so sorry that this has happened to you.'

'Happened to *us*,' corrected Puppy, running forwards

and hugging Crank. Perry glanced farther along the beach, however, and saw an enormous figure walking towards them.

'Nobody move!' bellowed Diablo's deep voice.

Chintu's quivering, shaking figure was between his fists. She muttered something that Perry could not hear, and Diablo wore a look of grim satisfaction. As with Yasha and Crank moments prior, the two figures were locked in a stoic embrace. They could not be separated by a spear, boomerang or dart.

'You judge me a fool?' said Diablo. 'Think again. A singular movement, and the wrench's neck shall be slit.' He raised a disc and held it to Chintu's throat.

'What do you want?' said Perry, as Ruffe yapped.

'You peasants think I have wants?' laughed Diablo, 'Nay! I make demands. You permit my leave from this island, or I'll slice her neck.'

Each person stood completely still, petrified. Perry stepped towards Diablo. Crank did the same.

'Why should we trust you?' demanded Perry. 'Why should we trust that you'll stick to your word – that you won't kill her?'

'You have no choice,' growled Diablo, smirking at Perry before turning to Crank. 'Aha! Now he presents himself – the traitor in our midst! I should've known.'

'Crank, no,' said Perry. 'No way.'

'It doesn't matter,' said Crank.

'What do you –'

'It doesn't matter!' he roared, charging across the sand. Diablo had not expected the attack, and released Chintu in shock. She fell to the ground, crawling through the sand towards Perry, as Crank lashed his Kraken at Diablo with all his might. He was too late, however; Diablo flicked his wrist, and a razor disc soared through the air and lodged in Crank's throat.

Diablo span around and leapt into a boat. Crank crumpled, blood pouring down his body and into the sand. The boat whirred to life and moved away, taking Diablo away from Hades Forest. Puppy threw one final spear, but it was insufficient to kill the escaping Demiurge. Diablo's long, black hair faded into the morning sun.

'No...' muttered Perry, running forwards with the rest of the rebels by his side. All eleven of them crowded around Crank's body, some screaming, others silent, as the Leagros king blinked up at the fading clouds.

'Why?' said Perry, 'Why did you do it?'

'You already – already won,' said Crank, pulling the disc from his throat. 'I needed to – needed to do it – for – for myself.'

'But this isn't over! We can – we can fight, we can – we can do something!' insisted Perry, tears streaming as his body convulsed with grief at the sight of his dying king.

'He was going to kill Chintu.'

'But there would've been a solution!'

Crank shook his head.

'I'm so sorry, kiddo. I was not cut – cut out for this world. I don't have your strength.'

'You've always had –'

'Listen to me, kiddo,' Crank interrupted. 'Go to Sleepers Den. Find the chest in the – the top room. Open it. It'll tell you everything you need to know.'

'I'm so sorry, Crank. It's all my fault. I couldn't stop you dying.'

'There's more to this than – than fighting,' said Crank. 'You have empathy and compassion. Fighting is the means, not the end. Remember that, Perry.'

Crank's head collapsed and his eyes rolled upwards. Perry's one and only king crunched a beetle between his teeth, and then, with the puff of a defeated soldier, his eyes frosted over and faded into the abyss.

# Chapter Twenty

# A Place to Hide

Crank's head shined in the golden sun. The scars seemed to vacate his face as the silent minutes wore on.

The group dispersed somewhat along the beach. Yozora, blood dribbling across her bruised body and her crocodile head mask lying in the sand, hauled Tovia and Paraskevas together and sat between them both. She did not vocalise her horror, but instead boxed her left ear. The rest of the group left her alone. A red fody, once again, perched on her shoulder.

Aruba and Florius lay beside Killua's body, staring up at the sky. Aruba muttered a flow of continual grievances through her swollen, purple lips. Florius nodded, dipping her mohawked hair into the dried blood stained in the sand.

The remaining warriors – Perry, Chintu, Kirito, Avanti, Puppy, Jonas, Fabe, and Kitten, all looking equally beaten and pained – formed a dismal circle around the Leagros king. Kirito stepped forwards to close Crank's eyelids.

'Perry,' said Chintu, peering at him with two puffy eyes. 'We have to get going. If we're going to find the –'

'I know,' said Perry, 'I just need a moment.'

The gravity of their loss – the immovable hurt contaminating Perry's heart – did not spawn ignorance of the task ahead. Crank's final words stuck with him, but so too did the sight of Diablo's escape over the waves. The Demiurge elsewhere would soon know that their troops were dead. Would they retrieve the bodies of their departed, or would they leave them to die, deserving of their fate at the hands of the lowly Crolax?

Perry suspected that an expedition would be sent to remove all bodies from the forest. The Demiurge would reuse this forest for future experiments.

'I need to check something,' mumbled Perry, standing up from the group. He sidestepped a crab and walked to the eight boats harboured on the shoreline. He turned back with a sudden idea, however, and reclaimed the crab he had just avoided. It flailed on either side as he picked up its body, trying to snap at his fingers as he dropped it into one of the boats.

Rods sprung out across the interior and clasped the creature, pinning its claws and sticking its body to the base of the vehicle. The motor kicked into life and the boat shimmied down the sand and into the water, propelling itself across the ocean.

'How did the shabby man do that?' said a voice behind him. Perry turned around and grimaced at Kirito, whose luminous spikes of hair now sagged with sand.

'I don't know. It must be automated.'

'At least the shabby man knows that, now,' said Kirito. 'Crocodile conquest?'

Perry shrugged and the pair fell silent, watching the

boat fade into the distance.

'You could've called me tubby, y'know,' said Perry after some time. 'Or chubby. Or big boned. Why always fat?'

'Perhaps the shabby man wishes that Kirito called him kiddo, instead.' Kirito placed a hand on Perry's shoulder. 'Where does the shabby man think the boat is going?'

'The Demiurge headquarters, probably. The question is: how do we hijack them?'

'By not touching the inside of the boat,' said Kirito.

'But the engine is on the interior.'

'Engine, shabby man?'

'You'd have to hijack the engine, so you could sit in the boat without it moving away.' Perry stared across the sea, filled with anger, bitterness, and frustration. A rough hand took his own, gritty and unlike Chintu's.

'Umm… Kirito?' said Perry, turning around.

'Sorry,' blushed Chintu. 'I still have sand on my hands.' She pressed her nose against his.

'Are you all right?'

Chintu nodded. 'Are you?'

'You lied to me,' he said, pulling away from her.

'About what?'

'When I arrived in Leagros, you told me a story. You said that you once saw Taveron raping a small parrot in the forest. That was a lie, wasn't it? I spent an hour with Taveron, and I don't think they'd do that.'

Chintu sighed. 'How else was I supposed to make you take them seriously?'

'By telling me the truth. By telling me that they were

trying to kill me.'

'That wouldn't have worked. You were still too worried about touching plants and hurting animals. I needed you to toughen up.'

'I don't want to toughen up,' said Perry.

'Nor did I,' said Chintu. 'But, if you haven't noticed, you already have. You're completely different now to when you first joined the forest. Would you be alive right now if I hadn't told you that story?'

Perry considered this for a moment, and then turned away. There seemed to be only one reason he was alive, and it was because of the woman lying dead in the distant forest. Miist had saved his life. Miist could have killed him, but didn't. Now she was dead, and Perry was stranded with the hollow grief left not only by her absence, but by Crank's as well.

'I just said to Kirito –'

'I heard,' said Chintu, 'and I think it's a trap. The boats will be designed so that they can't be hijacked. And even if they can, we won't be able to do it.'

'Crank said that the Demiurge technology isn't as superior as they have us believe,' pointed out Perry.

'True, but we can't risk getting this wrong. We need to hide, in case the Demiurge come back, but we don't need to get away from this island, we just need to make the Demiurge *think* we did. I've asked Yozora to take one of Taveron's boats and push it into the sea. If the Demiurge do come here, they will see it on the water, empty, and assume we've all drowned.'

'There's no way they'll believe that.'

'They think we're stupid,' pointed out Chintu. 'They don't think Crolax are logical like them.'

'But they'll still check the island, just in case.'

'True,' Chintu nodded, turning back to face a now largely vacated beach. 'But they won't find us. Puppy just told me about a hiding spot we can use – a bunker he built months ago beneath Sleepers Den. He says Dolphin didn't know it was there, and the rest of the Demiurge never really went to that part of the forest, so they won't know about it, either.'

As Perry considered this proposal, Puppy emerged from the distant treeline. His hair was as shaggy and sweaty as ever.

'We need to get going,' he said.

Perry nodded, and followed Puppy, Chintu and Kirito along the sand in melancholy silence.

'I'm sorry for calling you Chintabelle,' said Puppy.

'It's all right,' said Chintu. 'It made me feel like the woman in the relationship, for once.'

Chintu squeezed Perry's hand and kissed his cheek.

As they rounded the end of the beach, Broadfields came into sight. The different groups of animals – ostriches, horses and springbok – dispersed as the new arrivals waded through the grass. Puppy led them into the forest and over the East River bridge. Yozora appeared and caught up with Perry and Chintu.

'The boat is out on the ocean, as instructed. The planets say that your idea was a good one.'

'Thank you.'

Chintu took Perry's hand as they approached the

bamboo. He only shut his eyes as they passed through it – otherwise, despite his chest contracting, he felt numb to the fear. Compared to what he had just seen, the bamboo seemed suddenly less harrowing now.

After re-opening his eyes, it took only a few more moments for them to find their way to Sleepers Den.

'I'll take care of the tiger,' said Puppy. 'Anyone want to help?'

'I will,' said Perry, stepping forwards with renewed vengeance. Puppy handed him a spear as Kirito, too, marched up the steps towards the violet door. Puppy pushed the door inwards and slid against the wall. Perry and Kirito followed close behind.

'The brave man should stick with Kirito. Kirito suspects that the sweaty boy can kill a tiger on his own.'

Perry moved through a doorway to the right while Puppy stepped into a room on the left. Perry and Kirito stood close together, peering around wooden armchairs and tables in fear of the tiger. An enormous roar sounded from the adjacent room, followed by the shriek of a young boy.

'Got it!'

Puppy stood over a tiger in the next room, his bloodied spear in hand. He grinned at them both, sweeping his sweaty black hair from his eyes. The front door burst open and Chintu ran into the room.

'We heard a noise – is everything all right?'

'Yeah,' smiled Puppy. 'Perry killed it.'

Perry went to contradict him, when Puppy winked and left the room.

The rest of the warriors followed him up the stairs in the next room, before emerging in a setting unfortunately familiar to Perry, Puppy and Chintu. A woman and a tiger both lay in dried circles of blood on the wooden floor.

'Oh my,' exclaimed Kitten. 'How disgusting.'

Avanti stood against the back wall, coughing and sneezing, as the others scoured the area. After a few moments, however, it seemed pointless; the chest that Crank told them to find was clearly not in this empty room.

'It's not in the pit – I would've seen it when I was down there,' said Perry. 'Maybe there's another floor, above this one?'

'There isn't,' said Puppy. 'We're in the roof. It has to be here.'

'Well, clearly it isn't.'

'Don't you think I can see that?'

'Well, that's just typical,' snarled Kitten. 'The one bit of help we get, and it's nonsense. The chest isn't here. That Crank fellow lied to us.'

'Don't say that!' snapped Perry, but Kitten batted her eyelids and trudged back down the stairs. Aruba and Florius followed, and after a few more minutes of fruitless searching, Jonas and Fabe left the room. Only the surviving Leagros members remained, accompanied by Puppy and Yozora, the latter of whom Kirito glanced at hopefully.

'We're missing something,' said Perry. 'I'm certain we are.'

'We've looked everywhere,' said Chintu. 'There's nothing in this stupid room, besides a hole in the floor.'

A bang sounded as Puppy hit the blunt end of his spear

up against the ceiling in frustration. Splinters of wood fell down into his hair. The others looked on as Puppy continued hitting the spear against the roof, until he stopped and stared across at them all.

'Did you hear that? That one was different.'

Puppy stepped back and pushed the spear up into the ceiling once again. This time, Perry heard it too. The resulting sound was more hollowed than Puppy's previous attempts. The ceiling was not boarded up in this part of the room.

'It's hollow,' said Perry, leaping forwards.

'Crocodile conquest!'

Puppy span the spear around, and thrust the sharp end into the wooden ceiling. The spear pierced through the wood, and the plank was lodged onto the end of the weapon. He pulled the spear down, revealing a hole in the ceiling. In an instant, Chintu climbed onto Perry's shoulders and reached up into the hole, scraping her fingernails along the hollowed ceiling tiles. She let out a sudden shriek of glee and, using both her hands to clasp onto something, jumped down from Perry shoulders. She held out a small, moss-covered box in her hands.

'I don't believe it!'

All five of them froze, staring at the green chest. It was shaped like a cuboid, constructed out of wood and the size of a new-born baby in Chintu's arms. She placed it on the floor and they all stared down at it, dumbstruck.

'What now?'

'We open it, of course,' said Avanti.

'Kirito is concerned that something dangerous is in

there.'

'There won't be,' said Perry. 'Crank told us to find this, remember?'

Chintu scraped away the moss to reveal a thatched lid beneath. She displaced it and the group stared down into the chest. There was a thin, white sheet inside.

'That's – that's paper,' whispered Avanti. '*Real* paper, like the humanoids had. I remember destroying it in the Eradict factory.'

'But how can it be?' said Chintu. 'If the humanoids used it, then it can't have existed for –'

'Centuries,' finished Perry. He slid the paper out of the chest, holding it up to the ceiling. There was black writing printed across it, which he read.

Avanti: Anorexia

Killua: Schizophrenia

Miist: Vitiligo

Perry: PTSD

Florius: Anarthria

Fabe: Homosexuality

Bunny: Bipolar

Kirito: ADHD

Monosc: Arthritis

Puppy: Dyslexia

Paraskevas: Dwarfism

Tovia: Phobia

Yozora: Bisexuality

Chintu: Vaginismus

Hexen: Tourettes

Sorowitz: Vertigo
Aruba: Lesbianism
Kitten: OCD
Jonas: Anxiety
Malik: Depression

Each warrior in the forest was listed beside a strange word that Perry did not recognise. He noticed that the only people not listed were the Demiurge hidden within the forest. That was, until he spotted two more words written at the bottom of the paper in scratchy brown marking.

Crank: Amnesia

'I don't know any of these words,' said Perry.

The group went silent for a few moments, until Chintu spoke up.

'Crank kept forgetting things. Maybe that's what amnesia is. Why else would it be written there?'

'But why is it written at the bottom, and not printed in black on the paper?'

'Because whoever first wrote this list didn't know that Crank had amnesia when it was made. Someone must have figured out that Crank was different, too, and wrote it at the bottom as a note to themselves.'

'So, that means,' said Perry, 'all these other words are…'

'The disabilities that make us different,' concluded Chintu. 'That's why we're in here – all of us. We each have a mental or physical disability, and those differences are listed on this sheet.'

'But there's nothing wrong with us,' said Perry, looking around the group. 'We need to remember that. We're normal, just like everyone else. Who's to say what makes a person normal, and what makes them abnormal? All people should be accepted, no matter who they are.'

Everyone nodded, glancing across the room at each other. Their shared trauma bound them together, and Kirito grabbed Perry's hand on one side, and Chintu's on the other. Avanti, Puppy and Yozora followed suit, until the six of them stood in a circle, holding hands and looking into each other's eyes.

Finally, they left the room. Kirito clutched the scrunched-up paper in his hand. The remaining warriors waited on the forest floor, but before Perry could open his mouth to reveal the discovered note, Puppy guided them all into a dingy, damp area below the fortress. He pried open a camouflaged wooden square nailed into the floor, and gestured the group towards a wooden ladder running into the ground.

Kirito stepped down first. Perry followed, carrying Ruffe in his arms. He was reminded of Juniper as his head lowered into the earth.

He was amazed by the size and luxury of the bunker. Flames were lit across the walls, and the dirt flooring was unyielding to each person's footsteps. The roof ran four or five metres upwards.

'Puppy, this is amazing,' said Perry. He turned back as the young boy closed the square roof, shutting everyone inside. Puppy ran his hands through his sweaty hair, appearing close to tears.

'I made it when I first arrived here,' said Puppy. 'The others said they didn't want me sleeping on their island. They were going to abandon me altogether, until they realised how good at fighting I am.'

Standing in the corner, Kitten was not listening. She plucked a banana from a pile of food in the corner, but did not get the chance to eat it – Kirito ran across the bunker and knocked it from her hands. It fell to the floor and Ruffe rushed over, devouring it as Kitten stamped her feet and wailed. Puppy pinched some of the dirt-covered banana from the coyote's mouth, and placed it in his mouth.

'You are *disgusting*,' spat Kitten.

'Don't talk to him like that,' snapped Chintu, helping Perry lug piles of food into the centre of the room, and smiling at Kirito. The entire group tucked in.

They ate without discussion. Finally, Kirito cleared his throat and revealed the piece of paper to the rest of the group. They each looked over it in silence, as Kirito explained its contents to them.

Perry's thoughts went to the strange letters written beside his name on the list.

*PTSD. PTSD. PTSD.*

He had never heard of the term before. He had no idea what it meant.

The other warriors, having just read the list, now turned away. They were each in their own bubble, contemplating what the strange word beside their name meant. What did the state know about them, that they did not? The Demiurge remained omnipresent, even in this bunker.

Perry cleared his throat and pushed back his fringe. The four warriors, previously disconnected from the conversation in the room, all looked up at him. He smiled at each one of them, looked into their eyes in turn, and gave a subtle nod. Slowly, a crease formed in the eyes of Fabe, then Jonas, then Aruba and Kitten, and they all smiled back.

Perry squeezed Chintu's hand, watched Ruffe chase his tail in the corner of the room, and accepted some food from Avanti. To him, it mattered not whether they were in the bunker for two days, or two years; it mattered only that they stuck together. And although a long battle awaited him, filled with uncertainty and pain, Perry knew that this was the start of a new beginning.

He had finally found a home.

# Acknowledgements

To my parents: thank you for your continued support, no matter what I do.

To my two sisters, Pippa and Charlotte: thank you for always making me laugh.

To Tabitha: thank you for not only encouraging my promising ideas, but unequivocally telling me when I have a terrible one.

Printed in Great Britain
by Amazon